MW00579721

A MERRY LITTLE MURDER PLOT

A MERRY LITTLE MURDER PLOT

Jenn McKinlay

BERKLEY PRIME CRIME
New York

BERKLEY PRIME CRIME
Published by Berkley
An imprint of Penguin Random House LLC
penguinrandomhouse.com

Library of Congress Cataloging-in-Publication Data

Names: McKinlay, Jenn, author.
Title: A merry little murder plot / Jenn McKinlay.
Description: New York: Berkley Prime Crime, 2024. | Series: A Library
Lover's Mystery
Identifiers: LCCN 2024025587 (print) | LCCN 2024025588 (ebook) |
ISBN 9780593639368 (hardcover) | ISBN 9780593639382 (ebook)
Subjects: LCGFT: Christmas fiction. | Detective and mystery fiction. |
Novels.
Classification: LCC PS3612.A948 M47 2024 (print) | LCC PS3612.A948
(ebook) | DDC 813/.6—dc23/eng/20240624
LC record available at https://lccn.loc.gov/2024025587
LC ebook record available at https://lccn.loc.gov/2024025588

Printed in the United States of America
1st Printing

Book design by Laura K. Corless

For my plot group besties, Paige Shelton and Kate Carlisle. You are the only people I know who react to "I'm going to electrocute the victim" with oohs and aahs, insight and encouragement. I adore you both and am a better writer and person for having you gals in my life.

A MERRY LITTLE MURDER PLOT

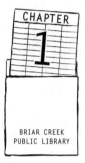

CHAPTER 1

BRIAR CREEK
PUBLIC LIBRARY

L *et it snow, let it snow, let it snow . . ."* a voice sang softly.

Library director Lindsey Norris glanced up from the computer monitor on the reference desk where she was working. Standing in front of her was a snowperson . . . sort of.

The faux snowperson was actually their children's librarian, Beth Barker, who also happened to be one of Lindsey's closest friends. Beth was wearing an oversize white T-shirt with three black felt buttons going down the front. Around her neck she wore a red scarf, and on her head was a white baseball cap that had two large google eyes glued on it, and a pointy nose made out of a batting-stuffed cone of orange felt attached to the front, just above the brim, to make a carrot-like nose between the google eyes. She looked adorable.

"Let me guess," Lindsey said. "It's a snow-themed story time today."

"What gave it away?" Beth scratched her head beneath the cap as if perplexed. Then she laughed and said, "We're reading *Little Fox in the Snow* by Jonathan London, *Making a Friend* by Tammi Sauer, and *A Thing Called Snow* by Yuval Zommer. Then we're crafting giant sparkly paper snowflakes to hang in the window. So fun!" Beth hopped up and down as if she couldn't contain her enthusiasm. No one promoted stories and reading like Beth. She was a treasure for their small public library in the shoreline village of Briar Creek, Connecticut.

"What are you working on?" Beth asked.

"I'm thinking of offering a website-building workshop, so I'm going over the possible free options, because I don't want to charge patrons. I just want to give them an idea of what's available and teach them how to get started," Lindsey said. "Our volunteer Ali McMahon is a website designer, and she's offered to teach the classes if I can come up with a curriculum."

"Sweet," Beth said. "I've considered taking a class on web design so I can create a webpage where I load up all of my story time information as a resource-sharing thing, you know?"

"I do," Lindsey said. "Potentially, we could link your page to the library's website as an additional resource, assuming I can get this class going. Honestly, the logistics are more complicated than I expected."

"You'll figure it out. And when you do, I'll be there." Beth nodded, making the felt carrot on her cap bob up and down.

"I appreciate your confidence." Lindsey smiled.

"Did you finish the book for our crafternoon today?" Beth asked. Thursday was their weekly crafternoon meeting in which they discussed a book they'd read, shared lunch and did a craft.

"Capote's *A Christmas Memory*?" Lindsey clarified. "Yes, I did. I've read it before, but there was so much I'd forgotten. It's really a wonderful story and I love the illustrated hardcover version we read."

"I thought so, too," Beth agreed. "Who's in charge of food this week?"

"Mayor Cole."

"Excellent." Beth pumped her fist. "She always brings meatball subs as soon as the temperature drops and stays in the thirties."

"With extra cheese." Lindsey felt her stomach rumble. She was more than ready for lunch. She glanced at the time on the top-right corner of her computer monitor. Another hour to go. Ugh.

"Library Lady!" A precocious little boy ran at Beth with his mother trailing behind him, carrying an armful of picture books and his coat. "Why are you dressed like a snow library lady?"

Beth glanced at Lindsey with a grin. "I love my job." Then she turned back to the boy. "Hello, Nate." Beth squatted down to be on his level and said, "Why do you think I'm dressed as a snow library lady?"

Nate leaned back, squinting his right eye as he studied Beth as if she were a riddle to be solved. After a few moments, his face cleared and he said, "Because we're reading stories about snow?"

"Yes!" Beth held up her hand for a high five, and Nate reached back and slapped her palm with his, giving it his all.

"Hi, Beth, Lindsey." Kaylee Bryce, Nate's mother, joined them. "He's very excited for story time today."

"So am I!" Beth cried. She held out her hand, and Nate took it without hesitation. As they departed for the children's section, where the story time room was, Beth called over her shoulder, "See you at lunch!"

Lindsey waved and turned back to her computer. The cursor on the blank document in front of her blinked impatiently. She glanced at the notes she'd made on the legal pad beside her. Surely, writing a class description and choosing software could not be more difficult than getting her master's degree in information science, right?

She studied her notes, felt suitably daunted, and decided she needed to get up and do a walkabout of the library. Avoidance? Yes. But as the director of the library, she tried to meet and greet as many patrons as she could during her short time on the reference desk. Also, it gave her a chance to browse the new books.

She passed through the adult reference area, which was quiet, and moved to the general fiction section. Three of the study carrels were in use by local college students, cramming for their fall semester finals, and several more patrons were browsing.

In the periodical area, Milton Duffy was in the corner in his usual position, standing on his head, while he did his yoga practice. His eyes were shut, so Lindsey didn't interrupt him. He was one of the town's biggest advocates of the library, led the chess club every Wednesday afternoon, and was dating Mayor Cole, so Lindsey was fine with him standing on his head wherever his heart desired.

She reached the prominently displayed new bookshelves by the front door and paused. The holidays were a little less than two weeks away, and the first December snow had fallen, leaving the town blanketed in white and fully representing the famed New England Christmas charm. She wanted something to read that matched the holiday spirit.

She supposed she could revisit a classic like *Little Women*, but there was so much more going on in the novel than the holidays, and she didn't want to overcommit emotionally. She supposed she could read a holiday thriller or just watch *Die Hard*. She picked up a Meg Langslow mystery set during Christmas by Donna Andrews. This definitely had the humor and heart she was seeking. She scanned the bookshelf for more and scored a holiday Royal Spyness mystery by Rhys Bowen. Christmas in England with Lady Georgie. Her evening was looking up.

Lindsey left the new books and approached circulation,

taking her place in line. She wanted to ask her colleague how things were going, but she didn't want to cut ahead of anyone to do it. There was only one person in front of her, and Lindsey tried to identify her from the back, which wasn't easy given that, like everyone else during this December cold snap, the patron was swaddled in winter gear.

From the back, she was a tall woman, almost as tall as Lindsey, with chin-length wavy dark hair. She was wearing a long, navy wool coat over wide-legged tweed pants and thick-soled brown lace-up boots. She had a Louis Vuitton handbag dangling from her elbow, and a pair of Ray-Ban sunglasses were pushed back on her head. When she turned, Lindsey recognized her profile.

It was Helen Monroe, who had just been installed by the Briar Creek Friends of the Library as the town's writer in residence. Helen had been working in one of the study rooms in the library for a little over a week, and other than the reception to welcome her, Lindsey hadn't had much of an opportunity to speak with her.

Lindsey had tried to engage Helen in conversation the few times their paths had crossed, but Helen hadn't been receptive. Still, Lindsey was always polite. She wanted anyone who used the library to know that they were among friends even if they wanted to keep their distance.

Paula Turner, the head of circulation, was manning the desk and assisting Helen. Paula was known for her elaborate tattoos—although they weren't currently visible beneath the turtleneck sweater she was wearing—and her colorful hair. Presently, it was a stunning shade of bright red, and she had fastened it into a thick braid that draped over her shoulder, tied with a scarlet-and-green-striped ribbon. Very festive.

"Here you are, Ms. Monroe." Paula pushed the short stack of books across the counter, and Lindsey glanced at the pile. She didn't mean to be rude, but she was curious to see what the writer in residence was checking out so she might be able to deduce what Helen was working on. So far, it had been kept very hush-hush.

In a move that had shocked the publishing world, Helen had declared that she had series fatigue and killed off the protagonist of her long-running thriller series. She announced she would no longer write the beloved Mallory Quest mysteries, which had rocketed her to iconic thriller writer status over the past decade.

The outcry among her fan base had been significant, and the reviews of her final book were mixed. Fans who couldn't forgive the abrupt demise of Mallory Quest vilified her for the betrayal while critics praised her for making a bold literary choice and elevating the genre. Lindsey could see both sides, but personally she had been very sad to see the end of the popular series.

When Carrie Rushton, the president of the Friends, had suggested that they host a writer in residence for the winter months in Briar Creek, no one had expected an author of Helen's caliber to apply. Wanting to launch what they hoped would be an annual program, the Friends naturally jumped at the opportunity to have Helen as their inaugural writer. It was particularly perfect because Helen lived in

Fairfield, just down the shoreline from Briar Creek, which basically made her a local author.

The post was fairly low-maintenance for Helen. She spent every morning in the library, writing in one of the glassed-in study rooms, where anyone could watch her at work. It was a bit like a fishbowl, and Lindsey was initially surprised that Helen, who seemed very private, was okay with it. Having watched her, Lindsey had noted that Helen did as much pacing as she did writing, and she spent long stretches of time staring off into space. It appeared the little room was fine for the pacing and the staring and the occasional flurry of typing on her laptop.

In addition to her in-house writing time, Helen was scheduled to do a short program every week where she talked about an aspect of writing, such as research, plotting or editing. Whatever Helen was in the mood to discuss would be the topic of the day. Because space was limited, patrons had registered for the first one, which was scheduled for Friday afternoon, in advance. It was fully booked—with a wait list—a half hour after registration had opened. Carrie had been thrilled and Lindsey was, too.

The books Paula pushed toward Helen didn't look familiar, and Lindsey studied the spines, which revealed them to be an assortment of information science technical manuals that Lindsey hadn't seen since getting her master's degree. Being academic resources, they definitely weren't items the public library owned, so Lindsey assumed that Helen had ordered them through their interlibrary loan service. Interesting.

"Thank you, Paula." Helen scooped up the books and turned, almost bumping into Lindsey.

"Doing a little light reading?" Lindsey asked. Helen didn't smile. She clutched the pile close to her chest as if she was trying to hide them. Was Helen concerned that Lindsey was judging her? Lindsey felt the need to explain. "It was a joke, you know, because the books are so big?"

Helen lowered her sunglasses over her eyes as if they were a shield. "Yes, I gathered that was the gist of your witty observation."

"Oh, good." Lindsey suddenly felt incredibly awkward and uncomfortable in her own skin. She didn't want to leave the conversation like this. "I'm happy to see you using our services. Is there anything else we can help you with?"

Helen lifted her sunglasses and stared at Lindsey. "That depends. Are you a skilled laborer as well as a librarian? I could use some tile work done in the bathroom of my cottage."

"Uh . . . no." Lindsey shook her head.

"That's a shame." Helen lowered her sunglasses again.

Given her deadpan demeanor, Lindsey had to assume that Helen was joking. There was no way she could be this frosty for real, could she? *Nah.*

"We do maintain a list of local handypersons in our files if you need some recommendations," Lindsey offered.

"I'll keep that in mind." Helen made a noise that sounded like an impressed humph.

Lindsey would take it as a win. Probably, she should let Helen get on with her day. She certainly didn't want to press her luck with the acerbic writer, but it was the holidays and Helen was new here, and Lindsey didn't want her to feel lonely.

"I don't know if you're interested, but—"

"I'm not," Helen interrupted her but Lindsey continued undaunted.

"We have a crafternoon group that meets every Thursday," Lindsey forged on. Helen sighed impatiently. "We have a book discussion, share lunch, and do a craft." She could see Paula making a slashing motion across her throat behind Helen's back. Lindsey ignored her. "We're meeting soon, and you're welcome to join us if you'd like."

Helen stood still for a moment as if considering. Then she tipped her head to the side and said, "That is a very generous offer considering I've never given you any indication that I would be even remotely interested in anything like that. So thank you, but no."

With that, Helen strode out the door without a backward glance.

"Lindsey, what were you thinking?" Paula hissed. "That woman is not crafternoon material."

"You don't know that," Lindsey said. "She could be aloof because she's shy."

"No." Paula shook her head. "She is not shy. She is antisocial, there's a difference."

"I think she's funny," Lindsey countered.

"Inasmuch as sharpened knives are hilarious," Paula said.

Lindsey raised her hands in surrender. She knew there

was no way Paula was ever going to agree with her about Helen.

"I'm going to keep the invitation open regardless," Lindsey said. "She's new in town and she's our writer in residence. She could probably use a friend."

She felt a patron approach from behind, and she moved aside so that Paula could help them. The woman was bundled in a puffy white coat with a pink-and-white-striped hat on her head topped by a huge pink pom-pom with a matching scarf looped about her neck.

"Can you believe she's here?" the woman asked. Her voice was high pitched with excitement as if she knew some juicy gossip and couldn't wait to share. Lindsey found that off-putting, but she didn't get a chance to answer as the woman plowed on. "That was H. R. Monroe, author of the Mallory Quest novels."

"We know," Paula said. She studied the woman as if trying to determine what she should say. No one liked spoilers, and maybe the woman didn't know the series had been concluded. "But she's working on something new now."

"Oh, that." The woman waved her hand dismissively. "She'll change her mind. She has to. The only thing she knows how to write is Mallory Quest."

Lindsey and Paula exchanged a glance. The woman had her mind made up, and there was clearly no debating with her. Maybe this was why Helen was so private outside of her residency. Perhaps she'd had her fill of fans and followers telling her what to do. That made perfect sense to Lindsey.

"I'm Jackie," the woman introduced herself, placing a stack of novels on the counter. Judging by the Friends of the Library stickers on the book covers, they were from the book sale shelf that the Friends maintained in the library lobby. One dollar per book was a bargain. "And I'm Helen's number one . . . fan."

There was a slight hesitation before the word *fan*, and Lindsey felt herself shift into high alert. There was something manic about Jackie's declaration that made her uncomfortable. Lindsey had dealt with a stalker of her own before, and she knew how fixated they could become.

"So, you've met Helen and she knows you?" Lindsey clarified. No need to panic. Probably Helen knew Jackie, and they were online buddies or something.

"Oh, yes, Helen knows me," Jackie said. There was something ominous in her tone that made the hair on Lindsey's neck prickle with unease. Something must have shown on her face, because Jackie threw back her head and laughed and added, "Relax, Helen and I go way back. When I heard she was going to be the writer in residence, I decided to come stay at the Beachfront Bed and Breakfast and see if I could meet up with her and give us a chance to catch up."

She winked at them, and Lindsey exchanged a concerned glance with Paula. This was not good. Jackie might be harmless, but the fact that she had followed Helen here was worrisome. This had been Lindsey's one fear when Carrie had proposed the writer in residence program. She hadn't wanted overzealous readers to take advantage of the author.

"Did you visit with her while she was here in the library today?" Paula asked. "Or register to attend her talk tomorrow?"

"No." Jackie looked annoyed. "I didn't want to interrupt her, and I missed the sign-up for her talk. But I'm certain she'll be happy to see me when we run into each other. Briar Creek is such a small village it would be impossible not to."

"I don't know," Lindsey said. "Helen seems to be a very private person."

"That's okay," Jackie insisted. "I told you, we go way back. I'm sure she'll be happy to see me."

Paula took the money that Jackie handed her and counted it. "Five dollars exactly. You're all set."

"Thanks." Jackie grinned and scooped the books up in her arms. "Byeeee."

Lindsey and Paula watched her step through the automatic doors and hunch into her coat against the cold winter wind that blew in from the bay. Jackie disappeared down the sidewalk, and Lindsey said, "We should warn Helen about her, don't you think?"

"I think we should mind our own business," Paula said. "Every time we don't, we end up in a murder investigation and it's very stressful."

"But I have a weird feeling about Jackie," Lindsey said. "You know, a stalker-like feeling."

Paula sighed. She lifted the end of her braid and adjusted the ribbon on the end. "I do, too, but we could just be over-reacting because of prior situations. Here's a thought, let's ask the crafternooners what they think."

"Good idea." Lindsey nodded. "I'm certain they'll be the voice of reason and agree we should warn Helen."

"Or not," Paula countered, giving Lindsey a pointed look.

CHAPTER

2

BRIAR CREEK
PUBLIC LIBRARY

Y ou have to tell her," Nancy Peyton declared. She was
somewhere in her late seventies with short white hair
and bright blue eyes. In winter, she favored turtleneck
shirts under brightly colored sweatshirts with jeans, all
three of which she ironed neatly before wearing.

"No, you can't. The woman didn't make a threat. She's
probably just a devoted fan who is overly enthusiastic," Violet LaRue reasoned. She was Nancy's best friend—one
was seldom seen without the other—and they very rarely
disagreed.

Violet was known for wearing flowing caftans, but with
the arrival of colder temperatures, she had opted for a
pretty lavender tunic sweater, accentuating her deep brown
complexion, over black yoga pants. She wore her silver hair

in a bun at the nape of her neck, and her reader glasses hung from a colorful beaded chain around her neck. A former Broadway actress, Violet ran the local community theater with her friend Robbie Vine, another actor and resident of Briar Creek.

"One for and one against," Lindsey said to Paula.

"I'm against and you're for, so that makes it two to two." Paula held up two fingers on each hand. She glanced across the table. "Mary, you haven't voted yet."

Mary was tapping her chin with her index finger as she pondered the situation. "I'm trying to decide what my brother would say and vote for him since whatever you decide will impact him much more than me."

Mary Murphy was Lindsey's sister-in-law as Lindsey had married Mary's brother, Sully, proper name Mike Sullivan, two years prior. Mary had the same bright blue eyes and wavy reddish brown hair as Sully, but where he was a quiet sort, Mary was not.

She ran the Blue Anchor, the only restaurant in the village, with her husband, Ian Murphy, who was also Sully's business partner in their water taxi and tour boat venture. Together they shuttled the inhabitants of the Thumb Islands, an archipelago of one hundred islands, if the big rocks were included, to and from the shore, while also providing tourists a look at the famed islands during the summer touring season.

"Sully would agree with me." Lindsey was fairly confident that he would but only after she talked him into it.

"Would he?" Mary narrowed her eyes at Lindsey. "He cares about you more than anything and would not want you to get yourself into another 'situation.'"

"I won't," Lindsey protested. "I'm merely informing a person I know that she might have a potential stalker."

"*Potential* being the operative word," Mary said. "You have no proof that Jackie is a stalker, so I have to say no. Don't get involved."

"Three to two," Paula said.

"What did I miss?" A snowperson dashed into the room. It was Beth. She tossed her cap onto an empty chair and pulled the extra-large T-shirt over her head. "Wait, where's the food?"

"Mayor Cole was detained," Paula said. "But she'll be here shortly."

"With meatball subs?" Beth asked.

"Yes, she confirmed the menu," Mary said.

"All is forgiven." Beth sat on the closest chair at the table. "What are we discussing? The book?"

"We haven't gotten to that yet," Paula said. She then told Beth about Lindsey's dilemma and asked her if she thought Lindsey should tell Helen about Jackie.

"Absolutely." Beth turned to Lindsey. "You have to let her know. What if this Jackie person is dangerous?"

"And now we're three and three," Paula said.

"Three and three what?" Mayor Cole asked as she entered the room pushing one of their book trucks. On top was a silver tray covered in foil and a large plastic bowl

with a tossed salad, and on the shelf below were two ca-
rafes, one with iced tea and one with lemonade.

The crafternooners all rose from their seats and helped
set the food on the table. While the subs and salad were
dished out, and the drinks poured, Paula explained the difference of opinion to Mayor Cole.

Eugenia Cole had been Ms. Cole when Lindsey first arrived as the new library director several years ago. Ms.
Cole, formerly called "the lemon" among the staff because
her personality had been rather puckered, had been an old-
school shusher of a librarian. Rules were rules and they
were meant to be upheld. Lindsey's more relaxed style had
not been a welcome change.

Glancing at the professional woman in front of her now,
it was hard for Lindsey to reconcile that it was the same
Ms. Cole she'd first met. Back then, Ms. Cole's personal
style had been to dress monochromatically, and while a
person might think that all shades of pink go together, they
do not.

When Ms. Cole made her bid for the position of mayor,
Beth had taken her in hand as her campaign manager, and
revamped Ms. Cole's wardrobe. Now the mayor dressed
for success in tailored pantsuits, regularly visited a mani-
curist and kept her hair professionally styled, leaving behind her former fat sausage curls and embracing a sleek
chin-length bob. Mayor Cole was a force of nature.

It had taken Lindsey years to find common ground with
Ms. Cole, but now she considered the formidable librarian
turned mayor a close friend.

The mayor nodded and munched her sub while she listened. When Paula had finished, Ms. Cole dabbed her lips with her napkin and asked, "Is there any reason to think that this Jackie person might harm the author?"

"No specific threat was made, if that's what you're asking." Lindsey drizzled dressing on her salad.

"I am. Do you know where the writer in residence lives?" Mayor Cole asked.

"No, the Friends of the Library are in charge of the program and arranged her housing. I know it's a cottage along the shore, but I'm not sure of the exact address," Lindsey admitted. She knew this was going to be a sticking point.

"You can't use the patron records to look it up," Ms. Cole said. "That's going too far. I'm afraid unless you run into her and have the opportunity to tell her about her admirer, you have to keep the information to yourself."

"Are you telling me this as my friend or my boss?" Lindsey asked.

"Both," Mayor Cole said. "You know how I feel about protecting patron privacy."

"At all costs," Lindsey acknowledged. "But Helen doesn't come back for her writer in residence shift until tomorrow morning, and who knows what could happen between then and now."

"Unless there was a direct threat, I don't think you can justify showing up at her house tonight. Tomorrow would be the appropriate time to tell her," Mayor Cole concluded.

"But—"

Mayor Cole shook her head. "No buts. Now, who read the book and what did you think?"

"The kites," Beth cried, slumping back in her seat with her hand on her heart. "They made each other kites for Christmas."

"Such lovely imagery," Violet agreed.

The discussion of Capote's *A Christmas Memory* and the joy found in his bittersweet childhood recollections took over the conversation. Lindsey listened but her mind was still on Helen. She knew what she'd felt when Jackie had talked about being Helen's number one fan, and it was concern bordering on alarm. She bit into her sub and tried to think of alternate ways to discover where Helen lived.

"Don't worry." Nancy leaned close and whispered, "I bet we can flush her out."

"Helen?" Lindsey asked.

"No, Jackie. We know she's staying at the Beachfront. We'll befriend her and get her to tell us what she's up to," Nancy said.

"You think she's going to admit to us that she's a stalker?" Lindsey asked.

"What are you two whispering about?" Mary asked. Her daughter Josie was a toddler, and she clearly had the hearing of a parent who knew mischief when she heard it.

"We were debating ways to befriend Jackie," Nancy confessed.

Mayor Cole glanced at them over the rim of her glass of lemonade. "I did not hear that."

"Befriend her?" Paula asked.

"Yes," Nancy said. "Then we could keep an eye on her, and maybe if she's busy helping us with all of the holiday activities around Briar Creek, she won't have time to stalk Ms. Monroe."

"I suppose that could work, but I'd be more comfortable saying something to Helen directly. I mean if something happens to her and I didn't warn her, then I'd be partly to blame," Lindsey said.

"No, you wouldn't. The person who does the harming is to blame," Beth countered. "I think Nancy's right. We should befriend Jackie."

"If by that you mean to invade this Jackie person's privacy, I can't condone that either," Mayor Cole said.

"From what Lindsey and Paula have said, Jackie offered up loads of information about herself." Beth speared a cucumber with her fork. "She told them who she was, what she was doing here and even where she's staying."

"That's true," Lindsey said. "We could invite her to—"

"Not to the crafternoon group." Paula cut her off. They all turned to look at her, and she grimaced. "Sorry, it's just that the group is perfect as is, and I don't think we should invite someone who may have a malevolent agenda into our circle just because we're trying to find out more about them. Crafternoon is a sacred space."

"She's right." Violet nodded. "There are plenty of activities happening in town that we could invite Jackie to, which would allow us to get to know her and determine whether Helen is in danger or not."

"We might find out she's harmless," Mary said. "And then you won't have to cause Helen any undue worry."

"That does seem like a solid plan," Lindsey said. "So what activities are happening this week?"

"There's the tree lighting and caroling at the town green," Paula said. "And everyone is welcome."

"The annual Christmas pageant at the community theater is happening," Violet added. "We're always looking for volunteers."

"There's the bake sale at the senior center," Nancy said. "Everyone turns out for that."

"Tomorrow is the ugly Christmas sweater party for the Friends of the Library," Beth said. "Carrie Rushton said that Helen has agreed to be one of the judges."

"Really?" Lindsey was surprised. "Mayor Cole and I are both judges."

"It's happening right after her program," Beth explained. "The Friends are funding her writer in residence situation, so I don't think Helen could refuse."

"All right," Lindsey said. "Jackie is staying at the Beachfront Bed and Breakfast. I can pop over and bring Jeanette Palmer the latest Anita Blake book by Laurell K. Hamilton. She's first on the list and we just finished processing it."

"Jeanette does love her vampires," Paula said.

Jeanette, who owned the bed-and-breakfast, was eighty-something and preferred her vampires to be smoking hot, which was against type, given that she was a petite grandmotherly-looking lady who wore her snow-white hair in a topknot and was partial to comfortable shoes and cardigans.

"Yes, she does," Lindsey agreed. "Maybe Jeanette has gotten to know Jackie a bit and can vouch for her being okay."

"Which she probably is," Mayor Cole said.

Lindsey and Paula exchanged a glance, and Lindsey knew Paula was as doubtful as she was.

"Now that that's settled, what is our craft this week?" Beth asked. "I was so consumed with making my snowperson outfit for story time, I didn't have a chance to work on anything else."

"I'm so glad you asked." Paula stood up and grabbed a very large plastic storage container from the floor beside her chair. "We're making paper ornaments using all of the book covers from the titles we read this year."

Paula pulled several baggies out of the tub and a handful of glue sticks. The crafternooners quickly finished eating, and the craft materials were passed out. Lindsey glanced at the baggie full of paper circles about the size of a silver dollar. She could see each one had a small picture of the cover of the different books they'd read, but she had no idea how they were supposed to be made into an ornament. Paula took a couple of finished ornaments out of the tub and put them on the table.

"Oh, I see!" Beth opened her baggie of circles and dumped them on the table. "You fold three sides of the circle, making it a triangle, and then glue the folded sides together until the triangles form a ball."

"Exactly." Paula beamed at her. "Five circles glued together make the top, ten make the middle, and five the bottom, so you need twenty in all."

Lindsey opened the bag and spread the circles out. She had no idea what Beth meant but figured if she copied what everyone else did, she'd be able to fake it. Or maybe she could avoid the whole thing by discussing the book that they'd read.

"I think my favorite line in *A Christmas Memory* was 'It's fruitcake weather!'" Lindsey said.

"Oh, I loved that," Nancy agreed. "And how Buddy and his friend made all of those fruitcakes not just for people they knew but for people they felt were kind or interesting."

"That was lovely." Violet held the folded sides of two circles together while the glue dried. "We should have a fruitcake-making day."

"Ugh, no thank you, fruitcake is the worst," Mary chimed in.

"That's only because you haven't had my fruitcake cookies," Nancy retorted. "How is that possible?"

"I don't know but it's clearly an oversight." Mary glued another circle to the ring she'd crafted. She glanced up and smiled at Nancy.

"I will rectify it posthaste." Nancy put her hand on her heart. "Promise."

"I read that the story is autobiographical. That 'Buddy' in the story is Capote, and his unnamed 'friend' in the story was his cousin Sook," Beth said.

"I read that, too," Mayor Cole confirmed. "The story is set in the late nineteen thirties. It was such a different time. The dire poverty of the Depression era is hard to imagine."

Mayor Cole had almost finished her ornament, and

Lindsey hurried to catch up, managing only to get glue all over the tips of her fingers, which made the paper stick to them. Seeing Lindsey's dilemma, Paula handed her a wet paper towel and gently took the project away from her, finishing the gluing for her before handing it back.

"It was a brutal time," Violet agreed. "Speaking of those in need, the Briar Creek Fire Department is running their annual food and toy drive. We're collecting for them at the theater as well."

"We have a collection bin at the library, too," Lindsey said. "Is it wrong that I'm hoping people will donate books?"

"Never! Books are food for the mind." Beth held up her finished ball of circles. Crafting just came naturally to her. "We could put the Friends of the Library book sale cart next to the donation bin and encourage patrons to buy those books and donate them."

"Genius!" Lindsey declared. "I'll move the bin after crafternoon."

Paula handed her the finished ornament that Lindsey had unsuccessfully started, and said, "All you have to do is attach the ribbon."

Lindsey gave her a dubious look.

Paula smiled. "I believe in you."

Lindsey sighed. She watched Violet use a metal yarn needle to thread the ribbon through two of the glued edges. She picked up her needle and ribbon, threaded the ribbon in the needle, poked a hole in the glued section and pulled the ribbon through. Achievement!

Lindsey tied off the ribbon, making it a hanging loop for the ornament, and held it up. It really was a festive decoration, and she loved seeing the tiny images of the front covers of the books they'd read. Paula had chosen the perfect craft.

"We should make these to decorate the library," Lindsey suggested.

"Way ahead of you, boss," Paula said. "Our teen volunteers will be working on these to hang all over the building, and we were thinking that at our annual Christmas Eve open house, we'd let people take them home. That'll save us from having to store or discard them."

"We are not paying you enough, Paula," Lindsey said.

"Agreed," Mayor Cole said. "Remember that at your annual review."

Paula grinned. "Oh, I will. And now I have witnesses."

The meeting ended with a confirmation of next week's book. They were going to stick with the holiday theme and read Jennifer Chiaverini's *Christmas Bells*, and Beth had already acquired the copies from interlibrary loan.

As promised, Lindsey moved the gift donation bin next to the Friends of the Library book sale truck. Ann Marie, the adult services librarian, was manning the reference desk while Paula returned to the circulation counter, joining their part-time clerk. With the library fully staffed, Lindsey figured this was as good a time as any to drop in at the bed-and-breakfast.

She grabbed her long wool coat from her office and looped her scarf about her neck. She'd worn her leather boots today and was as prepared for the cold as she could be, given that the temperatures had been steadily dropping all week. She checked out the book to Jeanette and tucked it safely into a canvas book bag.

As she stepped outside, she collided with a patron coming in. Instinctively, he caught her by the arms before she fell.

"Oh, no, you've got that determined look in your eyes," he said. "What are you up to now, Lindsey?"

CHAPTER

3

BRIAR CREEK
PUBLIC LIBRARY

R obbie!" Lindsey clutched the lapels of his jacket and
steadied herself. "What makes you think I'm up to
something, and why are you charging into the library as if
it's on fire?"

"I have *big* news," he said.

"I only have a few minutes for my break and I have to
run an errand. Walk and talk." Lindsey gestured for him to
follow her as she started down the sidewalk.

"Really?" His British accent thickened with his disap-
pointment. "I pictured us sharing a pot of tea and some
biscuits whilst I told you my news."

"Places to go, people to see." Lindsey continued walking.

"Fine." As he hurried to catch up to her, he huffed a
breath, and it came out in a plume. Robbie adjusted his flat
cap with a gloved hand and tightened the scarf he wore

beneath the collar of his coat. "It's bloody cold out here. Where are you going that's so important?"

"To the Beachfront," Lindsey said. "I need to see Jeanette."

"More smexy vampire books for her?" he asked.

Lindsey laughed. Jeanette's literary taste was well known in the village. "Smart and sexy? Yes. Jeanette says she keeps her standards high in her fictional boyfriends."

Robbie squinted at her as they turned onto Main Street. The road ran along the water, and a bitter wind blew in from the bay. Lindsey felt the sting of it against her cheeks, and she lowered her face into her scarf, trying to keep warm.

"I feel like you're leaving out pertinent details," he said.

"Such as?" Lindsey asked.

"I don't know, because you're leaving them out."

Lindsey shrugged. "Tell me your news, then."

"Well, I was inspired by our writer in residence, H. R. Monroe," he began.

"You're going to write a novel?"

"No." He shook his head. "I am, however, going to option the rights to the Mallory Quest novels to make a short streaming series out of them. What do you think?"

Lindsey had no idea what to think. When she'd done her research on the author after Helen accepted the residency, Lindsey had read an interview where Helen stated that she loathed the film industry, because they never respected the vision of the writer, and she vowed she would never sell the rights to her books. Lindsey couldn't imagine that she'd changed her mind, as Helen didn't strike her as a person who waffled once a decision was made.

"You know she's not a fan of the film industry?" Lindsey asked.

Robbie waved a dismissive hand before quickly tucking it back in his coat pocket to keep warm. "She just needs the right person to execute her vision."

"I'm not so sure about that," Lindsey cautioned him. "I get the feeling that Helen is done with the Mallory Quest series and that's that."

"What's she working on now?" Robbie asked. "I still can't believe she walked away from her series at the top of her game."

"I admit that I'm going to miss Mallory Quest." Lindsey turned onto a side street, and Robbie turned with her. "She hasn't told us what she's working on. Apparently, there is supposed to be a big reveal at the end of her residency."

"Are you sure she's not going to bring Mallory back?"

"I don't see how she can when she killed her off."

"Maybe it wasn't really Mallory but an evil twin," Robbie suggested.

"Please make sure I'm with you when you tell her that theory," Lindsey said. She turned up the walkway to the Beachfront. "I want to see her reaction."

Robbie gave her the side-eye. "I feel like you're setting me up."

"Me?" Lindsey blinked innocently.

"Yes, you," he said.

She laughed and climbed the steps of the front porch

and rang the bell. She stomped her feet on the doormat while they waited.

In moments, Jeanette appeared, opening first the heavy wooden front door and then the storm door. "Lindsey, Robbie, what a nice surprise! Come in, come in, you'll freeze to death out there in the cold."

Lindsey entered the cheery bed-and-breakfast, and Robbie followed.

"I brought you the latest Anita Blake, Vampire Hunter novel." Lindsey took the book out of the bag and handed it to Jeanette, who promptly hugged it to her chest. "The weather forecast says a snowstorm is coming, and I thought you could use a good book."

"Oh, thank you," she said. "I was hoping to get to the library today, then I got sidetracked by chores. But here you are offering delivery service. How wonderful. I hope you can both visit for a bit."

Lindsey smiled. "Of course."

They toed off their boots and hung their jackets on the coatrack in the foyer. Jeanette led the way into the front parlor. It was a large room, painted a soft butter yellow, with a fire crackling in the redbrick fireplace. Small groupings of furniture filled the room, inviting the guests of the bed-and-breakfast to settle in and stay awhile.

"I was just making some hot cocoa," Jeanette said. "Join me?"

"Yes, please." Lindsey nodded.

"Sounds lovely," Robbie agreed.

"Make yourselves comfortable," Jeanette said. "I'll be right back." She put the novel on the coffee table and departed for the kitchen at the back of the house.

"All right, what gives?" Robbie asked, sitting in one of the armchairs by the fire.

Lindsey took the one across from him and said, "I have no idea what you're talking about."

"Right." He rolled his eyes. "This is me, love, I know you. Did someone die?"

"What? No," Lindsey retorted. "At least, not yet."

"The plot thickens," he said. "Is Jeanette a suspect?"

"Of course not!" Lindsey shook her head. She lowered her voice to whisper, "But there is a person staying here that I am interested in knowing more about."

There was a pause, and Robbie rolled his eyes at her and said, "Because?"

"Because—" Lindsey began, but Jeanette stepped into the room, bearing a tray that had three steaming mugs and an open cookie tin.

Robbie rose and crossed the room, taking the tray from Jeanette and placing it on the coffee table for her.

"Thank you, Robbie. I hope you like shortbread."

"Love it." Robbie helped himself to a napkin and plucked a shortbread in the shape of a Scottie dog out of the red-and-black-plaid tin. He lifted his mug and dunked the cookie in the hot cocoa, devouring it in one bite.

Jeanette smiled in approval. She turned to Lindsey and said, "Other than the book, what brings you by?"

"Nothing specific." Lindsey lifted her mug and took a sip. The cocoa was thick and rich with a hint of orange. "Oh, this is delicious."

"Thank you." Jeanette smiled. "Secret family recipe."

"It's exceptional," Robbie complimented her.

Jeanette bobbed her head in acknowledgment. She then turned to Lindsey with a speculative gaze and asked, "Now would 'nothing specific' have to do with a certain guest of mine named Jackie Lewis?"

"Jackie Lewis?" Lindsey blinked. "The author?"

"Yes, she writes a very steamy space police series." Jeanette wagged her eyebrows with excitement. "You could have knocked me over with a feather when she called and booked a room."

"I had no idea," Lindsey said. Which was true. Although she *had* come to find out more about Jackie, she hadn't expected this bit of information. She blinked, trying to look innocent. Robbie shook his head. It was well-known that Lindsey was a terrible actress. "What makes you think I came because of her?"

"Because it's the off-season and she's my only guest at the moment," Jeanette said. "Also, as wonderful as you are as the director of the library, I have never known you to deliver books being held for patrons, unless they're ill or living out on the islands."

"She's got you there," Robbie said.

"Is Jackie in at the moment?" Lindsey asked.

"No," Jeanette said. She glanced at the front door as if

she was expecting it to open at any moment. It didn't, and she continued, "She said she had some reconnaissance to do. Whatever that means."

Lindsey exchanged a glance with Robbie, who raised his eyebrows.

"Is she a military person?" he asked.

"Not that I'm aware of," Jeanette said. "I do know that she's here because she wants to visit with your writer in residence, H. R. Monroe. She said they go way back."

"She said the same thing to me," Lindsey said. "But weirdly didn't identify herself as a writer at the time."

"She's certainly not keeping her reason for being here a secret," Robbie said.

"No, she was very clear on her purpose," Jeanette agreed. She nibbled a shortbread.

Lindsey stared into the fire and sipped her cocoa. She didn't want to influence Jeanette against her guest, but she wanted to know if Jeanette had gotten a cautionary feeling about Jackie.

"You have hundreds of guests here each year," Lindsey observed.

"I do." Jeanette sipped her cocoa. "The income is welcome and I'm a people person—every stranger is a friend I haven't met yet."

"That's a lovely philosophy, Jeanette." Robbie took another shortbread.

"Are there some guests that you haven't clicked with over the years?" Lindsey asked.

Robbie sent her a knowing look, which she ignored.

"Absolutely," Jeanette said. "Human beings are complicated. I can usually cajole a guest into a better frame of mind, but I've had a few curmudgeons that couldn't be budged out of their negativity."

"Would you say you're good at reading a person's character, then?" Robbie asked.

He had obviously figured out Lindsey's circuitous route for extracting information and was giving her an assist, which she appreciated.

"I think so," Jeanette said. "I've had a few people call to make reservations, and I could tell by our phone conversation that I wouldn't be comfortable having them stay here, and weirdly I'm always booked up on the dates they request."

"What a coincidence." Robbie grinned and Jeanette returned it.

"What about Jackie?" Lindsey asked. "What sort of vibe do you get off her?"

"And now we're at the heart of it." Jeanette waved a cookie at Lindsey.

"I suppose we are," Lindsey conceded.

"Do you mind if I ask why you're interested?" Jeanette asked.

"It's just a feeling I had." Lindsey set her mug down and leaned forward. "I can't explain it, but when Jackie said she and Helen went way back, it made the hair on the back of my neck stand on end."

"Given what happened to you with that stalker you had

a while back, it's small wonder." Jeanette reached across the space between them and patted Lindsey's knee.

Lindsey appreciated the sympathy, but she also wondered if that was why she reacted so strongly to Jackie's obsession with Helen. Mayor Cole was right. It wasn't any of Lindsey's business. And maybe Jackie was just a very enthusiastic reader, and being a writer herself, she must admire Helen's success. Lindsey had certainly read books that had changed her life, and she was ever grateful to the authors who'd written the stories that captured her imagination.

Of course, Lindsey didn't follow them to a small village on the shoreline and do reconnaissance as she planned how she would run into them . . . and there it was. The prickle of unease that had put her on high alert was back, insistent in its warning that something wasn't right with this situation.

"As far as I can tell, Jackie is just a die-hard Mallory Quest fan," Jeanette said. "I mean, who isn't? Even I loved that series, despite its unfortunate lack of vampires."

Lindsey huffed a small laugh, which she was certain was Jeanette's intention. She took a cookie and dunked it in her hot chocolate. "Maybe I am just being oversensitive."

"No one would blame you." Robbie chomped on another cookie, putting a nice dent in the quantity in the tin.

"I'm sorry to have interrupted your day," Lindsey said.

"Not at all." Jeanette waved a dismissive hand at her. "You brought my book, which saved me a trip."

They were all silent for a beat, enjoying the cocoa and

the fire, and Lindsey knew she should let it go but she just couldn't.

"I am probably being ridiculous, but if you notice anything suspicious about Jack—" Lindsey began but was cut off by Robbie when he had a sudden coughing fit, which was odd because he'd already swallowed his cookie.

"Jack or Jackie?" a voice asked from the doorway.

Lindsey whipped her head in that direction and saw Jackie Lewis standing there, staring at her with an intensity that almost made Lindsey squirm.

CHAPTER

4

BRIAR CREEK
PUBLIC LIBRARY

Jack," Jeanette said. "He's the raccoon who lives in the woods across the street." She smiled at Jackie as she continued, "You didn't hear him banging around on the neighbor's trash cans last night?"

Jackie lifted her eyebrows and shook her head.

"He's been a real menace in the neighborhood. Very smart, very sneaky, very suspicious."

Robbie raised his eyebrows as he watched Jeanette tell her fib as if it were an actual fact. Even Lindsey, who knew better, started to believe the neighborhood was being terrorized by a raccoon.

"Don't raccoons hibernate?" Jackie asked. She pulled off her pink-and-white-striped hat and unzipped her puffy white coat.

Busted! Lindsey glanced out the window at the cold

winter's day. There was no way a raccoon with any sense of self-preservation would be out in that.

"No, they don't," Jeanette said.

Lindsey turned back to her in surprise. Was this true? How did she not know this?

"When it gets really cold, they enter a dormant state called a torpor," Jeanette explained. "It only lasts a few weeks, and judging by Jack's shenanigans last night, he's not there yet."

"Oh, well, if that's the case." Jackie's shoulders visibly dropped, and she chuckled. "I thought . . . well, it doesn't matter."

"Would you like some hot chocolate?" Jeanette asked.

Jackie looked as if she was considering it. "I'd love to, but I have to go get ready."

"Hot date?" Jeanette asked.

Jackie smiled. It was a closed-lip smile, the sort that held secrets. "Something like that."

She turned and headed for the stairs. "Thanks for asking though."

Lindsey felt her opportunity to get to know Jackie slipping through her grasp. She stood up and said, "You're an author?"

"That's right." Jackie paused on the bottom step. She glanced at Jeanette and asked, "Did you mention me?"

"Lindsey recognized you." Jeanette sipped her cocoa.

"Really?" Jackie asked.

"Librarian," Lindsey said with a shrug. She did not like how this was going.

Jackie's eyes lit up. "Are you a fan of my work?"

"Uh . . ." Lindsey knew there was no way she could pull off a lie—especially if Jackie asked her what her favorite book of Jackie's was—so she said, "Sadly, you've been on my to-be-read pile, but I haven't gotten there yet. Of course, now that I've met you . . ."

"My books will get moved up?" Jackie asked with a laugh. There was a bitterness in it that made Lindsey wince. "I guess my trip was well worth it, then."

And awkwardness filled the room like a bad smell, and Robbie stood up and said, "We love our holiday season around here, don't we, Jeanette?"

Jeanette sent him a confused glance but said, "We sure do."

"You should join us in some of our activities, Jackie," Robbie said. "Right, Lindsey?"

"Yes! We're having some really fun events this weekend," Lindsey said. "And we are very much a 'the more the merrier' community."

Jackie looked surprised and said, "I don't know. I have a lot of plans of my own."

There it was. The warning bell in Lindsey's head, telling her that Jackie was up to something.

"Of course you do," Robbie agreed. Lindsey heard his British accent thicken as he poured on the charm. "A lovely lady such as yourself is bound to be booked weeks in advance."

Jackie flushed a deep shade of pink and self-consciously tucked a loose strand of blond hair behind her ear. "No, it's nothing like that. I am planning on attending the ugly Christmas sweater party tomorrow evening at the library, so I'll see you then."

"Oh." According to Paula, Helen was judging the contest for the Friends of the Library. Lindsey tried not to let her panic show. "Don't you have to wear an ugly sweater to attend?"

"Not to worry," Jackie said. "I have the most obnoxious sweater in the history of ugly Christmas sweaters. I'd show it to you, but I don't want anyone to see until the moment of truth. I am absolutely positive that Helen will be suitably . . . impressed."

"Do you think she'll even be there?" Lindsey asked, hoping she sounded authentically doubtful. Judging by Robbie's aggrieved expression, she did not. Lindsey hoped to plant the seed of doubt in Jackie's mind, and maybe she wouldn't go.

"Definitely," Jackie said. "I got it from a very reliable source that she's one of the judges."

So much for that ploy, Lindsey thought.

"Is there a prize involved?" Jeanette asked.

"Bookstore gift card for one hundred bucks," Jackie said.

Jeanette sat up straight. "Well, that's incentive. I'm going to have to examine my closet. I think I have a green sweater with a Rudolph head on it, and the nose even lights up, or 'you could even say it glows.'"

"Mercy." Robbie laughed.

"That sounds perfect, but I think I still have you beat," Jackie said. "I guess I'll see you all tomorrow, then."

"Guess so," Lindsey said.

Jackie spun on her heel and shot up the stairs to the second floor. They all watched her go, and when Lindsey heard her door shut, she turned to the others. Before she could say a word, Robbie held up his hand, stopping her.

"No, and just to reiterate, let me say it again. No."

"No?" Lindsey asked.

"No, I will not wear an abomination of a jumper just to keep an eye on a woman who may or may not be a stalker."

"But . . ."

"Nope." He shook his head. "A man has to keep some of his dignity. I will do just about anything for my friends, but I will not sacrifice my self-respect."

I f anyone posts a picture of me in this, I'll have to go into seclusion for the rest of my life," Robbie moaned. "I'll be living in the bay on one of those islands that's really a rock, residing in a tent and eating cans of cold beans to survive."

"Someone's feeling very dramatic tonight," observed Emma Plewicki, the chief of the Briar Creek Police Department and also Robbie's partner.

"I'll say," Sully, Lindsey's husband, muttered as he tugged the sweater Emma had given to him over his head, wrestling the scratchy acrylic fabric into place. He leaned close to Lindsey and said, "Although, right now, I'm really glad that our parents took a holiday cruise together. The moms would blackmail us forever if they got pictures of us in these."

Lindsey laughed. He wasn't wrong.

The four of them were crammed in Lindsey's office at the library, dressing for the ugly Christmas sweater party being held in the large meeting room on the other side of the building. The library was officially closed, but the Friends of the Library were hosting their annual party, and anyone who purchased a ticket was welcome to attend.

When Lindsey had called Emma to express her concerns about Jackie, Emma had zeroed in on the sweater party. She told Lindsey to get Sully and meet Emma and Robbie at the library. They were all dressing up and going to the party, she declared. Lindsey tried to bow out, as she was one of the judges, but Emma was adamant, and Lindsey felt that when the chief of police told you to do something, you did it.

"I don't know why you're fussing, Vine," Sully said. "You only have to wear it for an hour, two, tops."

Robbie moaned. "How did this happen? One minute I was planning to option a book series and the next I'm dressed like a . . . a . . . what exactly am I supposed to be, love?"

"Just give me a second," Emma said. "I have to find the missing piece."

Surprising everyone, Emma had ditched her police uniform and gone all in on the ugly Christmas sweater challenge. Apparently, the police department had an annual contest with a cash prize as incentive, and Emma had a closet full of the sparkly, jingly, sight-impairing knitwear that she was more than happy to share.

"You need to wear the matching hat to really capture the spirit," Emma said. She pulled a bright yellow hat out of the plastic tub where she stored her sweaters, and tugged it over Robbie's reddish blond hair. It was a very floppy star that immediately fell over his forehead, but it definitely paired with the sweater, which was a bold shade of green with a red garland woven into the fabric. That and the bright-colored baubles hanging off it made it clear that Robbie was a Christmas tree.

"I think you just need to get into character, you know, be a tree." Lindsey held out her arms in a tree pose, while pressing her lips together to keep from laughing.

Robbie glared at her.

"I think you look amazing," Emma said. "Oh, but here's the best part." She tapped one of the plastic ornaments on the sweater, and suddenly they all lit up.

Robbie let out a high-pitched yip of terror, and Sully could no longer contain himself. He doubled over as the guffaw he'd been holding back erupted out of him.

"What are you laughing at?" Robbie cried. "You're dressed like an enormous biscuit."

It was true. Sully was wearing the only sweater that fit his broad shoulders, and it sported a huge frosted ginger-bread man on the front. Still, it was positively demure compared to Robbie. Emma had chosen to wear a fluffy white puff of a sweater that, when she spread her arms out wide, made her resemble a large snowflake. This left Lindsey with a bright red number that was decorated with presents all topped with large three-dimensional bows, which sparkled so much she felt as if she'd been glitter bombed. She checked the ground around her feet just to see if she was leaving a trail. She was not, which was weirdly disappointing.

"How do you rank in the annual police department's sweater contest, Emma?" Sully asked.

She grinned. "I win every year. Everyone hates me. It's awesome."

"My girl clearly has a competitive streak," Robbie said. He beamed at her with pride.

"I'm glad you feel that way because for this year's party, we're wearing matching sweaters," Emma said.

"Matching?" Robbie's voice went up with his degree of horror.

"Yes!" Emma clapped her hands in front of her. "We're going to be Dasher and Dancer or Donner and Blitzen."

"Not Comet and Cupid?" Robbie asked. "I think I'd make an adorable Cupid."

"Making me Comet?" Emma paused to consider it. "I could live with that."

"Come on." Lindsey nudged them all out of her office. "The party is about to start and I'm one of the judges, which is why I really don't feel like I need to wear a sweater."

"Oh, no." Sully shook his head. "Our vows were very specific, for better or worse, in ugly sweater solidarity, until death we do part."

"Weird, I don't remember that line." Lindsey raised an eyebrow at him.

"You were probably too nervous." He tapped the bow just under her chin, and glitter sprinkled down onto her industrial carpet. The cleaning crew was going to hate her.

"Focus, people, focus." Emma clapped. "I want to get a look at this potential stalker you mentioned. Does Carrie know that you think her writer in residence has an over-zealous fan?"

"No, I didn't want to sound the alarm until I was certain," Lindsey said. "As president of the Friends of the Library and the person overseeing the writer in residence program, Carrie already has enough to manage."

"Probably just as well," Emma said. "You wouldn't want to get hit with a lawsuit for slander."

"Does that seem likely?" Sully raised his eyebrows as he glanced in Lindsey's direction.

"No." Lindsey shook her head as she shut and locked her office door. Then she glanced at Emma. "Does it?"

"Depends upon whether this Jackie person hears what you've said about her and takes offense." Emma shrugged.

They left the staff area of the library and made their way out to the main floor.

"Having met the person in question, and given that I've had an overly attached fan or two in my time, I can back Lindsey up on the red flag feeling Jackie gives out," Robbie said.

"Thank you," Lindsey said.

Several members of the Friends of the Library were stand-

ing beside the front door, letting attendees in, while Carrie
Rushton stood beside the circulation desk with her partner,
Dale Wilcox. An ex-con and fisherman, Dale was known
for being rough around the edges, but he and Lindsey had
bonded over Hemingway and she'd watched his relationship with Carrie bloom, mellowing the tough guy out
enough that Lindsey had gotten him to read Cormac Mc-
Carthy among a few other favorite authors.

"Hi, Carrie, Dale," Lindsey greeted them. It was then
that she noted they were in matching Nordic sweaters.
Dale's said *I don't do matching sweaters*, while Carrie's
read *I do*.

"Clever!" Emma pointed at the couple and then turned
to Robbie. "See? Dale's wearing a couple's sweater."

"Not one word." Dale looked at Sully and Robbie with
a death glare.

Both Sully and Robbie raised their hands in the air.

"Wouldn't think of it," Robbie said. "At least yours is
subtle."

"There is that," Dale agreed. His lips twitched, which
was the equivalent of a grin from him.

Carrie rolled her eyes. "Honestly, you'd think I asked
the man to donate a kidney with the fuss he made."

"I'm sorry about that," Dale said. He glanced at Robbie,
taking in the lights and the hat. "Now that I've seen Vine's
hideous sweater, I can appreciate that you went easy on me."

"You know I can hear you, right?" Robbie asked. The
lights on his sweater started to twinkle. He turned and
frowned at Emma. "You have got to be kidding me."

She grinned. "It's a real showstopper, isn't it?"

"You're forgiven," Carrie said to Dale. She turned to Lindsey and said, "It's a full house, and some of the sweaters are amazing. I don't envy you having to choose."

"Is Helen here?" Lindsey asked.

"Yes, as well as the other judges, Mayor Cole and Betty Caruthers."

Lindsey's eyes went wide. "Betty Caruthers? Really?"

Carrie nodded. "I know. I didn't want her to be one of the judges either, but she's the president-elect since I'm stepping down at the end of the year. She made a motion to make herself the judge in this year's sweater contest, and the new board approved it."

Lindsey frowned. She'd had several confrontations with Betty over the library's acquisition policy. To put it simply, Betty was a book banner who believed if a member of the community had a problem with one of the books, then the book should be removed. Period. Full stop. And for some inexplicable reason, the books she wanted to ban were Helen's Mallory Quest books. In fact, Lindsey suspected that Betty had been driven to run for president of the Friends after Helen was named the Friends' choice for their writer in residence. Betty was opposed to the program, and to Helen, and had actively tried to shut it down before it even began.

Sensing the drop in her mood, Sully put an arm around her shoulders and said, "Don't worry, in an hour this will be all over, and we'll be out of these toxic sweaters and on our way home."

"I heard that," Emma said.

"I'm sorry, Lindsey," Carrie said. "Honestly, I'm still not clear on how she won the election. As far as I can tell, other than her mean girl squad, no members of the Friends like her."

"Bribes?" Robbie hypothesized.

"Makes as much sense as anything else," Carrie said.

Lindsey noted that a crowd was forming behind them. She reached out and squeezed Carrie's arm. "Let's not worry about it now. We'll talk more later."

Carrie nodded, and their group made their way into the large meeting room where the party was being held. The room had been decked out in holiday lights and had a buffet table on one side of the room and a red carpet running right down the middle of all the tables and chairs.

The buzz of conversation was loud, and there was a decided air of excitement. Who knew a gift card to a bookstore could motivate so many people? Lindsey took it as a good sign that the love of books was alive and well in her community, despite book banners like Betty. She blinked as she took in the party guests. There was one member of the Friends who was dressed as a gnome, from his pointy hat and long white beard to his tunic sweater that went all the way to his feet. Not exactly a Christmas sweater but definitely festive.

A band was playing at the far end of the room, and they, too, were dressed in an assortment of holiday sweaters. The lead singer, who was belting out "Rockin' Around the Christmas Tree," had an enormous fruitcake embroidered onto the front of his green sweater. The group paused to watch the band as they rolled into their next song.

Lindsey squinted. Yup, the singer was her former neighbor Charlie Peyton. He'd been pursuing a music career with marginal success for as long as Lindsey had known him, but it hadn't dampened his enthusiasm at all. As they watched, he ripped into a guitar solo in the middle of "Rudolph the Red-Nosed Reindeer," and only when the entire party came to a standstill and stared at him did he pull it back and return to the melody with a sheepish shrug.

Lindsey glanced at Sully and found him bobbing his head to the music. Charlie worked for Sully part-time during the summer's high season, running the tour boat and water taxi around the islands. He was the little brother Sully never knew he wanted, and the two of them were very close. Lindsey saw the thumbs-up Sully sent to Charlie and the grin Charlie sent back.

"I think Mrs. Kowalski made her famous eggnog," Sully said. "Want some?"

"The one with extra nog? Yes, please." Lindsey pointed to the cloth-draped table on the other side of the room. "I'm going to report for judging duty. Meet me over there?"

"Will do." Sully kissed her quickly and headed for the refreshments.

Emma and Robbie had already left them behind to go dance in front of the band with a crush of partygoers, and all Lindsey could see were the lights on Robbie's sweater. Emma had outdone herself with that one.

She greeted several of the members of the Friends group

as she made her way across the room. She was relieved to see Mayor Cole and her partner, Milton Duffy, standing beside the judges' table. Milton was wearing a suit that resembled an enormous red-and-white-striped candy cane. Lindsey wondered where a person shopped for something like that. It had to be online. In contrast, Mayor Cole was wearing a very reserved sparkly blue sweater.

"You are aware that as judges, we can't be entered in the contest, yes?" Mayor Cole asked as she took in Lindsey's vibrant bow-laden sweater.

"I am," Lindsey said. "This is a loan from Emma, who insisted on participation. Apparently, she has quite the collection."

"I was feeling very good about my ensemble until I saw Robbie." Milton stroked his goatee thoughtfully. "Lights really do up the ante, don't they?"

"He's going to be hard to beat," Lindsey agreed. She glanced around the room. "Has anyone seen Helen? I heard she's one of the judges."

"She was here a moment ago," Mayor Cole said. "She went to get some refreshments."

Lindsey nodded. She turned and scanned the room, but with the array of bold sweaters catching her eye, it was impossible to spot the author.

"You know who the other judge is, right?" Mayor Cole asked.

Lindsey sighed. "Betty."

"The book banner?" Milton asked. "How? Why? She hasn't even been sworn in as president yet."

"I have no idea," Lindsey said. "Carrie said Betty passed a motion and that was that. Carrie was out and Betty was in as tonight's judge."

"Because the next year won't be long enough. Why not get her reign of terror started early?" Milton huffed. He turned to Mayor Cole. "We're going to have to be vigilant, Eugenia. She's going to try and do everything she can to ban books and gut programs—anything she doesn't like will be a target."

Mayor Cole patted his shoulder comfortingly. "Let's just take it one day at a time. We have plenty of precedents to block her if need be."

"Talking about me, I presume?" Betty Caruthers appeared behind them, making them all start.

CHAPTER

5

BRIAR CREEK
PUBLIC LIBRARY

Betty Caruthers had moved to Briar Creek from New York City during the pandemic. Newly divorced with three teenagers, she'd arrived in town to live in what was formerly her husband's aunt's house by the water. She made it quite clear that it was a step down from the life she had come to expect, and anyone who crossed her path was treated to her tale of woe about being done wrong by her ex.

Mr. Caruthers had yet to make an appearance in town, preferring to send a car and driver when it was his turn to see his children. Betty had rejected the local public schools, choosing to hire private tutors instead. She claimed that the curriculum at the school was subpar, but most of the locals believed that it was just one more way to stick it to her ex financially.

With the public school no longer in her sights, Betty turned on the community itself. She was at all of the town meetings, inserting her opinion about the library, the parks, the police department—even the sanitation department was under her scrutiny as she lobbied to have trash pickup on her street changed to a later time because she liked to sleep until ten o'clock in the morning and the trucks woke her up.

Lindsey had never met anyone quite like Betty. She was petite with long blond hair, enormous blue eyes and acrylic nails that resembled weapons. She was known for label dropping in every conversation, so it was never "hand me my scarf, please," but rather "hand me my Burberry scarf"—with no "please." From what Lindsey observed, Betty viewed the world through the lens of her personal preferences. All thermostats should be set to her preferred temperature, no other cars should be on the road or in her way when she was driving, and she should never have to stand in line and wait for anything ever. Betty wanted the world to accommodate her, and she was irate when it didn't.

Lindsey wondered what it was like to wake up every day, gearing up for battle. It exhausted her just thinking about it.

Mayor Cole looked Betty up and down, taking in her pale blue silk blouse and pearls. "How very festive, Betty."

"Is that a slam?" Betty narrowed her eyes. "Just because I refuse to dress like the bargain rack at a low-end department store doesn't mean I am lacking in holiday spirit. I'll have you know my blouse is Chanel and my pearls are Yvel."

"Bah! You wouldn't know holiday spirit—" Milton began, but Lindsey interrupted.

"Of course no one is saying you lack spirit." Lindsey stared at Milton until he harrumphed and glanced away. "I believe we need to take our places for judging. Why don't we do that?"

She led the way to their designated table. Name cards were placed at each seat, and Lindsey found hers and sat down. Mayor Cole was on her right, and Betty was the seat beyond her. Helen's card was on Lindsey's left, and just as they all settled in, Helen appeared, carrying a glass of wine in one hand and a thick piece of cake in the other.

"Hi, Lindsey. You should grab some refreshments before they're all gone," Helen advised as she sat. Picking up her fork, she tucked into the decadent slice.

Lindsey was surprised by the friendliness Helen was showing her. Frankly, she was stunned that Helen even remembered her name. Then again, maybe it was the festive atmosphere causing her joviality. That or the wine and cake. Yeah, that was probably it. In Lindsey's experience, there was nothing a slice of chocolate cake couldn't improve.

The band finished their song, and Carrie stepped up on the stage. She instructed the partygoers who were entering the contest to form a line, walk in front of the judges' table and strut their stuff. There was some good-natured teasing as the contestants took their places, and Lindsey found herself smiling as she watched Robbie and Emma trying to act out their sweaters, with Emma twirling like a snowflake and Robbie standing tall like a tree.

She glanced at Mayor Cole and saw her smiling, but then noticed Betty was glaring in their direction, as if she resented the entire event. Why was she here, then? She didn't have to be here tonight. She could have let Carrie finish out her term as president and be the one to judge the sweaters. Why participate in something she obviously took no pleasure in? Was Betty that determined that no one enjoy themselves?

Sully strode across the room, carrying a glass of eggnog. He set it down in front of Lindsey and said, "Good luck, darling, the competition is fierce."

"Thank you." Lindsey toasted him with her glass. "Who knew everyone was going to take the ugly sweater competition so seriously."

"Emma knew." He laughed.

"Hi, Sully," Betty called from her seat down the table. She sent him a little finger wave, a hair toss and a few blinks of her big eyes surrounded by her massive eyelashes, and he nodded.

"Evening, Betty." He glanced at Lindsey. "I'm going to go catch up with some of the guys."

"Are you running away?" Lindsey asked in a low voice so that only he could hear.

"As fast as my feet can carry me," he admitted.

"Go." Lindsey smiled.

Sully leaned down and kissed her quickly. Then he winked and said, "I'll find you after."

Lindsey nodded, watching him until he disappeared into the crowd.

She couldn't blame him for bolting. The few times Sully's path had crossed Betty's, she had made it abundantly clear that she felt more than neighborly toward him. Lindsey found it interesting that Betty, having been tossed aside by her own husband, was so flirtatious with a married man. But Lindsey had no worries about Sully since he was as constant as the tide. Maybe Betty could see that, too, and that was why she liked him.

"How did Sour Face get picked for this gig?" Helen asked. Her gaze was on Betty, who was checking her lipstick in the reflection of her phone, making it clear whom she was talking about.

"She's the incoming president of the Friends and managed to pass a motion," Lindsey said. "I take it you've met?"

"She stopped by on my first day and told me she wanted my books banned from the library." Helen took another bite of cake.

"Oh, I'm so sorry," Lindsey said. "That must have been awkward."

"Not really." Helen shrugged. "I told her she was welcome to try."

"Well, she took that to heart," Lindsey said.

"It'll never happen. There's nothing about them that warrants banning," Helen said. "It doesn't look like she wants to be here. Frankly, I don't want to be here either, but I try not to make it obvious. Wine helps."

Lindsey smiled and said, "From what I can tell, Betty is not a fan of the library or, well, anything in our village for that matter."

"Then why go for the president of the Friends position and not run for office or something?" Helen asked. "That makes no sense." She chewed thoughtfully and then said, "And I don't mean to be paranoid, but with the way she is glaring at me, I feel like she loathes me in particular, but I don't even know her."

"If it's any consolation, you're not alone," Lindsey said. "Betty has a lot of hostility to give."

"So this should be fun," Helen quipped.

Lindsey laughed. She tried to be open-minded about the members of her community, but Betty was a challenge. Lindsey appreciated that everyone had individual wants and needs specific to their lives, and it was the job of the library to reflect those needs in its collection and programming. But Betty wasn't interested in any of that. She had made it clear when she tried to ban Helen's books and residency that she only wanted the library to carry books and offer programs of which she approved. She didn't see a need for her tax dollars to be funding anything she didn't like, and she was very, very vocal about it. At least Helen didn't seem to take it personally.

"All right, judges." Carrie spoke into the microphone, drawing their attention. "The contestants are numbered and ready to walk the carpet. Please list your top three by their number on the pad in front of you. We will then have a finalists' round to declare the winner."

The band began to play a quiet holiday beat for the contestants to walk across the room. The first up was Jeanette from the bed-and-breakfast. She wore leggings under a bedazzled tunic sweater that was so loaded with sparkling gems, her shoulders drooped from its weight. The crowd cheered, and Jeanette did a pirouette in the middle of the floor that tipped her perilously over to one side, but she righted herself and exited the red carpet.

"Strength of character kept her upright," Helen observed.

Lindsey and Mayor Cole laughed.

"You're not wrong," Mayor Cole said. "Jeanette Palmer was born and raised in Briar Creek. In fact, the Palmers were one of the founding families of the village."

"Which just means that she's as interesting as a barnacle," Betty said.

They all swiveled their heads in her direction.

"What?" Betty asked. "It's true. What has she ever done with her life that is even remotely interesting?"

A fierce surge of protectiveness blasted through Lindsey. Jeanette wasn't just a patron of the library, she was Lindsey's friend. Lindsey leaned forward and said, "I don't know, I think that affair she had with Jimi Hendrix was the stuff of legend."

Mayor Cole glanced at Lindsey with one eyebrow raised. Without looking at Betty, she said, "That was nothing. Remember when she modeled for Andy Warhol?"

Lindsey looked thoughtfully at her bedazzled friend. "Jeanette is something special."

"She is indeed," Mayor Cole said. She turned to Betty and gave her a dismissive look. "You wouldn't know anything about that though, would you?"

Betty's nostrils flared as her lips compressed into a thin line. She opened her mouth to retort, but Mayor Cole held up her hand in a *stop* gesture. "The next contestant is coming."

Betty's face turned a mottled shade of red. She looked like she was going to have a temper tantrum, but instead she closed her eyes and took several deep breaths. Then she focused on the contestant in front of them. It was the fire marshal, wearing a blue sweater with a very large teddy bear in a red bow tie on the front.

"That was all made-up, wasn't it?" Helen whispered to Lindsey.

"Was it?" Lindsey asked. "People have layers."

"True," Helen agreed. "But a person who is born and bred somewhere and runs the local bed-and-breakfast is not likely to have an affair with a rock star or be a model for a pop art genius, is she?"

"You just never can tell." Lindsey pointed to the next contestant.

"I suppose not." Helen turned back to the parade of sweaters but not before Lindsey noticed that the corner of her mouth turned up just a little bit.

They were halfway through the lineup when a commotion broke out at the door. Lindsey could hear the angry voice of a woman, although she couldn't see her through the crowd.

"What do you mean I can't enter?" the woman demanded. "I spent a lot of money on my outfit, and I want to be in the contest."

"We can't let you in," Carrie said. "One of the rules is that all entrants must be signed in before the parade starts."

"But that's not fair," the woman wailed.

"No. Unfair is letting people enter after the event has started," Carrie said. "If you saw what people were wearing, you could have left to make your sweater even more ugly just to win."

"I will not be denied!" the woman announced.

"There seems to be a lot of that going around," Lindsey said.

Helen snorted, making Lindsey feel as if she were the cleverest person in the world for making the award-winning author laugh.

Just then the band stumbled to a halt as a woman jumped up onto their raised platform. She was wearing the ugliest Christmas sweater Lindsey had ever seen. It was a green-and-white-striped minidress with faux white fur trim and a wide black belt that she paired with red leggings and white go-go boots and a green Santa hat. No question about it, this was the worst.

It took a moment for Lindsey to look beyond the outfit and recognize the person. When she did, she gasped. It was Jackie Lewis.

"Oh, no," Helen muttered. "No, no, no, no. This can't be happening."

Lindsey glanced from Jackie to Helen and asked, "Do you know her?"

"I used to," Helen said. "I never thought I'd see her again. Ugh."

"Was she a friend?"

"At one time I thought so." Helen picked up her glass and lifted it to her lips.

Lindsey glanced back at the stage, where Carrie was trying to wrestle the mic away from Jackie.

"Ma'am, you are not allowed on the stage. You need to go now," Carrie said.

Jackie pivoted away from her and then jumped off the stage, striding through the room with a determined look in her eye. She was headed straight for the judges' table.

"You!" she bellowed into the mic as she pointed at Helen. "You took everything from me."

"Here we go," Helen said. She downed the last of her wine and pushed the remainder of her cake away.

Jackie had a manic light in her eye, and she stared at Helen as if she were some exotic creature that she'd been hunting and had finally caught. Jackie stopped in front of their table, panting for breath, probably because the acrylic nightmare she was wearing did not allow for good airflow.

"I took nothing from you," Helen said. Her voice was incredibly calm in the face of Jackie's outrage. "You can try and spin it however you like, but my success is my own and had nothing to do with you."

"Nothing to do with me?" Jackie spluttered. Carrie took the opportunity to snag the mic out of Jackie's hand and return to the stage with it.

"So sorry for the interruption, next contestant, please." Carrie waved at the line of participants.

It should have worked. That should have been the end of it, Lindsey thought, but it wasn't. No one paid any attention to Carrie; instead, they stared past her to watch the drama unfold between the two visitors to Briar Creek.

Lindsey scanned the room until she saw Sully trapped beside the refreshment table. When their gazes met, he raised his eyebrows as if to ask what was happening. Lindsey shrugged. The only thing that was loud and clear was that Jackie was not the worshipful fan she had pretended to be, as the hostility pouring off her in waves was palpable.

Ignoring Carrie and the crowd that was watching, Jackie doubled down. In a voice that carried to every corner of the room, she yelled, "You stole my idea! I'm the one who wrote a mystery series first. I'm the one who should be on the bestsellers lists, interviewed on television, and hosted as the writer in residence."

No one in the room moved. All eyes turned to Helen to see how she'd react. She didn't seem shocked or dismayed by Jackie's accusation. Rather, she looked bored.

"Jackie, I don't know how to break this to you, but you are completely delusional," Helen said. "We were in a critique group together three years before I wrote the first Mallory Quest. I hadn't even thought of the story yet."

"You didn't have to think of it, because you stole it from

me." Jackie pounded her fist against her chest in indignation.

"Stop saying that," Helen said. "It's simply not true, and repeating it over and over and over won't make it so. You tried to sue me. It was thrown out of court. The judge even said there was no evidence of any infringement of your intellectual property. You write a science fiction series about intergalactic police stationed on planet Balthusa, not a mystery series featuring a FBI agent as the main character."

"They're not just science fiction. They have crimes in them, too," Jackie declared. "You know, for years I've listened to everyone rave about the depth of character in your series. I gave you that depth."

Helen rolled her eyes. "No, you didn't. And you have spent years accusing me of something I simply didn't do. Just think, if you had spent that time actually working on your own writing, maybe you'd be on the bestsellers list now instead of stalking me and accusing me of ruining your career."

"You did ruin me. You stole more than my ideas, and you know it." Jackie's chest was heaving, and her face was cranberry red, but her glare was steady, and she never took her gaze off Helen.

"Yes, well." Helen glanced away first. "Either you leave or I do, but this scene you're causing isn't fair to any of the participants in the ugly sweater contest." She paused to glance around the room. "And it appears there was a lot of effort put into some of these . . . er . . . sweaters."

"Since when have you ever cared about fair?" Jackie hissed.

Helen narrowed her gaze at Jackie but didn't respond.

"I think you need to go now, ma'am," Emma Plewicki said as she joined them. "You can take up your issue with Ms. Monroe on your own time, but she's here to judge and there are people waiting."

Jackie turned her head to take in Emma in her snow-flake costume. She scoffed and said, "Who are you to tell me what to do?"

"Don't let the fabulous sweater distract you," Emma said. "I'm the Briar Creek chief of police."

Jackie's mouth dropped open and then snapped shut.

"Shall we?" Emma asked as she gestured to the door.

Jackie turned back to Helen. "This isn't over."

"Yes, it is." Helen picked up her fork and stabbed the last bit of cake with the tines. She closed her lips over the morsel, chewed and swallowed. "You see, you're just like that slice of cake, Jackie. All gone."

Jackie looked like she wanted to take a swing at Helen. Emma must have thought so, too, because she took Jackie by the elbow and steered her toward the door.

"Well, well, well." Betty leaned around Mayor Cole. "It appears someone has a few skeletons in her closet."

"Hardly." Helen sat back down. "What I have is a bitter former friend who is trying to tarnish what I've achieved because she isn't talented enough to succeed herself. From what I understand, that should be quite relatable for you, Betty."

Betty blinked. "What are you insinuating?"

"Oh, I'm not insinuating anything," Helen said. "I'm stating it plainly. You and your book-banning buddies are just as sad and pitiful as Jackie. You have no creative spark, no imagination, so you try to take it away from those who do. You won't succeed. Good people and other creators won't stand for it."

"How dare you!" Betty seethed.

"I said what I said." Helen shrugged. "No daring required."

"I am personally checking out every single copy of your books and burning them," Betty said.

"Oh, no, you're not," Lindsey and Mayor Cole said together.

"No, I think you should let her," Helen said.

"What?" Lindsey cried.

"Think of the bigger picture," Helen instructed. "I will personally replace every volume she destroys, and you will be able to remove her as president of the Friends of the Library, because clearly they can't have someone who would do such a thing as president. I imagine you can vote her out and replace her with someone more library friendly, don't you think?"

Both Lindsey and Mayor Cole turned to Betty.

"Obviously, I was just joking," Betty snapped.

"Right," Mayor Cole said. "Because burning library books is such a funny bit."

"I'll be following up on what your little friend said."

Betty glared at Helen. "I think she might be onto something."

"Knock yourself out." Helen shrugged. "The lawsuit is public record. My favorite part is where they dismissed the entire thing and advised Jackie to get on with her life. I like to read it right before I go to bed at night. It comforts me."

"Hello? Judges?" The sound of snapping fingers brought them back to the contest. "What's a Christmas tree got to do to get your attention?" Robbie strutted by them with his hands on his hips. He gave a little shimmy and a little shake before jumping up and kicking his heels together. The crowd behind him cheered, and Lindsey glanced at Carrie. Her relief that Robbie had brought the party back to its purpose was obvious in the way she sagged against Dale.

For that alone, Lindsey would have chosen Robbie as the winner, but when he performed the running man and the star hat on his head bobbed up and down, she had to give it to him for sheer salesmanship. She jotted down his number and noted that the other judges did, too. She just hoped Robbie wasn't insufferable about the win.

Where do you think we should keep my trophy?" Robbie asked Emma.

They were standing with Lindsey and Sully at the holiday light ceremony on the town green the evening after the ugly Christmas sweater party. It was dark and cold, and Lindsey used her thick paper cup of hot chocolate to keep her hands warm as she burrowed into her scarf.

"The trophy you won with the sweater I lent you?" Emma gave him a pointed look.

"Would I be wrong to suggest the tank on his toilet as the perfect place?" Sully whispered to Lindsey.

"Not wrong." Lindsey laughed. "But I think we should let them work it out."

"How does he manage to work his win into every sentence?" Sully asked.

"Robbie loves his awards," Lindsey said. "Remember when he won that Tony?"

"We had to hear about it for months." Sully sighed.

"On the upside, I don't think his bragging for this one will last longer than the holiday season," Lindsey said.

"Another couple of weeks, then?" Sully asked.

"Give or take." Lindsey hid her smile by sipping her cocoa.

"Have you seen Jackie Lewis?" Emma asked Lindsey.

"Not since you escorted her out of the party last night," she said. "Why?"

"I heard from a reliable source that you and the crafternooners were planning to befriend her to keep her from stalking Helen Monroe," Emma said.

"What? I . . . that's . . ." Lindsey's voice trailed off under Emma's unwavering stare. It didn't help that she was dressed in her police uniform. "It was just a thought."

"Uh-huh." Emma lifted the lid off her cocoa and sniffed the contents before taking a cautious sip. "Unthink it."

"But . . ."

Emma shook her head, and Lindsey said, "Fine. Jackie didn't seem like the friend-making type anyway."

"What happened after you walked her out last night?" Sully asked.

"She went back to the Beachfront," Emma said. "I had one of my officers make sure of it. I was hoping she'd decide to pack up and go home, but no. I talked to Jeanette this morning, and Jackie was planning to stay through the holidays. I expect she's here in the crowd somewhere."

Lindsey glanced at the people around them, looking for a puffy white coat and a pink-and-white-striped hat with a large pink pom-pom. She recognized most everyone in the crowd, and the few that she didn't weren't Jackie.

"What do you suppose she wants?" Lindsey asked. "I mean, according to Helen, Jackie lost her lawsuit. What could following Helen to Briar Creek do for Jackie?"

"If she wants to make trouble, this is the perfect situation," Robbie said. "Helen is stuck at the library every day in that glassed-in room. Jackie can find her and accost her anytime she likes."

"You'll let me know if that happens," Emma said to Lindsey.

"Of course, we won't let her be harassed by anyone, never mind a person with an apparent grudge," Lindsey assured her.

"Is Helen here tonight? Because Jackie has arrived." Sully pointed across the green to a woman identifiable by her coat and hat. It was Jackie, all right. Lindsey would recognize that pink pom-pom anywhere.

"I don't know if Helen was planning on attending," Lindsey said. "On the one hand, I'm sure she'd prefer to avoid crowds after last night, but on the other, she might want to make an appearance just to prove that whatever Jackie says doesn't bother her."

"Let's keep an eye out, and if we see Helen, let's run interference," Emma said. "I don't want a repeat of last night."

"I do," Robbie said. "Especially if it means I win

another award. You know, something in the 'Perfect Boy-friend to the Chief of Police' category would look great between my Tony and Ugliest Sweater Awards."

Emma rolled her eyes, and Robbie grinned. It was clear he was teasing her. "Okay, perfect boyfriend, earn your keep and spot Helen in the crowd."

Robbie saluted her and began to study the people around them, as did Lindsey and Sully. Being an introvert, Lindsey knew that she personally would be on the outskirts of an event like this if it weren't for her friends dragging her right into the heart of it.

Helen had been keeping to herself for most of her time here, so maybe she was on the perimeter. Then again, she was also an international bestselling author who was used to crowds, so where would she choose to be, assuming she was even here?

Helen didn't know many people yet, so it would make sense that she'd be in a spot where she stood a chance of running into someone she'd met before, like Carrie, or Lindsey—or Mayor Cole, who was about to turn on the light display. Lindsey's eyes darted to the people in front of the gazebo.

"There she is!" Lindsey pointed to the group. "She's in the dark coat with the purple hat."

"Let's go," Emma said. "We can be a human shield be-tween her and Jackie."

"I don't know that Jackie is her biggest problem right now," Sully said. "It looks like she's having beef with the people standing next to her."

Lindsey glanced back at Helen. Sure enough, a middle-aged man and a young woman had Helen trapped with her back against the gazebo with no viable exit. From the looks on their angry faces, they were not fans of Helen's.

Emma cut through the crowd, using her chief's voice to order people out of the way. Robbie, Sully and Lindsey followed in her wake.

"You're a ghoul, that's what you are!" the young woman shouted at Helen. "You take other people's tragedy and you twist it into your stories, and for what? Fame? Fortune?"

Helen stared at the woman in confusion. "I'm sorry. Who are you?"

"Lisa Campbell." The woman tipped her chin up. "But I expect you are more familiar with my father, Jeffrey, and my mother, Diane."

Helen's eyebrows lifted in surprise.

"Jeffrey Campbell?" Helen turned to the man in a fleece-lined red plaid flannel coat and a navy beanie who accompanied the young woman. "The . . . uh . . ." She stopped talking, and an awkward silence fell between them.

"Say it, I dare you." The man glared at her from beneath the edge of his beanie. Helen said nothing. "That's what I thought. Come on, Lisa."

"That's right!" Lisa snapped, resisting her father's urge to leave. "I'm the baby you wrote about in your first Mallory Quest novel, all grown up. Did I turn out like you expected?"

"I'm sorry, but I write fiction, not true crime," Helen said.

Lisa barked a laugh that caused everyone in the vicinity to turn and stare. "Did you hear that, Dad? She writes fiction. But it doesn't change things. I was the baby found in the woods with her murdered mother," Lisa said. "Everyone who read your book knew it was me. It kept the rumors and gossip alive when they should have died out."

Jeffrey muttered a curse. "You can call it whatever you want, but when you base your 'fiction' on real lives, you hurt people like my daughter." He paused and put a protective arm around the young woman's shoulders.

Helen pursed her lips as if to keep herself from responding. She failed. "Please let me explain. My process begins with a news story that I can't stop thinking about. Yes, in this case it was you, Lisa, a baby in the woods. But I didn't write specifically about you or your parents, not really. It was just me trying to process the horror of what happened. I strive to make sense of it all, you know?

"It was never my intention to hurt you." Helen turned to Lisa. "I'm very sorry."

Lisa glared at her. It was clear she'd come for a fight, not an apology, and she had no idea what to do with the latter.

"Again, I'm—" Helen began again after a beat of silence, but Jeffrey interrupted.

"Save it," he snapped. "I hope someday you know exactly what it's like to be accused of something you didn't do and that it ruins you. Then and only then will we be square.

"Lisa, we drove all the way here so you could confront her and find closure, and now you have. It's time to go."

Lisa looked as if she'd add to what her father had said, but he shook his head, and she nodded before he led her away. The crowd parted for them, and Lindsey could hear people whispering as they walked by.

"Was that Jeffrey Campbell, the guy who was arrested for murdering his wife and abandoning his baby girl in the woods like fifteen years ago?" Emma asked Helen.

Helen nodded. "Apparently."

"What's he doing in Briar Creek?" Robbie asked.

"Sounds like he brought his daughter here just to see Helen," Lindsey said.

The group all turned to the author, and she shrugged. "Lucky me."

Her face was pale, and her gaze darted around the crowd as if she was looking for another threat. Lindsey studied her, noting that the usually calm, cool and collected writer in residence appeared . . . rattled. Even Jackie's public spectacle hadn't fazed the author's usual serene demeanor as much as this.

"Is what they said true?" Robbie asked. "Do you base your novels on real crimes?"

Helen waved her gloved hand in a so-so gesture. "Somewhat. I mean, current events are usually a stepping-off place for me. Diane Campbell's murder happened a few years before I got the idea to write a female FBI investigator as a lead character. At the time, it was believed that Jeffrey had murdered his wife, so I wrote the story that way. But I changed the names and dates, the setting, and the method of murder. I even made the baby a boy in my book, but anyone who had followed the case closely probably saw a slight similarity."

"I never heard of that case," Lindsey said. "Where did it happen?"

"Over in Danbury," Emma said. "I remember because I was enrolled in the police academy at the time. Diane's body was found in the woods. A blunt trauma caused her death, and four-month-old Lisa was found sleeping peacefully nearby. Jeffrey, being the husband, was the chief suspect, and after a speedy, emotion-loaded trial, he was sent to jail.

"His attorney didn't quit, however, and finally, after demanding that a strand of hair found at the crime scene in the victim's hands be DNA tested, his lawyer proved that there was another possible killer. After more evidence turned up, the real murderer confessed and is now in prison. Jeffrey was set free."

"Who did it, then?" Lindsey asked. "Who killed Diane Campbell?"

"Ashley Santos, the coworker Jeffrey was having an affair with," Helen said.

"Ohhh," the group said together.

"I followed the case after Ashley was arrested, but of course, it was too late to rewrite the book, and I wouldn't have done so anyway. It was fiction, not true crime. I did portray the husband in my novel as the killer, but he was vastly different in personality and appearance from Jeffrey Campbell. And while I used the part about the child being found with her mother, I made it much more dramatic and had the mother in the story holding her sleeping child."

"But the taint of being accused of murder remained for Jeffrey even after he was released, and he probably blamed your novel for keeping the suspicion alive," Robbie said. "Clearly, he's bitter."

"I am sorry about that," Helen said. "I feel for him and what he went through, but my deepest sympathies are for Lisa and Diane. By all accounts, Diane was a wonderful person and a devoted mother. It's a miracle Ashley didn't kill Lisa as well."

"The daughter seems to blame you for ruining her father's life," Emma said.

Helen sighed. "Again, I think her father has more to answer for in that regard than I do."

The group was silent as Mayor Cole took to the podium for the official lighting. Unlike her predecessor, she kept her speech short, congratulating the cooperation between the parks department and facilities on their hard work to decorate the park and Main Street. The village green boasted displays for all of the major holidays happening in December, and lights had been strung up and down Main Street, giving the center of the village a festive vibe that helped combat the shorter days and winter chill that had arrived a few weeks ago.

This was one of the things Lindsey most loved about village life, especially since she could enjoy the light display from the comfort of the library just across Main Street.

When the display was taken down in January, she was always sad to see it go.

She glanced at the back of the crowd and noted that Jackie was standing exactly where she'd been before, but now her gaze was locked on Helen. That couldn't be good. Lindsey wondered if Jackie had overheard the Campbells chewing Helen out. There was no way to tell.

"Thank you, everyone, for coming out tonight," Mayor Cole said. Lindsey turned her attention back to the bandstand. "It's a wonderful thing to have a community that appreciates the small joys in life."

Milton stood beside Mayor Cole and handed her the ceremonial power button that was always used to turn on the lights. Mayor Cole didn't hesitate. She pressed the big red button, and the town green was immediately illuminated with thousands of twinkling lights. Every tree had been outlined, along with the gazebo and the large Christmas tree that had grown beside the gazebo as if it knew this was its purpose.

In the center of the park, there was a tall tunnel made of arches of lights that ran the length of the park and was synced to holiday music that came from several speakers built into the arches. There were shrieks of joy from the children in attendance and several oohs and aahs from the adults. The band from the Elks Lodge began to play carols in the gazebo, and volunteers passed around trays full of hot chocolate and cookies to the crowd.

"Isn't it beautiful?" Nancy Peyton asked as she approached their group, holding out a tray of cookies.

The cold had given Lindsey an appetite, and she happily took two festively decorated sugar cookies. She noted that Helen didn't. Instead, Helen stared through the crowd in the direction that Lisa and Jeffrey had gone. Lindsey wondered if Helen was feeling guilty about writing about what had happened to Jeffrey and Lisa. Their hostility had been palpable, and Lindsey doubted that was the sort of thing even a seasoned writer like Helen could just shake off.

Nancy pushed more cookies on them, which Sully and Robbie were happy to take, while the elementary school choir took the stage to lead the crowd in a selection of winter songs. Helen took the opportunity to excuse herself.

"It's late," she said. "I have to give a talk to a Girl Scout troop tomorrow, so I think I'll go home."

"Robbie and I will escort you," Emma said. She glanced across the park to where Jackie had been standing. She was no longer there.

"That's not necessary," Helen demurred.

"Did it sound like it was optional?" Emma asked.

Helen blinked. It was clear she wasn't used to being told what to do. Still, she inclined her head and said, "All right. As long as you're going my way."

"Of course we are," Robbie said. "Um . . . which way would that be?"

Helen smiled, and with a wave, the three of them departed.

Lindsey and Sully watched them disappear into the crowd. When they were out of range, Lindsey turned to her husband and said, "Is it just me, or was this light ceremony weird?"

"Not you." He took her empty paper cup and threw it in the bin with his. "Ready to go home?"

"Yes, please."

He slipped an arm around her, and together they made their way through the proud parents, watching their children sing, to the sidewalk. It was a short walk down the street to the spot where he'd parked his pickup truck.

On the way, Lindsey saw Betty Caruthers standing beside her Mercedes, parked just beyond Sully's truck, talking to a person who was blocked from view by their vehicle. Lindsey immediately turned her head away. She wasn't one to avoid people generally. As the director of the library, she felt that she was the face of the library and always wanted to be perceived as friendly. But Betty was more than she wanted to deal with at the moment, so she kept her gaze averted.

It worked right up until she heard a snippet of the conversation and recognized the voice of the woman talking to Betty as belonging to Jackie Lewis.

"You promised me," Jackie said. She sounded angry.

"I didn't promise you anything," Betty retorted. "I said I'd try to do what you want, and I have, but it's been more difficult than I anticipated."

Lindsey slowed her walk. Betty and Jackie? How did they know each other? And why did it sound like they were . . . conspiring?

CHAPTER

7

BRIAR CREEK
PUBLIC LIBRARY

"Y ou good?" Sully asked as he noticed Lindsey's decrease in speed. She nodded, not wanting to answer and draw attention to herself.

"Frozen toes," she whispered.

"Uh-huh." Sully glanced past her to where the two women stood just up the street. "I've never heard that euphemism for eavesdropping before."

Lindsey widened her eyes and put her gloved index finger over her lips, signaling for him to be quiet.

Sully nodded and fussed with retrieving his keys from his pocket in an obvious effort to give Lindsey more time to hear the conversation. She generally wouldn't listen in on another person's private talk, but given that both Betty and Jackie had issues with Helen, and the library was hosting Helen's writer in residence program, she felt it was part of her job to look out for their author. It was a thin rationalization, but she refused to dwell on it.

"You were supposed to humiliate her, ban her books and shut down her program," Jackie said. "So far I am seeing none of that. She just goes on her merry way and nothing ever touches her."

"It'll touch her, don't you worry about that," Betty said.

"You'd better be right," Jackie said. "I'd hate to have to share what I know about your recent election win with the powers that be."

"Are you threatening me?" Betty asked. "Need I remind you that you're the one who approached me?"

"It's not a threat. It's being put on notice," Jackie said. "Get it done."

She stepped back from Betty, and before she glanced their way, Lindsey threw her arms around her husband and planted a kiss on him that made him drop his keys.

Sully kissed her back with enough enthusiasm to distract Lindsey from her purpose. When they broke apart, Sully grinned and said, "Feel free to eavesdrop anytime."

Lindsey felt her face grow warm, and she glanced over her shoulder just in time to see Betty drive off, while Jackie walked away from them toward the bed-and-breakfast. Lindsey took this as a positive sign that neither of the women had noticed her and Sully.

"Here they are." Sully pulled his keys out of the small drift of snow. "Crisis averted."

"For now," Lindsey said, thinking of the two women and their plan to humiliate Helen.

As he opened the door for Lindsey and she climbed into the truck cab, she wondered how it was that Jackie and Betty had come to be plotting against Helen together. And how did Jackie think Betty was going to be able to ban Helen's books and end the writer in residence program? As president of the Friends, Betty would have some power, but not that much.

There was really only one thing to do. On Monday morning during Helen's writing shift in the library, Lindsey would have to share with her what she'd overheard, just so that Helen was prepared should either Jackie or Betty attempt to make trouble for her.

The question, though, was how did Jackie and Betty know each other? Betty said that Jackie approached her, but how did Jackie pick Betty as an ally? And why did they both seem to have it in for Helen? Jackie had already made it clear why she disliked Helen, but what possible motive could Betty have? Betty had come from New York City, so it was unlikely that she and Helen had crossed paths before. As far as Lindsey knew, Helen had never set a book outside the state of Connecticut. On the surface, there was simply no reason for Betty to have an issue with Helen. But clearly she did. Lindsey knew there was only one way to get the answers to her questions . . . ask.

D id you know Betty Caruthers before you agreed to come and be our writer in residence?" Lindsey asked Helen on Monday.

"That's to the point, isn't it?" Helen asked. She put her laptop case on the table and took off her coat. She draped it on the coatrack in the corner of her workspace, then stuffed her hat in one of the pockets and her gloves in another.

"Sorry, let me start again," Lindsey said. "Good morning, Helen, do you know why Betty Caruthers wants to ban your books and tried to shut down your residency before it began?"

Helen took her laptop out of the bag and flipped open the lid. She pressed the power button, and while it fired up, she gave Lindsey her full attention. "Because she's a mean girl?"

Lindsey was surprised by Helen's flippancy. If Lindsey were a writer and someone tried to ban her books or have her programs canceled, she'd be furious, but Helen didn't seem to care.

"So, you haven't met her before?" Lindsey persisted.

"I honestly don't know." Helen shrugged. "I mean, I might have met her at a book signing, but if I did, I have no recall. And as to why she dislikes my work so much that she wants my books banned, I haven't a clue. Some people think their opinions on certain books are the only ones that matter. Maybe Betty is one of those types."

"All right, I'll give you that," Lindsey agreed. She remembered the course she'd taken in library school about how to deal with book banning. One notable case they studied was a school board in Ohio that tried to ban *Harriet the Spy* on the grounds that it encouraged children to lie, spy and talk back to authority. Thankfully, it didn't go through, but Lindsey could still remember the absolute fit

Beth had upon studying the case, as Louise Fitzhugh was one of her all-time favorite authors.

"Can I ask why you have so many questions about Betty Caruthers?" Helen took one of the books she was using for research out of the lower drawer in her desk and placed it beside her laptop.

"I overheard a concerning conversation between Betty and Jackie last evening when Sully and I were leaving the park."

Helen glanced up with an expression of surprise. "Betty and Jackie? They know each other?"

"It seems so. And they were talking about you. More specifically, Jackie was telling Betty that she expected her to humiliate you, and Betty said she was trying," Lindsey said.

"Interesting."

"I would emphasize *concerning*," Lindsey said. "How do they know each other? Did they meet here? Why was Jackie asking Betty to humiliate you? And why was Betty agreeing to try?"

"No idea." Helen shook her head.

"Aren't you worried that they might try to damage your career or cause you harm?" Lindsey asked. She hated saying it out loud, but she didn't feel as if Helen was taking the situation seriously enough.

"Who knows how they found each other," Helen said. "There might be a troll site online, dedicated to hating on my work. I've heard that some authors have to deal with that sort of thing. I don't see why I should be immune."

"But they seem to have actual plans in play to humiliate you," Lindsey said.

"They're welcome to try," Helen said.

"But—" Lindsey started to protest but Helen interrupted her.

"Don't worry, Lindsey. As far as I can tell, Betty and Jackie have one thing in common. They are both supremely dissatisfied with their lives, and for whatever reason they are striking out at me. Probably because I'm actually happy. Miserable people hate that."

"Maybe." Lindsey didn't think it was that simple. "But I think you'd be wise to keep your wits about you."

"Noted." Helen turned back to her computer, and Lindsey knew she was dismissed.

She had her hand on the doorknob when Helen said, "Thank you, Lindsey. I appreciate your concern."

"You're welcome." Lindsey left Helen to her work, hoping that she was wrong and that Helen was right.

At the end of the day, when the library was closing, Lindsey thought Helen might have been right all along. There had been no sign of Jackie or Betty. Maybe Betty had thought better of aligning herself with Jackie, and that was the end of it. Lindsey certainly hoped so.

She was on duty to close the library that evening. Sully was working late as well, and they had agreed to meet at the Blue Anchor for dinner. Lindsey had spent most of the afternoon dreaming about the order of clam fritters she planned to have. The only dilemma was whether she wanted to pair Ian and Mary's famous clam chowder with the fritters or their equally revered lobster bisque. It was a co-nundrum.

The staff gathered by the back door, and they all walked out together. Paula headed straight for her car while Ann Marie loitered, walking slowly, taking deep breaths of the cool evening air.

"Everything all right?" Lindsey asked her.

"Yes, I'm just soaking in the peace and quiet before I go home," Ann Marie answered. She was a mom to two ram-bunctious tween boys, and while she and her husband loved their sons to distraction, they could be exhausting. "The weeks before the holidays can be a lot. Sometimes when I get home, I just sit in my car and listen to the quiet for a few minutes before I go inside."

Lindsey smiled. She'd seen the same frenetic energy in their younger patrons lately, and she expected they'd only ratchet up even more as the holiday loomed closer.

"Take all the time you need. I won't tell," Lindsey said. "See you tomorrow."

"Bright and early," Ann Marie confirmed.

She climbed into her car, and Lindsey continued down the walkway to the side of the building. She followed the sidewalk to Main Street. Across from the library, the park was all lit up with its holiday decorations, and beyond that was the pier where Sully's water taxi company had a small office and where his sister and her husband ran their restau-rant. As she got closer, Lindsey could smell something fry-ing at the Blue Anchor, and she felt her stomach rumble.

She looked both ways and crossed the street, planning

to cut through the park to the restaurant. She was just stepping onto the town green when there was a horrible crackling noise like a giant bug zapper, followed by a shriek, and all the lights went out.

Lindsey stood in the middle of the village square in the dark, knowing that something had just gone horribly, horribly wrong.

"Hello?" she called out into the darkness. No one answered.

She glanced past the park and noted that all of the other lights in town were on. The streetlights, the businesses, everything looked perfectly normal. The power outage was just the green.

Lindsey pulled her phone out of her shoulder bag and turned on the flashlight. It illuminated the area around her but not much. She knew she had heard a shriek, and it sounded as if it had come from the gazebo.

She hurried across the green, circling the arch, and climbed the steps. As far as she knew, this was the only place an electrical outlet could be. She moved her light in a circular direction, not wanting to be surprised by someone appearing out of the darkness.

"Hello? Is anyone here?" She stood still on the top step and listened. There was no sound except for the soft swoosh of the waves on the public beach on the other side of the green. She assumed it must be high tide, as the waves were loud, which indicated they were close to the large rocks that barricaded the park from the bay.

"Lindsey! Everything all right?" a voice called to her from across the green.

Lindsey swiveled around to face the person. She could only see their outline against the backdrop of the streetlights, and she didn't recognize the voice. It sounded muffled, as if the person had their scarf up over their mouth.

"I don't know," she said. "I was walking by the park when I heard a shriek and the lights went out."

Lindsey started down the steps to meet the person halfway, when she was slammed from behind. The hit was right in the middle of her back, and it sent her airborne over the steps. Her phone shot out of her hand, and her shoulder bag fell from her arm. She barely had time to get her arms up to protect her face and head before impact. She hit the frozen ground so hard it knocked the wind out of her.

"Lindsey!"

She could hear the sound of feet running toward her and away from her at the same time. It was disorienting, and she sucked in a gulp of air, trying to inflate her lungs and get some oxygen in her system.

The person running toward her dropped to their knees beside her. "Are you all right? Who can I call? Do you need an ambulance?"

Now that she was closer, Lindsey recognized Helen Monroe.

"No, I'm fine," Lindsey wheezed.

"I don't mean to be argumentative, but no, you're not," Helen said. "Someone pushed you. I saw them run past."

"Did you recognize them?" Lindsey asked. She pushed herself up to a seated position. Thank goodness for her thick coat cushioning her impact, or she was certain she'd have been covered in bruises tomorrow. She probably would be anyway but not as badly.

"It was too dark to make them out," Helen said. "They looked like a big dark shadow, and I was more concerned with you and how hard you hit the ground."

"Thanks." Lindsey glanced around the green. It was still dark, and as far as she could tell, she and Helen were the only people here.

"Let me help you up," Helen offered. She scooped up Lindsey's bag and her phone. "You can sit in the gazebo for a bit and get your legs back under you, unless you want me to call for an ambulance. Do you think you broke anything?"

"No, nothing's broken." Lindsey took the hand Helen offered. Together they made their way up the steps, taking a seat on the bench that ran along the inside of the bandstand.

Lindsey leaned back, trying to get a grip on what had just happened. Had she startled the person who rammed her? Were they the person who had screamed? Was it the lights going out that had caused their fright? She had no idea.

"I think the person who screamed might have been the same person who bumped me," Lindsey said.

"Bumped you?" Helen's voice was gently mocking. "By the light of your phone, I could see the person had their shoulder lowered before they hit you, clearly with intent to harm."

"Well, maybe they thought I was going to hurt them, so they struck first," Lindsey said.

"Possibly, but why run away?" Helen sounded dubious. "Why do you suppose the lights are out?"

"I don't know," Lindsey said. "Perhaps the timer is wonky."

"Does the electricity come from the gazebo?" Helen stood up.

"Yes, it has power."

"If it's that simple, I'm sure we can fix it." Helen reached into her purse and pulled out her phone. Just like Lindsey had, she turned on the flashlight app and swept the faint beam around the gazebo.

"I think the outlet is over there." Lindsey pointed to the far side.

Helen walked in that direction, shining the beam along the wall where the outlet would be. When the light illuminated a pink-and-white-striped hat with a large pink pom-pom, Lindsey gasped. She knew who belonged to that hat.

Helen's beam of light moved from the hat to the puffy white coat and then to the face under the hat. She spun to face Lindsey and said, "It's Jackie Lewis, and I think she's . . . dead."

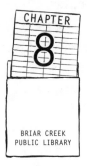

CHAPTER

8

BRIAR CREEK
PUBLIC LIBRARY

Lindsey jumped to her feet. She wobbled but forced herself forward. She crouched beside Jackie. Her face had a ghostly pallor, and her vacant eyes were staring up at the gazebo ceiling as if she were looking for something, a string of lights clutched in her hands.

"Call the police," Lindsey said.

"Oh my God, oh my God, oh my God," Helen muttered as her fingers fumbled with her phone. "This can't be happening. It just can't."

Lindsey knew better than to touch Jackie so as not to contaminate the scene. Instead, she lifted her phone and turned on the light, which thankfully still worked. She aimed the beam at Jackie's body, looking for any signs of injury or bleeding. There was nothing.

"This is Helen Monroe, yes, there's been an . . . accident?"

She glanced at Lindsey in dismay. "At least, I think it was an accident."

"The place, Helen, tell them where we are," Lindsey said.

"I'm at the park, in the gazebo, with Lindsey the librarian," she said. "No, Lindsey is fine, but we found a body. It's Jackie Lewis and we think she's dead."

Lindsey could hear the muffled voice on the other end. They sounded calm as they asked questions.

"No, we haven't touched her." Helen glanced at Jackie's body. Her face was pale and her voice sounded shaky. She was clearly struggling with the reality of someone she knew lying dead at their feet. "No, she's not breathing. She's just staring . . ." With a sob, Helen handed the phone to Lindsey. "I can't."

"It's okay." Lindsey took the phone. "Hi, this is Lindsey."

"Lindsey, are you safe? Are you all right?" It was Molly Hatcher, the administrative assistant and dispatcher for the Briar Creek Police Department.

"I'm fine," Lindsey said. "But Jackie Lewis isn't."

"The chief was here when the call came in," Molly said. "She's on her way."

"Thank you, Molly." Lindsey glanced at the park, hoping to see Emma appear.

"Do you want me to call Sully and let him know what's happening?" Molly asked.

"No, thanks," Lindsey said. "It'll be better coming from me."

"Lindsey!" Emma Plewicki appeared at the edge of the park.

"Up here!" Lindsey said. "Chief's here. Thanks for your help, Molly."

"Of course," Molly said.

Lindsey returned Helen's phone to her and stood up. She was relieved that she'd caught her breath and her legs seemed steadier. She raised her phone to illuminate Jackie's body so that Emma could see.

"And here I thought we were going to have a quiet holiday season," Emma muttered. She unclipped the Maglite from her belt. It was much more powerful than Lindsey's puny phone flashlight, and the entire gazebo was immediately bathed in light.

Emma ran the beam over Jackie's body, pausing on her bare hands. She jumped back and grabbed Helen by the arm and shoved her toward the steps and then did the same thing to Lindsey. "Get out of the gazebo. Now!"

"Why? What's happening?" Helen asked.

"Go!" Emma shooed them away. The urgency in her voice did not invite dawdling.

They dashed down the steps, only stopping when Emma did. They were thirty feet from the bandstand, and Emma pulled her phone out of her jacket pocket.

"What is it, Emma?" Lindsey asked. "What's wrong?"

"I'm not positive, but I think our victim up there was electrocuted," Emma said. "If the current is still live, one of you could have been next."

Lindsey and Helen gaped at each other. The horror of how close they'd come to joining Jackie hit both of them at the same time. To Lindsey's surprise, Helen reached out and grabbed her arm. Lindsey put her hand over Helen's and squeezed her gloved fingers with her own.

"Wait here, do not go any closer to the gazebo," Emma ordered. She had her phone to her ear, and Lindsey heard her giving commands in rapid-fire police chief–speak as she paced back and forth, glancing at the gazebo every few seconds as if she expected it to burst into flames.

"Electrocuted?" Helen whispered.

"Apparently," Lindsey replied. "How did she know? I couldn't see any marks on her."

Helen's eyes were wide, as if she couldn't believe what was happening. Lindsey was right there with her.

Emma ended her call and joined them where they stood. Her hands were shoved into her pockets, and she huddled into her thick uniform coat, trying to block the December chill.

"How do you know she was electrocuted?" Lindsey asked.

Emma glanced between them as if considering whether to answer. Finally, she nodded and said, "Her hands. Where the cord touched her palms, there were burns, deep crater burns, the sort a person gets from being electrocuted and having the current go through them, burning their tissues."

"Oh, Jackie." Helen clapped a hand over her mouth and spun away. From the shudder that ran through her, Lindsey suspected she was trying not to be sick.

"I had you two leave the gazebo because if my theory that Jackie was electrocuted by the holiday lights is correct then the current could still be live. I don't know enough about electricity to know if it's safe up there. If the current was still running through her, touching her could have caused any of us to be electrocuted, too."

Lindsey took a steadying breath. "But they're just holiday lights. They can't be strong enough to kill a person, could they?"

"That's a question for an electrician," Emma said. "All I know is burns like hers are really, really bad."

Emma's phone rang, and she lifted it to her ear as she turned away.

"Are you all right, Helen?" Lindsey asked. "Can I get you anything?"

"No." Helen shook her head. She swallowed and then said, "You know I write about all sorts of grisly scenarios, but I've never dealt with it on a personal level. Jackie and I might have been at odds, but I would never wish this on her."

"I'm sorry." Lindsey nodded. She remembered the first time she'd encountered a dead body at a murder scene. It had haunted her for months. Of course, there was no reason to think this was a murder scene. It was most likely just a horrible accident. "I wonder what Jackie was doing out here."

"She had to have been meeting someone, don't you think?" Helen asked. "I mean, it wasn't her ghost that flattened you while running from the gazebo."

"You're right," Lindsey said. "We have to tell Emma."

"Tell Emma what?" Emma asked as she joined them.

"Someone was with Jackie," Lindsey said. "Or at least someone found her before we did."

"What do you mean?" Emma asked.

"Lindsey was standing on the steps of the gazebo when I called out to her about the lights being out," Helen said. "She turned to come and meet me, and this shadow rose up behind her and slammed into her back, knocking her down the steps."

"Are you all right?" Emma studied Lindsey as if looking for damage.

"Yeah, they just knocked the wind out of me. Helen helped me up, and then we sat on the bench while I caught my breath. That's when we saw Jackie," Lindsey said. "Honestly, I forgot about being knocked down after that."

"Understandable. How much time passed between you being shoved and discovering Jackie?" Emma asked.

"A couple of minutes? Maybe five?" Lindsey looked at Helen.

"About that," Helen agreed.

"Well, hell, they could be anywhere by now." Emma frowned. "Helen, I want you to think about what you saw. Any detail about the person no matter how insignificant it might seem would help."

Helen nodded. "Of course. I'll do my best, but it was dark and I was so focused on Lindsey, I'm afraid I didn't see much."

"That's okay, just try," Emma said. She glanced at the

edge of the park, where two cars pulled up to the curb. One was a patrol car but the other was a black SUV. "I had Molly ask Ernesto Peña from facilities to come. He's the town electrician. He's the only one who'll know if the area is safe or not."

Ernesto was a spark plug of a man. Prepared for the assignment, he came across the grass wearing a hard hat with a light on it and carrying a toolbox.

"I hear you had a power outage, Chief," he said.

"A little bit more than that I'm afraid," Emma said. The officer who followed Ernesto was one of Lindsey's favorites on the force. A big, rawboned redhead with a calm demeanor, Officer Kirkland made every room he entered feel safer. Even now in the dark, Lindsey was reassured just by having him here.

"What do you need me to do?" Ernesto asked.

"Can you check to make sure there are no electrical currents live anywhere?" Emma asked.

"No problem." Ernesto glanced at the gazebo. "Looks like it's out but better safe than—"

"There's one more thing," Emma interrupted. "It appears a person was electrocuted in the gazebo. Medical personnel are on the way, but I don't want you to disturb the body if at all possible."

Ernesto's eyebrows rose. "There's a person up there? A dead person?"

"Yes." Emma nodded.

"I . . . uh . . . I don't think . . ." Ernesto swallowed as if he was already anticipating being sick to his stomach. He glanced up at the dark night sky overhead and then at the chief. "I've never seen a dead body before." He looked embarrassed to admit this.

"The first is the worst," Officer Kirkland said.

"I wouldn't ask this of you, Ernie, if we didn't need you. Officer Kirkland will go with you," Emma said. She looked at Kirkland, who nodded. "Do whatever he says. Do not touch anything that might have a live current."

"Roger that," Kirkland said. "Come on, Ernie, I'll be with you. It'll be all right."

Together the two men headed for the gazebo. Lindsey watched them go with a feeling of dread.

"Lindsey!" Sully shouted from across the green. She could just make out his shape under the beam of the streetlight.

"Over here!" She lifted her arm and waved. Sully broke into a jog.

He didn't stop until he reached them, and he swooped her into a quick hug. "I saw the patrol car and knew you were walking this way. Is everything all right?"

Lindsey hugged him in return, taking comfort in his warmth. She leaned back and met his gaze and said, "No, it's not."

Sully took a deep breath and glanced at Emma and Helen and back at Lindsey. "What happened?"

"Jackie Lewis is dead," Lindsey said. "From what Emma could tell, she was electrocuted."

Sully's brows drew together in a frown. "Here?"

"As far as I can determine, she was zapped by the

holiday lights," Emma said. "But Ernie is making certain it's safe before we put anyone in danger and investigate further."

Sully nodded. He pulled Lindsey gently up against his side as if to reassure himself that she was okay. Lindsey leaned in.

They waited as the light on Ernie's hard hat lit up the area around the gazebo. There was the sound of a person retching, and Lindsey suspected Ernie had seen Jackie. Poor guy. Kirkland was right. The first was the worst.

"The area is safe," Ernie announced as he and Kirkland came back from behind the gazebo. He and Sully exchanged a nod of acknowledgment before Ernie continued. "I checked the circuit box and made certain all of the switches are off to the gazebo. I also unplugged the lights that the woman is holding. I have a portable floodlight in my truck if you need it."

"Yes, please," Emma said. Ernie started to walk away, when she called out, "Wait. Just to clarify, is it possible that the woman was electrocuted by a string of holiday lights?"

"Oh, yeah." Ernie turned around to face them. "Happens all the time. People don't usually die, but thousands end up in the emergency room every year with severe burns."

"Those little twinkle lights don't seem like they'd be strong enough to cause that much harm." Kirkland glanced around the park with a frown.

"That's why people get hurt, I expect. They don't realize it only takes one hundred milliamperes to stop a heart, and a string of one hundred lights runs about four thousand milliamperes," Ernie explained.

"But aren't these lights safe?" Helen asked. She gestured to the village. "I mean, they're all over the place."

"Yes, they're very safe, but missing or broken bulbs, frayed or exposed wires, standing water in the vicinity can all be factors," Ernie said. He glanced at the gazebo, and his face became grim. "The facilities department is very thorough when inspecting the holiday displays. We have several people go over the same strands just to be certain they're in good condition. There's no way they missed something. This had to be a freak accident or . . ."

"Or what?" Emma asked.

"Or someone messed with the lights." He turned and headed for his truck, leaving them to ponder his assessment.

S ully ordered takeout from the Blue Anchor and met Helen and Lindsey at the police station, where Emma was having them fill out their statements.

Helen scooped up some of the hot chowder while she read over what she'd written on the form. "It feels impolite to eat after discovering the body of someone I've known for years."

"Not eating isn't going to help Jackie." Lindsey picked at the clam fritter on her plate. She'd been looking forward to this meal, but now it was just sustenance.

"No, I don't suppose so." Helen sighed and rubbed her eyes with the tips of her fingers. "This feels like a bad dream. I keep expecting to wake up."

"You mentioned before that you and Jackie were in a critique group together?" Lindsey asked. "Were you friends then?"

"We were," Helen said. "There were four of us—Jackie, Melanie Starland, Liz Maynard, and me—we all had best-selling aspirations."

"Were you the only one who made it?" Sully asked.

Helen lowered her spoon into her chowder. "One of our group never got the chance. Cancer."

"I'm sorry," Lindsey and Sully said together.

"Thanks." Helen nodded. "It was the first crack in our foursome. Melanie was the glue that held us all together, and when she passed, well, the group sort of fell apart. Liz quit writing to become a legal secretary because she had kids and needed a more reliable income. That left just Jackie and me. We didn't last more than six months without the others."

Lindsey and Sully were quiet, letting Helen share as much or as little as she wanted. She glanced up at them and said, "And now she's dead."

"When she first introduced herself to me, Jackie said she was your number one fan," Lindsey said. "But she wasn't, was she?"

"No." Helen shook her head. "She was very bitter about the success of my series. I sold the books after our critique group broke up, and by then, Jackie had lost the ability to even pretend to be happy for me."

"That's too bad," Lindsey said. "It's hard when friend-ships end."

Helen gave her a wan smile.

"Were you the only author Jackie had a problem with?" Sully asked.

Helen shrugged. "I don't know. As I mentioned, we haven't been close in a long time."

Lindsey thought about her staff, the people she worked with every day. She couldn't imagine not knowing about their lives. Then again, Jackie and Helen had been critique partners, not coworkers, and it had been over ten years ago. If she left here and moved elsewhere, would she know what was happening with her former employees? Probably not. And a critique group wasn't even as formal as coworkers. She couldn't fault Helen for not knowing what was happening in Jackie's life. Especially when Jackie had been so fixated on Helen's success. Why would Helen keep in touch?

"Have you finished your reports?" Emma asked as she entered the room.

"Just reading them over before we sign," Lindsey said.

"I appreciate your cooperation," Emma said. "I do have a few questions for you, Ms. Monroe, if you don't mind?"

"Not at all," Helen said.

"Great." Emma reached into the satchel she was carrying and pulled out a large clear plastic evidence bag. There was a thick sheaf of papers inside. "Do you think you can tell me why Jackie had what appears to be the start of your current manuscript in her shoulder bag, which was found at the scene?"

CHAPTER

9

BRIAR CREEK
PUBLIC LIBRARY

T hat's mine!" Helen rose from her seat and leaned over the table. She went to grab the bag, but Emma pulled it away. "Sorry. It's evidence and will remain in police custody. You are certain it's yours?"

"Yes!" Helen frowned. "But why would Jackie have it? I keep it locked in the study room with my other research materials." She looked at Lindsey in panic. "Could someone have broken into the library? Into my workspace?"

"I don't see how," Lindsey said. "I know the staff checks the doors and would have noticed if someone had tampered with your room or it was left unlocked at closing."

"How many keys are there to the room?" Emma asked.

"No keys," Lindsey replied. "It locks with a keypad. Helen has her own code. We had her set it for her exclusive use. No one else can get in unless the door is left unlocked."

"I need to go and see if anything else is missing. Some of the books I'm using are through interlibrary loan," Helen said. She glanced at Lindsey with an alarmed expression.

"You can go as soon as you're done here," Emma said. "I'll have Officer Kirkland meet you there just in case there is something to report, such as other missing materials or damage."

Helen stood up and started to pace, clearly anxious to get to the library.

"Can you tell me about anyone in Jackie's life who might have wanted to harm her?" Emma asked.

"You think she was electrocuted on purpose?" Helen gaped.

Emma shrugged. "Someone pushed Lindsey down the steps as they were fleeing the scene. If they had just stumbled upon the body, why would they run?"

"Panic," Helen suggested. "Who knows what they were doing in the park? Maybe they were doing something unrelated but also illegal, found Jackie and freaked out."

"Maybe," Emma conceded. "Still, I have to rule out all possibilities. It's my job."

Helen nodded. She blew out a breath and crossed her arms over her chest. "I was just telling Sully and Lindsey that I'd lost touch with Jackie several years ago, so I really have no idea what was going on in her life or who she was involved with. She was divorced and had no children. She might have stayed in contact with Liz, our other critique partner, who quit writing to go back to work, but Liz has never mentioned her to me when we've spoken."

"So all you know for certain is that Ms. Lewis believed you stole her work and your success should have been hers," Emma said.

"Her *idea*. Jackie said I stole her idea." Helen met Emma's gaze. "She was a bit fixated on that, but it's not true. I got the inspiration for my series after I left our critique group, which was down to just the two of us and wasn't going well. Jackie had a book deal for her intergalactic police procedural series, which doesn't resemble my thrillers in any way."

"Would you say it's your word against hers?" Emma asked.

"No, because my agent and editor helped me develop the Mallory Quest series, so they know the idea was mine as it evolved from my initial proposal into a much bigger story with their input. As I said at the ugly sweater party, she was writing a science fiction novel with space police, not a thriller about an FBI agent."

"There doesn't seem to be much crossover there," Emma admitted. "Can you give me the name of your editor and agent?"

Helen looked surprised and very resistant.

"No, I'm not going to pitch an idea for a book to them," Emma joked.

Helen sighed. "Sorry, I get that a lot, as you can imagine. Of course you can have their contact information. Can I ask why?"

"Would I be wrong in assuming Ms. Lewis reached out to them after your series proved so successful, using you as a point of contact?" Emma asked.

"No, you wouldn't," Helen said. "Jackie had hoped my agent would represent her and my editor would publish her, but they don't work in the genre she writes . . . wrote . . . so they passed."

"I'm guessing that didn't go well," Emma said.

"Understatement," Helen said.

"Do you have a record of any harassment you've been on the receiving end of from Ms. Lewis?"

"Nothing recent. I did have a restraining order at one time, but I blocked Jackie on social media and moved to a new home in an undisclosed location. It's been refreshingly peaceful for the past few years."

"Why did you take the residency, then?" Emma asked. "You had to know she'd find out and show up."

Lindsey sat silently, her head swiveling from Emma to Helen and back. Emma was asking all of the questions Lindsey wanted answers to. She noted Sully was doing the same, and she exchanged a brief glance with him. He raised his eyebrows, signifying he was as interested in Helen's responses as she was.

"Honestly?" Helen paused. "I've been struggling since I ended my series. I thought the accountability of a writing residency would make me more productive, and this was the first one that popped up."

"And has it helped?" Emma asked.

Helen glanced away before she said, "No."

Lindsey felt her breath catch. She hadn't really considered the ramifications of the writer in residence struggling to finish their novel. She had just assumed that they'd have something to show for their time. From the grim set of Helen's features, that was not going to be the case here.

"All right." Emma pushed off the edge of the table. "You are free to go, but I might be calling on you at any time with more questions."

"That's fine," Helen said. "Are you ready, Lindsey?"

Lindsey took the last bite of her fritter and final spoonful of her chowder. "I am now."

"I'll have Kirkland meet you at the staff entrance to the library," Emma said. With a curt wave, she left the room.

Lindsey pulled on her coat, as did Sully and Helen. They quickly signed their statements and dumped their empty food containers in the trash. Lindsey grabbed her bag on the way out the door, looping the strap across her shoulders, which were still sore from her fall.

It was dark and cold as they walked down the sidewalk from the police station to the library. Lindsey glanced across the street at the park, where she saw the medical examiner's van parked at the curb. The floodlight that Ernie had set up illuminated the gazebo with a glaring bright white light, and Lindsey could see the crime scene technicians in their Tyvek suits examining the area. Little yellow markers were set up all over the floor of the gazebo, and a photographer was taking pictures, their flash popping every few seconds.

Helen glanced at the park and then away, walking faster.

It was a furtive look, and Lindsey felt a sense of urgency coming from her that she didn't understand. Helen wrote thrillers about suburban murders that were ranked high on the terrifying scale. She said she'd never dealt with a grisly death on a personal level. Did that also mean this was the first time she'd had anything like this happen in her own life?

"Helen, is this the first time you've ever seen a dead body?" Lindsey asked.

"Yes, unlike you, it's not a hobby for the rest of us," Helen said. Lindsey recoiled at the harshness of her tone. Helen glanced at her and said, "Sorry. That was out of line. I'm just a bit freaked out. I mean, of course, I've seen a dead body before, but it was always in a casket prepared for burial, not tripped over in a gazebo with her eyes open and staring . . ." She shivered.

"It's not a hobby for me either," Lindsey said. She gave Helen the side-eye. "It sounds like you know I've been involved in some investigations before."

"I did some research on the town before I came," Helen admitted. "The librarian who stumbles across bodies and solves murders came up several times in my online search."

"Oh." Lindsey didn't know what to say to that.

She exchanged a look with Sully, and he appeared equally stymied as to how to explain. Briar Creek was a lovely place to live, they just had a very small police force, and the village residents frequently helped when something bad happened, be it a stolen bicycle or a homicide.

"Is it like that?" Helen gestured at the gazebo.

"Pretty much," Lindsey conceded. "These things just seem to happen, and the community feels compelled to help."

"But you're a librarian," Helen protested. "You don't work with dead people, unless your side hustle is extra shifts as an undertaker?"

"No." Lindsey shook her head with a small smile. "And it's not just me. Everyone pitches in where they can."

"Including when the bodies are discovered?" Helen asked.

"Occasionally." Lindsey slipped her gloved hand into Sully's, and he squeezed her fingers in reassurance.

"Silly me. I thought small towns were about Little League, yard sales and community gardens," Helen said.

"We have those, too," Sully offered.

Helen gave him an arch look, but whatever she was about to say was interrupted by Officer Kirkland as he stepped forward from the alcove where the library's rear door was set back from the parking lot.

"Hey, Sully, Lindsey, Ms. Monroe," he greeted them.

"Ah!" Helen let out a yelp and stepped back. She put her hand over her heart and glared at him. "You might have warned us that you were there."

"Apologies." He held up his hands in a gesture of innocence. "I didn't want to interrupt."

Helen looked marginally mollified. Lindsey moved forward and unlocked the library door, using her key, and then disarmed the alarm once they were inside. She switched the lights on for the main part of the library and gestured for Helen to go ahead.

Helen strode down the hall and across the building to the line of study rooms. She was about to grab the handle of the room, when Officer Kirkland said, "Wait, let me." He pulled on a blue latex glove that he had in his pocket. "It's best not to touch anything. If we discover more items missing, we'll want to dust for fingerprints."

"Of course." Helen stepped aside and Kirkland tried the door. It was locked. Helen glanced over her shoulder at Lindsey to be certain she knew it, too.

"I'll check with my staff to make certain it was locked when they closed the building," Lindsey said.

"Thanks, Lindsey, that'd be a big help," Kirkland said. He handed Helen a pair of gloves. "Put these on, please, just in case we find something and want to check the room for fingerprints."

Helen pulled on the gloves and punched her code into the keypad beside the door. The distinct click of the door unlocking broke the silence. Kirkland turned the handle and pushed the door open.

Helen went inside and Kirkland followed. Lindsey and Sully stayed outside the office, not wanting to get in the way. Lindsey watched through the glass wall and saw Helen's relief when she opened a bottom drawer on the right side of the desk and all of the books she'd borrowed for her research were there. She sent Lindsey a thumbs-up, and Lindsey felt her tension ease, too.

"What do you think happened today?" Sully asked.

"Meaning to Jackie?" Lindsey asked.

"Yeah," he said. He dropped his voice so that only

Lindsey could hear him. "After that scene at the sweater contest, it wouldn't surprise me if Helen had a beef with Jackie."

"And electrocuted her?" Lindsey asked.

"Not on purpose," he said. "It could have been an accident."

Lindsey pulled him a few feet from the room while Helen and Kirkland checked it over.

"You think Helen and Jackie were fighting before I got there?" Lindsey asked.

"You said in your statement that Helen appeared right after the power went out," he said.

Lindsey frowned. "But someone else knocked me down. Helen was on the sidewalk and was walking toward me when I got hit from behind."

"Yes, but she could have left the gazebo before and walked around the park in the dark, coming out on the street," he said. "It would make her look innocent."

"Then who shoved me down the steps?"

Sully shrugged. "Someone who was already there who saw what happened to Jackie and was afraid they'd be next?"

"I don't like thinking Helen had anything to do with it."

"We can't rule her out just because she's an author whose work you enjoy."

"I know," Lindsey agreed. "But I just don't see her hurting anyone. She was absolutely shocked at the gazebo when we found Jackie. I don't think she could fake that sort of horror."

"Who else had a reason to murder Jackie?" he asked.

"I don't know," Lindsey said. "But I do know that we overheard Jackie arguing with Betty the night of the holiday light ceremony."

"We did," Sully agreed.

"And it sounded like they had some sort of deal brokered," Lindsey said. "As in Jackie expected Betty to help her out by humiliating Helen."

"I remember," Sully said. "Are you thinking that Betty is the one who electrocuted Jackie?"

Lindsey shrugged. "I think it's worth mentioning to Emma, don't you?"

"Definitely," he agreed. "But I sense you want to do some investigating of your own before we go to Emma, am I right?"

"Would that be so bad?" Lindsey asked. "I mean, it's the holidays and Emma is going to be swamped. If we can rule out Betty ahead of time, we can save Emma so much work."

"Uh-huh. I take it we're getting involved?" His bright blue eyes did not hold a bit of surprise.

"I think we have to," Lindsey said. "I mean, why did Jackie have Helen's manuscript? Don't you think that's suspicious?"

"It's odd, for sure." Sully put his arm around Lindsey's shoulders and pulled her into his side. He kissed her head and said, "Tell me what you need me to do."

"Help me investigate Betty's alibi for tonight, assuming she has one," Lindsey said.

"Oh, boy." Sully sighed. "You know I'd do anything for you, but . . ."

"I know."

"If I do this, you have to promise me you won't leave me alone with her," he said.

"Michael Sullivan, are you afraid of Betty Caruthers?" Lindsey asked.

"As any sane man would be," he countered.

"That's fair," she said. "I promise I won't leave you alone with her, but we're going to have to move quickly. I think our best chance is to catch her off guard at the senior center cookie sale."

"At least there will be cookies," Sully said, consoling himself.

CHAPTER

10

BRIAR CREEK
PUBLIC LIBRARY

"How many tubs of cookies did you bake, Nanners?" Charlie Peyton asked as he used a handcart to deliver three more enormous plastic tubs of cookies. Sully followed behind him with a second handcart.

"I think I closed in around a thousand this year," Nancy said. "This fund-raiser is what keeps the senior center going. I have to do my part."

"I'd say you've done yours and everyone else's," Sully said. He helped Charlie unload the tubs, and they headed back to the parking lot, where the rest of Nancy's cookies were loaded in the back of her car.

"How are you feeling?" Nancy asked Lindsey. "If this is too much for you after last night, you don't have to help. I have the rest of the crafternooners taking shifts all day, and Charlie is here to help, too."

"No, I'm fine," Lindsey said. "This is one of my favorite holiday activities. I get dibs on all of my favorites. Besides, did you see the look on Monique Wallace's face when we rolled in with these tubs?"

"I did not. I bake out of the goodness of my heart," Nancy said. "I would never stoop to competing over who baked the most cookies. Although, I heard from a very reliable source that Monique topped out at seven hundred and fifty cookies. Amateur."

Lindsey turned her head to hide her grin. She lifted the lid off the tub closest to her and began to plate the cookies, using the paper-lined plastic trays and the food prep gloves Nancy had provided.

"Did you ever consider opening up a bakery?" Lindsey asked as Nancy arranged decorative sugar cookies on her own tray.

"No." Nancy shook her head. "I never wanted my hobby to become a job. It would suck the joy right out of it."

Lindsey thought about the library and realized her love of books had never been a hobby. It had been her entire life. An avid reader as a child, she had always known that she would work with books; she'd just never known in what capacity. When she discovered library science, it had been the perfect fit.

"Nancy, you have outdone yourself again," Sarah Costas, the senior center coordinator, said as she approached their table.

Nancy preened a little before she said, "I have already

put aside a tin of your favorites. It's my way of saying thank you for all of your hard work."

"Yay!" Sarah cheered. "Your gingerbread cookies make it all worth it."

"Sarah! Sarah!" Betty Caruthers waved from the long table next to theirs.

"Well, almost worth it," Sarah muttered. With a forced smile, she waved and said, "Be right there." Then she turned to Nancy and Lindsey. "Do you really want to be next to Betty? I had people offering to pay me to make certain they weren't within three tables of her."

"We're fine here," Lindsey said. She ignored the doubtful look Nancy sent her.

"If you say so. Usually, no one wants to be in her vicinity," Sarah said. She adjusted her apron and met Lindsey's gaze with a questioning glance. "You actually made my job easier with this sacrifice, so thank you for that."

"Happy to help."

Sully and Charlie returned with the last of the tubs and assisted Lindsey and Nancy in the placement of the cookies. A glance at the clock informed them that the doors would be opening in five minutes.

"Take your places, crew," Charlie said. He fastened his shoulder-length black hair into a ponytail. Like the rest of them, he wore an apron and food service gloves. "What's going to be the hot ticket this year, Nanners?"

"It's a toss-up," she said. "We have the ever-popular raspberry linzers over there or the pecan shortbread that my friend John Charles gave me the recipe for—trust me, they're to die for. They're also my new favorite, so I'm showcasing them in the center."

Nancy was known throughout the village for her cookie-baking skills, and Lindsey had been the grateful recipient of Nancy's annual tin of cookies every year since she moved here, but she also attended the cookie sale, because one could never have enough Christmas cookies. Still, every year she was stunned by the sheer volume of cookies Nancy managed to bake for the event.

As they settled into their stations, Lindsey watched Betty out of the corner of her eye. Aware of Betty's fondness for Sully, they had given him the section closest to Betty's side of the table. Knowing full well that Betty wouldn't be able to resist the opportunity to flirt with him, Lindsey hoped that Sully managed to get her talking, particularly about her friendship with Jackie and where she had been last night. He had reluctantly agreed.

The police hadn't released any details about Jackie's death, but Lindsey had heard from Robbie that Emma was treating it as suspicious. Footage from the security cameras in the park was in black and white and very grainy, so it hadn't helped to identify the person who shoved Lindsey. Also, the person in the footage was wearing a coat, hat and scarf, which hid their features.

As soon as the doors opened, Nancy's table had a line forming, and Lindsey was immediately busy bagging up orders. She glanced at Sully, who looked ill at ease. She almost felt bad for using him as a lure, but desperate times and all.

"Hi, Sully," Betty greeted him. She was holding up a plate of what looked suspiciously like store-bought cookies. "Do you want to try one of my cookies?" She giggled when she said it, as if she had suggested something naughty.

Lindsey forced herself to keep her head down and not roll her eyes. It was a struggle.

"Hi, Betty, those sure look good." Sully's voice sounded strained.

"I made them myself," she said.

"My aunt Fanny she did." Nancy leaned close and whispered to Lindsey, "That woman wouldn't know which side of a spatula to use if it slapped her."

"Let's just sell cookies," Lindsey said.

"Remind me again why Sully is trying to get information out of her," Nancy said.

Lindsey lowered her voice and whispered, "Because we overheard an argument between Jackie and Betty the night of the town's holiday light ceremony, and since Betty likes Sully, maybe she'll say something about the situation."

"Do you think the women knew each other before Jackie arrived in town?" Nancy asked.

"I think they had to," Lindsey said. "Jackie was very upset with Betty. It sounded like they had a plan to humiliate Helen, and Jackie didn't feel as if Betty had upheld her part of the agreement."

"And Sully is supposed to discover whether this is true?" Nancy sounded doubtful.

"He's going to try and get her talking and see if she says something suspicious," Lindsey said.

"Snickerdoodles!" A woman clapped her hands in delight, causing both Lindsey and Nancy to jump. "Can I have a dozen? It just isn't Christmas without your cookies, Nancy."

"Aw, thanks," Nancy said. "That's very kind of you to say, Tracy."

"Nothing kind about it," Tracy said. "Do you have your fruitcake cookies, too?"

"Of course!" Nancy started bagging the snickerdoodles, and Lindsey took the opportunity to eavesdrop on Sully and Betty.

"It's just tragic!" Betty cried. She tossed her long blond hair over her shoulder and stared up at Sully, blinking her overly large eyes.

"Did you know Jackie?" Sully asked.

"No." Betty blinked more rapidly.

Lindsey was surprised the woman's nose didn't start to grow, it was so obviously a lie.

"Really?" Sully asked. "Because the night of the holiday light festival, I could have sworn that I saw you talking to her. It looked tense."

"Well, she was very emotional about being escorted out of the ugly sweater competition." Betty put down her platter of cookies and began to play with her hair. She twirled it around her fingers as she said, "I'm sure I was just trying to console her. My heart is too big for my own good."

Lindsey had just bitten into an almond cookie and inhaled a bit of powdered sugar. She started to cough and choke. Nancy reached over and thumped her between the shoulder blades all while talking to her customer.

"I'm all right," Lindsey said. She took a sip from her water bottle and glanced over at Sully.

His features looked pinched, as if he couldn't take much more, and she was filled with sympathy. She couldn't put him through any more of this, no matter if Betty and Jackie had been up to no good. She'd find another way to get the information.

"Hey, Sully, can you grab the extra box of baggies from the car?" Lindsey called. "We're running low."

"Sure." Sully jetted forward as if he couldn't wait to run an errand for her. He turned to Betty and said, "Sorry. Gotta go."

He headed out from behind their table with a speed that rivaled an Olympic runner, and Lindsey wondered briefly if he even planned to come back.

"I know what you did," Betty said.

Lindsey glanced at her. Did Betty know that she had sent Sully over to her side of the table to try to get information? Should Lindsey even bother trying to deny it?

"I don't know what you mean." Lindsey decided to bluff.

"You don't need any more bags," Betty said. She gestured at the box of bags at Lindsey's feet. "You just wanted to get your husband away from me." She paused to perform yet another hair toss. "I get it. It happens all the time."

"I'm sure it does." Lindsey cleared her throat. She gave

Betty's cookies a pointed look and said, "I didn't know you were a baker."

Betty frowned. "I'm not. Unlike some people, I have better things to do with my time."

"Hey!" Nancy bristled, turning away from her customer to glower at Betty.

Betty shrugged. "Just sayin'."

"You were right. I did want to get my husband away from you," Lindsey said. "But not for the reason you think."

"Right. What other reason could there be?" Betty looked bored.

"I think you're involved in the murder of Jackie Lewis," Lindsey said. "And I don't want my husband anywhere near someone like that."

"Murder?" Betty gaped. "Who said anything about murder? I thought it was just a freak accident."

"Was it? Was it really?" Lindsey asked.

"If it was, it certainly wasn't me who did it," Betty said. "You should be looking at the person with a motive. The person who stole Jackie's ideas. Your precious writer in residence Helen Monroe seems the most likely candidate to me."

"You don't actually believe that, do you?" Lindsey asked.

"I do." Betty tipped her chin up.

"Convenient."

"What's that supposed to mean?" Betty snapped.

"That it's awfully convenient of you to believe someone

else has a motive when you were seen arguing with the victim a couple of days before she died by no less than two witnesses," Lindsey said. "I can't wait until Chief Plewicki gets here so I can tell her all about it."

Betty gasped. "Are you threatening me?"

"Nope." Lindsey shook her head. "Just stating facts."

"Listen, Jackie found out I was one of the judges, and she approached me," Betty said.

"Why?" Lindsey asked. The line at the table was long, but she was in no place to help Nancy right now.

"She said she wanted to humiliate Helen Monroe." Betty shrugged. "She knew that I wanted to have Helen's books banned—because they're trash—and that I didn't think Helen should be the writer in residence, so Jackie asked me if I'd help."

"And you agreed?" Lindsey asked.

"After I heard her reasons, of course I did," Betty said. Her eyes narrowed. "We jilted first wives have to stick together."

"Excuse me?" Lindsey raised her eyebrow in surprise.

"Oh?" Betty gave her a close-lipped smile, looking very self-satisfied. "You didn't know?"

"Know what?" Lindsey asked.

"Your precious author Helen Monroe stole Jackie's husband."

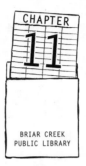

CHAPTER

11

BRIAR CREEK
PUBLIC LIBRARY

Lindsey felt as if all the air were suddenly sucked out of the room. *This couldn't be true. Could it?* Then she remembered what Jackie had said at the ugly sweater party, that it wasn't just her ideas that Helen had stolen. *Had Jackie meant her husband?* And if she remembered right, Helen hadn't said a word in argument. In fact, she had gone out of her way not to engage.

"Yeah, that puts a different spin on Jackie's death, doesn't it?" Betty sounded entirely too joyful about this. "Like maybe you're right and it was murder."

"Oh, now you're so sure it was murder and not a freak accident?" Lindsey asked. She was trying to remain calm, but if what Betty said was true, then this changed everything.

"You said it was murder first, and, yes, now that you

mention it, it does feel like Jackie's death was no accident."
Betty picked up one of Nancy's gingerbread men and bit the
head off.

"Hey!" Nancy cried. "Those are extra. That'll be two
dollars."

"Whatever." Betty dropped the cookie onto her table
and said, "It's dry."

Nancy gasped, as did the customers right in front of her
table. This was the deepest of insults to Nancy's baking.
Lindsey felt as if Betty had just executed the equivalent of
a glove across the face. No wonder no one wanted a table
near hers.

"Dry? Dry?! I'll give you dry, you shriveled-up prune,"
Nancy spat as she charged toward the other woman.

"Ah!" Betty gasped in outrage.

Charlie and Lindsey exchanged a look, and Charlie
swooped in between the two women. "Now, ladies, let's
remember that we're here to raise money for the senior
center."

"That's right." Betty tipped her head to the side and
studied Nancy. "Given your advanced years, Nancy, I really
need to be more charitable toward you. The senior center is
likely all you have, isn't it?"

"That's it!" Nancy looked like she was about to tackle
Betty to the ground and put a hurt on her, but thankfully
Chief Plewicki appeared on the other side of the table.

"Everything all right here?" Emma asked.

Charlie grabbed his aunt by the shoulders and gently
spun her around and pushed her back to her own table.

"It's fine," Nancy grumbled.

"Fine? It's fabulous," Betty said. The glitter in her gaze was triumphant when she glanced at Lindsey and then turned to the chief. "You should ask Lindsey about Jackie Lewis's murder. She knows some things."

Emma's eyebrows shot up, and she pushed her hat back on her head. "I wasn't aware that Jackie Lewis's death had been declared a murder."

"Oh, it totally is," Betty insisted. "Go ahead, Lindsey, tell her your theory about Helen."

Lindsey frowned. She refused to be needled by Betty. "I don't have a theory."

"No?" Betty put a hand on her chest in mock surprise. "You certainly seemed to have one when you accused me of being in cahoots with Jackie."

"Well, you were, you said so yourself," Lindsey said. And just like that, the tables turned, giving Lindsey no small sense of satisfaction.

"I said no such thing!" Betty protested.

The crowd at Nancy's table had paused to watch the exchange, and Lindsey could feel the weight of their scrutiny. She glanced at Emma to see if she noticed. She did. Emma glanced between Lindsey and Betty and said, "Why don't you two come with me."

"I would, but I can't leave my table unattended." Betty shrugged.

"I'm sorry. Did it sound like a request?" Emma countered.

"But my cookies." Betty pouted.

"Charlie, watch Betty's table," Emma ordered. Then she pointed at Lindsey and Betty and said, "Let's go."

"Now see what you did," Betty hissed as she stomped past Lindsey.

Lindsey saw Sully making his way through the crowd toward them. As they passed, he asked, "Everything all right?"

"Just clearing the air," Lindsey said.

"Call me if you need me." He squeezed her fingers with his before joining Nancy at her table.

There was a small office on the far side of the room, and Emma led Lindsey and Betty inside and closed the door after them. Emma gestured for them to take the available seats while she propped her hip on the edge of the desk, making herself taller than both of them. Lindsey recognized it for the power play that it was and respected it.

"All right, what's all this chatter about Jackie Lewis's death being a murder?" she asked. "Lindsey, you first."

"Why does she get to go first?" Betty protested.

"By all means, you go first," Lindsey said. She wanted to watch Emma's reaction to the news that Helen had an affair with Jackie's husband.

Betty narrowed her eyes at Lindsey suspiciously and said, "Well, I have it on good authority—"

"Whose?" Emma asked.

"What?" Betty blinked. The doe-eyed thing did nothing for Emma, and she stared at Betty unmoved.

"Whose authority?" Emma asked.

"Oh, well, Jackie told me," Betty said.

"Told you what?"

"That not only did Helen steal Jackie's ideas, she stole her husband, too."

Emma nodded as if she wasn't surprised, which confused Lindsey. Did she already know? Had Helen told her? She glanced at Betty, who looked put out that her bombshell hadn't caused so much as a ripple of reaction.

"Can you really steal a spouse?" Emma asked. "I mean if they want to go, don't they just go?"

"That's not the point," Betty said. "And, of course, a man can be stolen."

"Isn't that just the narrative the patriarchy wants us to believe so that we see all women as rivals, keeping us suspicious instead of supportive of one another?" Emma asked.

"I am not here to have a discussion on the patriarchy," Betty huffed. "The fact is that Jackie arrived in Briar Creek, found out I was one of the judges for the ugly sweater competition with Helen Monroe and asked me to help her humiliate Helen because Helen stole her career and her man."

"You never met Jackie before she arrived in town?" Emma asked.

"No." Betty rolled her eyes. "I mean, it's not like we move in the same social circles."

"What proof do you have that there was an affair?" Lindsey asked.

Betty sighed. "The victim told me. What more proof do you need?"

"Given that the victim also accused Helen of stealing

her work, which went to court and was found to be untrue, doesn't that mean that any accusation she made against Helen is probably a lie?" Lindsey asked.

Betty crossed her arms over her chest and turned away, looking at Emma. "So bored. Can I go now?"

"Is that all you have to tell me?" Emma asked.

"Yes." Betty rose from her seat. "I told you I don't know anything else, and I have cookies to sell."

Emma gestured to the door. She and Lindsey waited until the door shut after Betty, a bit more firmly than Lindsey thought was necessary, before Emma turned to her. Her expression was not happy.

"Are you really going around saying that Jackie Lewis was murdered?" Emma asked.

"No," Lindsey protested. "I mean I might have hypothesized about it, but I never declared it so."

Emma studied her. "What makes you think Jackie was murdered?"

"Her death just feels off," Lindsey said. "I mean, I know freak accidents happen, but an electrocution from holiday lights? And having it be the person who recently made a big public spectacle of herself? Not to forget that someone shoved me down those steps as they hurried away from the scene. It all just feels very homicidey."

"Is that even a word?" Emma asked.

"It could be," Lindsey said. "I mean, Merriam-Webster added *yeet* to the dictionary, so it feels like anything goes these days."

"And *yeet* came to mind as an example because?" Emma asked.

"I might want to yeet Betty Caruthers right out of this cookie sale," Lindsey said.

Emma laughed. "That's a mental picture. You tossing Betty out on her butt. Of course, I'm only laughing because I know you would never do it as it would be considered assault, and Betty would come after you and I'd have to arrest you."

"Of course I would never," Lindsey said. "But you can see the appeal."

"Betty does trigger most everyone she meets," Emma said. "Do you believe her about Jackie?"

"That she didn't know her before Jackie came to town?" Lindsey asked. "No."

"Me either," Emma said. "I'm going to see what I can find there. If their paths crossed before, it'll be interesting to see how Betty explains that."

"Do you think Betty might have an issue with Helen that we don't know about?" Lindsey asked.

"What do you mean?"

"Betty said that she and Jackie bonded over being jilted by their husbands," Lindsey said. "But what if that's not it at all? What if the thing Jackie and Betty have in common is a dislike of Helen in particular?"

"Interesting idea but why? I mean, Jackie I understand, but Betty? Why does she dislike Helen so much? It's weird." Emma tapped her chin with her index finger while she mulled it over. "When you were judging the competition with Betty and Helen, did you get the impression that they knew each other or had met before?"

"No. Helen showed up right as the contest was beginning, and Mayor Cole and I sat in between them, but they didn't greet each other as if they'd met before. In fact, Helen asked me who Betty was. Of course, it could be that they have but one of them doesn't remember."

"Helen?" Emma clarified.

"She must meet a lot of people on her book tours and such," Lindsey said. "Maybe she has met Betty and just doesn't remember her, which would undoubtedly be a deep insult to Betty."

"Perhaps," Emma said.

"Have you had any luck finding a next of kin for Jackie?"

"Her ex-husband is on his way," Emma said.

"Oh."

"Yeah, if what Betty said is true about Helen and Jackie's ex, then things could get very interesting," Emma said. "I'm trusting that you will not speak of this to anyone, most especially Helen."

"Are you planning to ask her about him?" Lindsey asked.

"Up until a few minutes ago, I didn't think I needed to, but now I'm planning to have her at the station when he arrives," Emma said.

"Wow."

"Maybe. It could be that Jackie made up losing her

husband to Helen just like she lied about Helen taking her ideas."

"What about the Campbells?" Lindsey asked. "Could they have been involved in Jackie's . . . accident?"

"Lisa and Jeffrey?" Emma asked. "Why would they harm Jackie? As far as I can tell, they didn't know her at all."

"No, I don't suppose they did," Lindsey said. "I just feel as if everyone who has an ax to grind has joined forces against Helen."

"Which is a very Agatha Christie sort of plot," Emma said. "But this isn't a mystery novel. In real life, it's usually the spouse or the ex-spouse, and they frequently get caught."

"Well, I hope it's that simple so that Helen can get on with her writer in residence and we can all go back to normal."

"Whatever that is for Briar Creek," Emma agreed. "I have to admit it would be nice to have this wrapped up by the holiday."

"I see what you did there." Lindsey laughed. "You've been spending too much time with Robbie."

"Did I hear my name?" a voice asked as the door opened and Robbie poked his head in. "It's almost as if you summoned me."

"I think you mean it's almost as if you interrupted," Emma countered. She gave him a wary look that Lindsey couldn't interpret.

"Actually, I was sent to fetch you," he said. "It seems there's a situation."

It was at that moment that Lindsey heard a shout from the cookie sale. Emma pushed off the desk and bolted for the door.

CHAPTER

12

BRIAR CREEK
PUBLIC LIBRARY

Unsurprisingly, the shout came from Betty's table. She was leaning over her side while Hannah, the school librarian for the high school, met her halfway from the other side.

"You do not get to tell me what books go into my high school library!" Hannah shouted.

"As a taxpayer—" Betty began, but Hannah interrupted.

"Who doesn't have any children in the school, because you don't think it's good enough."

Betty made a chopping motion in the air. "That doesn't matter. I still pay taxes. I have a say."

"No, you don't." Ann Marie Martin, the public library's adult services librarian, stepped up beside Hannah. "You get to decide what your teenagers read, you do not get to decide what everyone else's teens read, and the same thing goes for the public library. We are information specialists. We have degrees that teach us how to curate a collection, do in-depth research to find the *right* answers for information requests and to purchase materials that fulfill the needs of our *entire* community."

Betty lifted her phone and held it in front of Ann Marie's face. "Say that again. I plan to bring it to the library board, the mayor and the town council. I will have your job!"

"You didn't get video the first time?" a young teenage boy, whom Lindsey recognized as Ann Marie's oldest, asked from beside Ann Marie. He gave Betty a disdainful glance. "Lame."

Betty's mouth popped open, but before she could retort, his brother appeared on Ann Marie's other side. He looked at his sibling then shook his head at Betty. "Old people."

Betty let out a small yip. Her face turned bright pink, and she hissed through gritted teeth, "I am *not* old."

"If you say so, *ma'am*." The first boy emphasized *ma'am*, and Betty's upper lip curled. She looked like she might bite him. Ann Marie seemed to think so, too, as she put an arm in front of each boy and pushed them behind her.

Lindsey suspected Betty was about her age, which was to say somewhere just above or below forty. She could sympathize with Betty's horror at being called old, but given that Betty was trying to ban books and force her own agenda on the entire community, Lindsey suspected that the boys knew being called old was Betty's trigger and they were happily using it to wind her up.

"I would think that as the mother of young men, you wouldn't want them to have access to materials written by *that* woman," Betty said. "They're poorly written, depicting the worst of humanity, and they're just completely inappropriate."

Ann Marie's nostrils flared. "You would be wrong. I want my sons to read books from all sorts of authors in all sorts of genres. It teaches them to see things from different points of view so that they can learn empathy and understanding and become men that I can be proud of."

Betty sniffed as if she found Ann Marie's opinion to be offensive.

"Can you imagine if we hadn't been allowed to read *Bridge to Terabithia*?" the older of the boys asked his brother.

"Or *The Giver*?" the younger one responded.

"Or—" They started to list more titles, but Ann Marie cut them off.

"That's enough, boys," Ann Marie said. "We don't need to debate this here. Anything Ms. Caruthers has to say to me can be said at the library board meeting."

"And it will," Betty promised. "I'm coming for you, Ann Marie."

"Looking forward to it," Ann Marie replied. Lindsey knew from the gleam in her eye that she meant every word. Betty was in for a heck of a fight if she thought she was going to start banning books at either the high school library or the public one.

Ann Marie and her sons turned and left Betty standing at her empty table. If Betty had been the sort to be attentive, she might have determined that the bare area around her station indicated that the community at large did not agree with her book banning. But she wasn't, so she didn't.

"Everything all right, Ann Marie?" Lindsey asked as her librarian passed by with her two sons.

Ann Marie put an arm around each boy and gave them a quick squeeze before they could squirm away. "Everything is great. You know, whenever I worry about the state of the world, I look to this younger generation, and I know it's going to be just fine. They know what's important."

"It is reassuring," Lindsey agreed.

"Mom . . . cookies!" The teens pulled her along, and Ann Marie laughed and said, "See? Priorities." She waved as she disappeared into the crowd.

"Looks like that sorted itself," Emma said. She appeared relieved, and Lindsey didn't blame her, given that she had a potential murder to solve.

"It was lucky that Ann Marie arrived when she did," Hannah said. "Betty was informing me that she was planning to run for the school board and shut down my library. I might have lost my temper a teeny bit."

"Understandable," Robbie said. "Shut down a library? Who does that?"

"Betty Caruthers," Lindsey and Emma said together.

"Why is she so fixated on banning library books?" Emma asked.

"No idea," Lindsey said. "But it seems to be specifically Helen's books that she has issues with."

"That's too bad. The library belongs to the entire village," Emma said. "And one person doesn't dictate what the rest of us read. Like if one person decided there shouldn't be any vampire books because they don't like them or they think they're inappropriate, why do they think their opinion carries more weight than a person who likes vampire books? Where would that leave someone like Jeanette, who loves her vampire romances?"

"I imagine the people who wanted the vampire books gone would say that they were doing it for Jeanette's own good," Robbie offered.

"Well, that's just wrong," Emma said.

Lindsey shuddered. "I don't think I can talk about this anymore. It's going to give me a rash."

"Same." Hannah scratched at her arms through her sweater. "The idea that one person can dictate what information everyone else has access to makes me woozy."

"Ditto," Lindsey agreed. "I'm going back to my table to comfort eat some of Nancy's cookies."

"Excellent idea," Emma said. "For the sake of the bake sale, do me a favor and do not engage with Betty again. Please?"

"I will keep my distance." Lindsey glanced at the time on her phone. "I only have ten more minutes until the end of my shift. I can do this."

"I'm counting on it," Emma said. "Also, cone of silence on our talk."

"Of course," Lindsey agreed.

She watched as Hannah left with Emma and Robbie. Sully appeared at her side with a salted caramel cookie.

"This will help," he said. "Trust me."

Lindsey took a bite of the buttery caramel goodness and felt endorphins flood her system. Her husband was right. She felt a million times better already. She chewed the cookie, taking the water that Sully handed her to wash it down. Feeling someone's eyes on her, she looked over and found Betty glaring at her. It wasn't the stare of a rival or a person who had a difference of opinion. No. This was a look of stone-cold fury that made Lindsey's insides twist.

She did not doubt for one second that Betty was capable of murdering Jackie Lewis. The question was why.

What do we know about Betty Caruthers before she moved here?" Lindsey asked Sully on the ride home.

"Why?" he asked.

"There's something off about her," Lindsey said.

"You mean other than her desire to ban books, cut programs and ruin lives?" Sully asked.

"And here I thought you'd mention how she flirts outrageously with you," Lindsey said.

"Can't," he said. "I block it out in real time. But, yes, that is creepy, too."

It was midafternoon, and the sun was trying to burst

through the steel gray clouds overhead, but they appeared heavy with the snow that was predicted to start falling at any moment. The cookie sale was still going strong when Lindsey and Sully left, and Nancy was well on her way to selling out, which made it an incredibly successful fund-raiser for the senior center.

"I just can't shake the feeling that Betty lied about knowing Jackie before Jackie came here," Lindsey said.

"Is there a way to prove it?" he asked.

"Emma says that Jackie's ex-husband is coming to Briar Creek to identify and claim the body," Lindsey said.

"And you think he might know Betty?" Sully asked.

"Maybe." Lindsey shrugged. "If he does, then that will prove that Betty lied."

"Okay, suppose we actually get to talk to him without Emma finding out," Sully said. "How can we just ask him out of left field if he knows Betty Caruthers?"

"Just like that," Lindsey said. "Of course, we have to be able to run into him. I don't know if he's just going to be here for the day or if he's staying overnight."

"Either way, the man has to eat," Sully said. "Good thing my sister owns the only restaurant in town."

"Are we seriously going to stake out a man eating his dinner?"

"Yes," Sully said. "Unless you can think of a better way?"

"No," Lindsey admitted.

"Great, let's head over to the Blue Anchor," Sully said. "We can harass Ian while we wait and see if Jackie's ex shows up."

The restaurant was quiet when Sully and Lindsey entered. It was that perfect in-between time when it was too late for lunch and too early for dinner. Both Mary and Ian were in the restaurant. Ian was behind the bar while Mary sat at the end reading through some paperwork and enjoying a cup of coffee.

"Well, look who was blown in by the freezing temperatures," Ian said. "What can I get you two?"

"Coffee, please," Sully said.

"Same," Lindsey agreed. "It smells delicious."

They shrugged off their coats and draped them on the backs of two barstools.

"I put cinnamon in it," Mary said. She hopped off her seat and hugged them in turn.

"Even better," Lindsey said. "And where is our darling niece?"

"Being spoiled rotten by Ian's parents, no doubt," Mary said. "We're short-staffed, so I'm pulling a shift as hostess tonight. Three holiday parties and the usual crowd. It's going to be hopping."

Ian poured them each a mug of coffee and pushed them across the bar with a small pitcher of milk and several packets of sugar.

"How was the cookie sale?" Mary asked.

"Crowded," Sully answered the same time Lindsey said, "Informative."

"Do tell." Mary put aside her papers and gestured for them to sit down.

Knowing that she couldn't share anything that Emma

had told her, Lindsey kept to the situation with Betty Ca-ruthers and her desire to shut down the high school library.

"She's going to lose that fight," Mary said. "This is a town that loves its libraries. Besides, can you imagine tell-ing our community what they can and can't read? Heads would roll."

"I'm glad Mayor Cole wasn't there," Lindsey said. "It might have gotten violent."

Ian laughed. "No one protects libraries as fiercely as the lemon."

"Has there been any word on what exactly happened to that poor woman who was electrocuted?" Mary asked. "I haven't been able to look at the light display the same way since."

"I don't think it's been officially determined yet," Lind-sey said. "It could have been an accident, but . . ."

"But you were shoved down the stairs by someone," Ian said. "Which leads me to believe it was no accident."

Sully put his hand on Lindsey's shoulder as if to reassure himself that she was all right. They were both aware that if she had wandered into the gazebo just a few seconds ear-lier, it could have turned out very badly for her.

"As far as I know, Emma is treating it as a suspicious death," Lindsey said.

"What about that author the deceased woman accused of stealing her ideas?" Ian asked. "Could she have done it? You know, to protect her reputation."

"I don't think so," Lindsey said. She bit her lip. She wished she could say she absolutely didn't believe it, but the potential for Helen to have had an affair with Jackie's husband certainly changed things. If what Betty had said was true, then there was more than just a professional competition between the two women. It was personal. Very personal.

The door opened, letting the cold air in, and Lindsey picked up her mug to warm her hands. The man who entered was dressed in jeans and a fitted winter coat, and the standard New England winter wear of thick-soled lace-up boots, gloves and a scarf about his neck. His hair was gray and he wore glasses, giving him the look of an engineer. If asked, Lindsey would have placed him somewhere in his early sixties.

She glanced at Sully with one eyebrow raised, and he nodded in unspoken agreement. He thought the man was Jackie's ex, too.

"Good afternoon." Ian welcomed the man into the restaurant. "What can I get you?"

"Unfortunately, it's too early for a whiskey neat," the man said. He glanced ruefully at the wall of bottles behind Ian. "So I suppose I'll have a bowl of chowder instead. I hear yours is the best in the area."

"Best in all of New England," Ian corrected him with a disarming grin.

The man nodded. "Then I'll most certainly have a bowl of that."

"Have a seat," Ian said. "I'll be right back."

He disappeared into the kitchen. The man glanced at the nearly empty restaurant and chose to sit a few barstools down from Lindsey and Sully.

Lindsey nudged Sully and whispered, "Say something."

He widened his eyes at her and she sighed. This was the problem with two introverts being married to each other. No one wanted to take the conversational lead in public situations.

Mary, observing their turmoil, shook her head and turned to the man. "Hi, I'm Mary, and that was my husband, Ian. We own the Blue Anchor. Are you sure you just want chowder?" She lifted up a menu. "We have a whole menu to offer."

"Thank you," he said. He held out a gloved hand and took the menu, putting it on the bar in front of him. "I'll give it a look." He stripped off his gloves and stuffed them in the pockets of his coat before hanging it on the back of his chair. "I'm having a rough day, so I don't know that I have much of an appetite."

"I'm sorry to hear that," Mary said. She gestured to Sully and Lindsey. "This is my brother, Sully, and his wife, Lindsey. Is there anything we can do to help?"

"I'm Kenny. Kenny Lewis," he said. He shook each of their hands. Lindsey schooled her features so she didn't look overly eager to meet him. "Thank you, but I'm afraid there's nothing you can do."

Lindsey took his introduction as her opportunity to find out more and said, "Lewis? Forgive me, but are you any relation to Jackie Lewis?"

"Her ex-husband," he said. "We divorced several years ago, but as she didn't have any other family, I'm still her emergency contact." He glanced at them. "I take it you're aware of what happened to her."

"Yes," Lindsey said. "I was there when she was discovered."

"Right." Kenny nodded as if putting it all together. "Helen told me you were with her when she found Jackie."

He'd spoken to Helen?

"I'm sorry for your loss," Lindsey said. Sully and Mary echoed her sentiment, but Kenny shook his head.

"Jackie and I parted ways a long time ago," he said. "While I'm very sorry that she's passed, we weren't particularly close anymore. Mostly, I just feel sad for her. She didn't . . . it wasn't . . . it was not a life well lived."

"Here's your chowder." Ian came through the swinging kitchen door, carrying a tray with a large bowl of steaming soup and several packets of oyster crackers.

He set it on the bar in front of Kenny, when the front door opened and Helen came dashing in.

"You're here, oh, thank goodness, you're here!"

Kenny turned just in time, as Helen threw herself into his arms. Kenny caught her and hugged her tight. "How are you, sweetheart?"

"Better now," she said. She kissed him quick. "So much better now that you're here."

Lindsey felt her jaw drop. She glanced at Sully and Mary, and they wore matching expressions of surprise. The only one not shocked was Ian because he didn't know that Kenny was Jackie's ex-husband.

"Should I dish up another bowl of chowder, then?" Ian asked.

The couple broke apart, and Helen glanced over Kenny's

shoulder. Her eyes widened when she saw Lindsey and Sully, but she didn't step away from Kenny. If anything, she leaned into his strength.

She looked Lindsey right in the eye and said, "I take it you've met my husband."

CHAPTER

13

BRIAR CREEK
PUBLIC LIBRARY

Husband?" Lindsey repeated in an unnaturally high pitch. There was no way to make her voice sound neutral.

Helen nodded. "We've been married seven years. As soon as his divorce was final." She turned to Ian. "Chowder sounds lovely."

Ian glanced from Helen to Lindsey to Mary and said, "Someone is going to catch me up when I get back." He disappeared into the kitchen and they all sat down.

"You never mentioned that you were married to Jackie's ex-husband," Lindsey said. She tried not to sound accusatory, but she felt that it was a rather large chunk of information to leave out.

"We've done everything we can to keep it quiet," Helen said. "We didn't want to upset Jackie any more than we already had. I never wanted to fall in love with Kenny. It just happened."

Helen looked conflicted, and Kenny put his hand on her shoulder and gave it a quick squeeze. "Well, I for one am glad you did."

She smiled at him. She moved in close and pressed her forehead to his and whispered, "I've missed you."

"Same," he said. He leaned back and pressed a kiss on her hair. "It's so strange to be able to be in public with you."

"It is," she said. "I keep feeling the need to look over my shoulder, but we don't have to anymore, do we?"

"No."

They stared at each other in wonder.

"You've been married for seven years, and you haven't been able to go out in public together?" Lindsey asked.

"It was difficult." Kenny spoke slowly as if choosing each word with care. "In the beginning, when we were just dating, Jackie would show up wherever we were—restaurants, movies, a wedding—and make such awful scenes. It became so miserable that we broke up for a year."

"Worst year of my life," Helen said.

"Mine, too," he agreed. They shared a long look of affection and mutual pain.

Lindsey glanced at Sully and couldn't comprehend someone coming between them like that.

"During our year apart, I was officially divorced from Jackie. After which, I was determined to spend the rest of my life with the love of my life," Kenny said. "But I knew that Jackie could never find out that we were together or the nightmare would start all over again, so we agreed to keep it a secret."

"We've been long-distance married ever since," Helen said. "We live two towns apart, we never go out in public, and if we go on vacation, we go separately. It's not been ideal but so worth it to not be relentlessly stalked and threatened day after day."

"But now all of that is in the past," Kenny said.

"Does Chief Plewicki know this?" Lindsey asked. She imagined Emma was going to have some thoughts about this situation. Then again, Emma hadn't seemed very surprised when Betty said Helen had an affair with Jackie's husband.

"Yes, she knows." Helen glanced down at her hand in Kenny's. "I told her when Jackie's body was found that I was married to Kenny and that Kenny was still Jackie's emergency contact."

"I'll bet that was an interesting conversation," Sully said.

"It definitely moved me up to a person of interest," Helen said. "But if there's one thing I've learned in all my years of crime writing, it's that not disclosing pertinent information to law enforcement never goes well."

"You're not wrong," Mary said.

Ian arrived with a tray with several bowls of chowder. When Lindsey and Sully glanced at him in question, he said, "I brought some for everyone so I don't have to leave again. Now catch me up."

They tucked into their soup while Mary told her

husband everything they'd learned. Ian made all of the appropriate sounds of shock and dismay. When Mary was finished, he looked at Helen and Kenny and said, "But given that your life is significantly improved—sorry, I don't know how else to say it—doesn't that make you two the prime suspects?"

"Suspects?" Kenny asked. "I thought Jackie's death was ruled an accident."

"Not officially. Until the medical examiner gives his report, it's being considered suspicious." Lindsey sprinkled her crackers onto her soup.

"Oh, I suppose I can understand that," Kenny said. "I mean, it is an unusual way to . . . die."

"It wasn't unusual." Helen shivered with a glance at Lindsey. "It was grisly."

Lindsey nodded in agreement. It had been awful. "If you don't mind my asking, why did you take the writer's residency, Helen? Seriously, if you were trying to keep a low profile from Jackie, you had to know the residency would have gotten her attention."

Kenny ran a hand over his neatly trimmed hair. "We believed Jackie had moved on. It'd been years since Jackie accosted Helen with her wild accusations. Filing a restraining order and losing the lawsuit no doubt helped. After Helen ended her series, we both hoped that would be the end of Jackie's obsession."

"And instead Jackie followed you here," Lindsey said to Helen.

Helen nodded. "I was shocked. I couldn't believe it."

She glanced at Kenny. An expression of fatigue passed over his face and he said, "When Helen told me that Jackie had arrived in town, I told her to quit the residency, but she didn't want to."

"I felt that I'd made a commitment I had to honor," Helen said.

"Neither of us expected things to end like this, however," Kenny said.

They were all silent for a moment, and Ian rapped the top of the bar with his knuckles. "Eat your chowder, all of you; sounds like you could use it."

Kenny picked up his spoon and tucked in. Helen, Lindsey and Sully did the same. It was delicious, and Lindsey could feel the trail of heat it forged through her chest to her belly.

"Have you met with the chief yet?" Mary asked.

Kenny swallowed and shook his head. He glanced at the watch on his wrist. "I'm supposed to meet her in thirty minutes."

Mary pointed at the door. "Looks like she's early."

Kenny's head turned to the door, and Helen peeked around him.

Emma strode into the restaurant on a blast of cold December air. She stomped the snow off her boots on the doormat and glanced at everyone sitting at the bar.

"A bit early in the day, isn't it?" she asked.

"I believe we've become a chowder bar," Ian replied, gesturing toward the bowls lined up on the bar. "Get you some?"

Emma started to shake her head and then thought better of it. "A cup would be great. It's freezing out there."

Ian nodded and slipped into the kitchen.

Emma unzipped her coat, letting it hang open. "Are you planning on introducing me to your husband, Helen?"

"Yes, of course." Helen smiled but her lips were wobbly with nerves. "Kenny Lewis, this is Chief Plewicki."

Kenny shook hands with Emma, meeting her assessing gaze with one of his own. "Helen says you've been very helpful."

Emma shrugged. "I try."

Ian came back through the kitchen doors with a small bowl of chowder and several packets of crackers. "Here you go. What did I miss?"

Emma sent him a quelling look, and he raised his hands and backed away. "Sorry. I get it. I'm just a chowder boy and should mind my business."

"Thank you." Emma opened her crackers and sprinkled them on top of the chowder. She then picked up her spoon and scooped a mouthful of the tasty broth.

While Mary collected the empty bowls from the rest of them, Emma finished her meal, dabbing her lips with a paper napkin. Mary collected hers, too, and Emma turned to Kenny and Helen and said, "Are you ready?"

Kenny nodded. "Are we going to the morgue?"

"Yes," Emma said. "I just need a positive ID from her closest family member and we can release her to the mortuary. Do you know if she had a will?"

"I don't," Kenny said. "We didn't really share that

information after our divorce. My alimony payments to her were directly deposited. I think the last time I saw her was three years ago when her mother passed away and I went to the funeral."

"That was considerate of you," Emma said.

Kenny winced. "Not really. She asked me to go, and I couldn't think of a reason quickly enough to get out of it." He sighed. "I sound like a jerk."

"No, you don't," Helen protested. "You sound like a man who ended a very toxic relationship and was trying to avoid getting sucked back in."

"And did you?" Emma asked.

"Did I what?" Kenny looked confused.

"Did you avoid getting sucked back in?" Emma asked.

"Oh, yeah." Kenny looked pained. "The funeral was over the top, especially for a crotchety old woman who ignored her only child her entire life, and when she wasn't ignoring her, she was incessantly criticizing her. It wasn't a healthy mother-daughter relationship, and yet, Jackie spent a fortune on the casket, the flowers and the service. Even her mother's headstone was a monument to excess. To put it mildly, Jackie's issues had issues, and I couldn't get out of there fast enough."

"Hmm," Emma hummed. Her phone chimed, and she pulled it out of her jacket pocket. She slid her thumb across the screen and read the message she'd received. Her lips compressed into a thin line, and she glanced at Helen and asked, "Do you mind if we take a look at your car?"

"No, of course not, but why?" she asked.

"We just got an anonymous tip that there is evidence of your connection to Jackie's murder in the back of your car."

Helen's eyes went wide. "What? That's crazy."

"I don't like this," Kenny said. "It feels as if someone is trying to cause trouble."

"You're probably right. It's most likely a prank," Emma conceded. "You can't believe how many of these we get during an investigation. I swear people have nothing better to do than impede our work. Still, if we can take a peek, I can scratch it off my to-do list."

"Don't you need a warrant?" Kenny asked.

"If Helen refuses to let me look, yes," Emma said. Her tone was matter-of-fact, but Lindsey knew Emma better than that. She did not take her job lightly. Lindsey wondered if Emma was banking on Helen giving her permission since they were in a group and Helen wouldn't want to appear to have anything to hide.

"I don't see why not," Helen said. "I have my car right outside. We can check it before you go to the morgue."

"Thank you," Emma said. "With the holiday looming, I'd love to declare this case closed and move on."

Sully glanced at Lindsey with one eyebrow raised, and she knew that he, too, felt that Emma was being a bit blither than usual about a potential homicide.

They settled their bill with Ian, pulled on their coats and walked outside. As Lindsey fell into step beside Emma, the police chief looked at her and asked, "What?"

"Just wondering if you're feeling okay," Lindsey said.

"Of course I am," Emma insisted. "It's the holidays. I love Christmas and everything about it."

"Do you? Really?" Lindsey asked. "Because you sound very . . . aggressive about it."

"It's not aggression, it's joy," Emma insisted. But the look on her face was less joyous and more grim determination.

"Here it is." Helen approached her fancy SUV and circled to the back. She didn't unlock it; instead she just reached down and lifted the back hatch. "The lock is broken on the back. My mechanic ordered the part weeks ago, but we're still waiting."

"We'll talk more about your mood later," Lindsey said to Emma.

"Nothing to talk about," Emma countered.

Lindsey frowned. She tried to remember how Emma had dealt with the holidays in previous years but could not recall her ever being a Christmas enthusiast. Something was definitely up with the chief. It was almost as if she were throwing herself into festivities and activities to try to avoid something . . . or someone.

Lindsey and Sully stood back while Emma, Helen and Kenny stared into the back of the car.

"What's this?" Emma asked. She reached into the interior and pulled out a carefully wrapped string of lights.

"Those aren't mine," Helen said. "I don't have any lights on my cottage or in my cottage or anywhere. I had planned to go home and celebrate the holiday with Kenny, so I didn't do any decorating."

"And yet, these were in your car?" Emma said. She turned them over in her gloved hand and examined them.

Helen looked nervous, and she cleared her throat and said, "I swear—"

"It's all right," Kenny said. "We believe you."

"Unfortunately, it's not a matter of whether we believe you," Emma said. She turned the string of lights so that they all could see the tag that was taped to the cord. "These are clearly marked as belonging to the town of Briar Creek."

"So?" Kenny frowned.

"So the string that caused Jackie's death didn't belong to the facilities department," she said. "It was a non-town-owned replacement, which according to our electrician had been tampered with so that wires were exposed. Which means someone swapped them out. Someone who planned to murder Jackie Lewis."

"I didn't . . . I wouldn't . . . I don't know how those got into my car," Helen protested. She glanced at everyone around her, imploring them to believe her.

"I'm sorry, Helen," Emma said. "When we add this to the fact that Jackie had your manuscript when her body was discovered, it looks very bad. I'm afraid I have to bring you in for formal questioning."

Helen closed her eyes and let out a breath. "I'm going to call my attorney."

Emma nodded. "I think that would be wise. I'm going to have an officer escort you to the police station, while I take your husband to the morgue. Once we have the body released, I'll come back and question you. That should give you time to have your attorney present."

Helen and Kenny exchanged a horrified look.

"This is serious, then?" Helen asked.

"Deadly serious," Emma confirmed. "Excuse me while I call this in. We're going to have to go over your car as well."

"That's good though, right?" Kenny asked. "Whoever planted those lights might have left some fingerprints."

"Let's hope so." Emma strode a few feet away to make her call.

Sully and Lindsey stood in the cold with Helen and Kenny. Lindsey had no idea what to say to comfort the writer. There was no getting around the fact that this looked very, very bad.

"It's going to be all right," Kenny reassured Helen. "There's no way they're going to find any evidence linking you to Jackie's death."

"Except for the string of lights in my car and the fact that she had my manuscript on her when she was electrocuted," Helen said.

"There has to be an explanation," Kenny insisted.

"If I say what I'm thinking, I'm going to sound paranoid," Helen said.

"Say it anyway," he said.

"I think someone is trying to frame me for Jackie's murder," Helen said. "But who? And why?"

CHAPTER

14

BRIAR CREEK
PUBLIC LIBRARY

indsey, I hate to ask, but I know that you've investigated several murders in Briar Creek and have successfully discovered who the killer was. Is there any way . . . no, I'm sorry. It's not fair of me to put you in that position." Helen shook her head, and Lindsey heard her teeth chattering. She suspected it wasn't the cold causing it.

"Not at all," Lindsey said. "You're our writer in residence. I'll help in any way I can."

Helen looked relieved. She licked her lips and glanced at Kenny, who nodded and said, "You should probably tell her, then."

"Tell me what?" Lindsey asked. She had the sinking feeling that Helen was about to confess something even more damaging than the fact that she was married to Jackie's ex-husband. She braced for it.

"The subject of my current book." Helen paused. She glanced at Sully and then Lindsey. She shifted on her feet.

"Go ahead, she's going to find out anyway," Kenny said. "In fact, I'm surprised the chief hasn't already told her."

"Right. What with Chief Plewicki having my manuscript, I suppose it's only a matter of time," Helen said. She turned to face Lindsey full on. "The subject of my current book is you, well, you and the crafternooners."

"Me?" Lindsey blinked. "But you write thrillers with an FBI protagonist. I'm a librarian."

"A librarian who has been instrumental in solving multiple murders," Helen said. "That's why I took the writer in residence, that's why I've kept my distance. I didn't want to get too close to you and have it influence my writing."

"When you say me, you don't actually mean *me* though, right?"

"No, I suppose a more accurate description would be that the main character is *inspired* by you," Helen said. "My sleuth is a librarian in a small coastal town, and she solves murders. Oh, and she's married to a boat captain."

"Huh." Lindsey was gobsmacked. "I don't know what to say."

"Well, you don't seem upset, so that's encouraging," Helen said.

Lindsey looked at Sully. He seemed nonplussed as well. She glanced back at Helen and asked, "But you did change our names and such?"

"Oh, absolutely, and you're both younger and hotter," she confirmed.

"Well, I can't argue with that." Sully shrugged.

"Me neither." Lindsey laughed, still feeling a bit off-kilter. "Thank you for telling us."

"Thank you for not being mad," Helen replied. "And you're still willing to help?"

"Of course," Lindsey said. "You're our writer, so we have a vested interest in clearing your name."

"No, no, no." Emma joined them. She pointed at Lindsey. "You are not getting involved in this."

"Me?" Lindsey raised her eyebrows and feigned an innocent look.

"Yes, you," Emma said. She glanced at Helen. "You told her about your current book, didn't you?"

"I had to," Helen said. "I was afraid it would get out, and I wanted to explain."

"I read it. Her sleuth is way hotter than you," Emma said.

"So I heard," Lindsey said.

"And the local chief of police is a badass," Emma added with a grin.

"Of course she is," Sully said. He glanced at Helen. "Does the police chief have an annoying British boyfriend?"

"I haven't developed her character that far," Helen admitted. "But it's under consideration."

Lindsey, Sully and Emma exchanged wide-eyed glances. They all spoke at once. "Do not tell Robbie that."

"I hadn't planned on telling anyone anything until the book was finished," Helen sighed. "Now I may have to scrap the whole thing."

"Don't do anything hasty," Emma said. "Let's just see where this investigation leads us." She glanced at Lindsey and said, "*Us* as in the police, not you."

"I got it," Lindsey said.

A squad car pulled up and parked beside them. Officer Kirkland climbed out and strode over with an evidence bag in hand. Emma dropped the string of lights into it.

"They were found in the back hatch," Emma said. "Ms. Monroe says they aren't hers, so I want you to go over the car, particularly the back, and see if you find anything that indicates another person might have planted the lights."

"Fingerprints?" he asked.

"If you can find any, we can try and run them, but you know the lab takes forever," Emma said. "Stray hairs, bits of clothing, food wrappers, anything of note that you find, bag 'em." Kirkland nodded and headed back to his car to retrieve his fingerprint kit.

"We could pay a private agency to check the fingerprints," Kenny offered. He looked sheepish. "I know we're fortunate to have the means to do that, and I hate to jump the line but . . ."

"But like everything else, justice is also impacted by have and have not," Emma said.

"Sorry." Kenny shook his head. "My desperation is making me say stupid things."

Helen patted his arm. "It's going to be okay. You have to believe that."

Kenny nodded but his drooped shoulders indicated he was far from believing that things would turn out all right.

"Are you ready, Mr. Lewis?" Emma asked. "The morgue will be closing soon."

"Yes, let's get this over with." He leaned forward and kissed Helen's cheek. "I'll meet you back at the police station."

"Okay." She hugged him. "Despite everything, this is going to be hard for you. Call me if you need me."

"I will." He squeezed her hand and followed Emma to her squad car. Helen looked troubled as she watched him leave. Lindsey wondered what she was thinking but didn't have the nerve to ask.

"Lindsey." Helen turned to her. "Hypothetically speaking, if you were going to try to discover who killed Jackie, where would you start?"

"I suppose from the beginning." Lindsey met Helen's questioning gaze and explained, "I'd most likely reach out to the other member of your critique group. Liz somebody?"

"Liz Maynard," Helen said. "A legal secretary with Dixon, Carter and Suffield in New Haven. I pop in to see her when I'm in New Haven, which isn't very often, I'm afraid."

"Yeah, I'd start with her," Lindsey said. "You know, to see if she'd been in contact with Jackie recently. Maybe Jackie confided in her?"

"Interesting." Helen smiled at her.

"It's going to be dark soon. I'll need more light to do this properly," Officer Kirkland said. "I can escort you to the police station, Ms. Monroe. You can wait for the chief out of the cold, and I'll get lighting equipment so I can finish up here."

"Thank you." Helen shivered in her coat. "It would be nice to be warm." She turned to Lindsey. "I'll see you at the library tomorrow?"

"I'll be there," Lindsey said.

She and Sully walked to his pickup truck while Helen and Officer Kirkland made their way across the street to the police station.

"What sort of law firm do you suppose Dixon, Carter and Suffield is?" Lindsey asked as she climbed into her seat.

"No idea," Sully said. "I do know I've never seen an ad for them featuring a bear or an eagle or any other sort of wildlife, so they have that going for them."

Lindsey smiled. Sully shut her door and walked around the front of the truck to sit in the driver's seat. Lindsey took her phone out of her purse and did a quick search. The law firm came up immediately. "Family law."

Sully turned to look at her. His gaze was amused when he said, "Well, that certainly gives us a few options."

"That's exactly what I was thinking," Lindsey said. "I'm free tomorrow morning since I'm working the evening shift; how about you?"

"I can clear my schedule," he said.

"Thank you." Lindsey squeezed his arm. "I feel in my bones that Helen is innocent, and it would bother me if I didn't do everything I could to help her."

"It does feel imperative, given that she's basing her new series on you," he said.

"I'm not sure how I feel about that," Lindsey admitted.

"Me either," Sully agreed. "Do you think she'll let us read it first before it's released into the wild?"

"We can ask."

"Let's do that, then." He glanced out the windshield at their small village and said, "I've always considered Briar Creek and the Thumb Islands my sacred space. I'm not sure I want to share it with the world."

"I know what you mean," Lindsey said. She, too, studied their surroundings as they passed through town. Mr. Hicks, the local hardware store owner, was standing outside his shop, talking to Mr. Cowell, the postal delivery-man whose route was the center of town. They were both laughing, and as the watery gray afternoon light gave way to the deepening dusk, the streetlights came on, as did the holiday lights on the town green.

There had been some debate about not fixing the lights after Jackie's body was found, but Mayor Cole had decided that the village needed the cheer that the holiday lights offered, especially after such a tragic death. Ernie had fixed them, and now they glittered against the incoming darkness.

Lindsey knew that Mayor Cole was right, but she also knew that it would be a long time before she was able to look at the town gazebo with anything other than horror.

Sully parked the pickup truck in front of their detached garage. Lindsey glanced at the house, and sure enough, her best pal Heathcliff, a hairy black stray dog that she'd adopted when he'd been dumped into the book drop at the library, had his snout pressed to the window beside the front door. She couldn't see his tail, but she knew it was wagging.

"Brace yourself," she said to Sully as she reached the front door first and unlocked it. The second she pulled it open, Heathcliff barreled out of the house to greet his people.

Heathcliff was a hugger, and he stood on his hind legs and grabbed Lindsey just above the knee while he barked his joy at having his people home. As soon as she scratched his ears sufficiently, he bounded down the steps and caught Sully in a similar hug. Then he was off to patrol the yard with his nose to the ground.

"Go ahead," Sully said. "I'll wait for him."

Feeling the December air chill her all the way to her bones, Lindsey happily went inside. The warmth of the house embraced her as she shed her coat and boots, leaving them in the foyer. She switched on the lights as she entered the living room, taking a second to see that their cat, Zelda, was in her usual spot, sprawled on the top of the convector under the window.

Lindsey crossed the room and scratched the feline's ears, taking the opportunity to switch on the Christmas tree that she and Sully had set up in the corner. The soft white lights soothed her, as did the scent of pine that filled the air.

The front door opened, and Sully came in with Heathcliff, who sprinted into the living room as if afraid he'd missed something—namely, dinner. He did zoomies around the couch and then collapsed on the floor in front of the fireplace, where he rested his head on his paws and gave them his most pitiful look.

"I'll get his supper," Sully said. "As he's clearly going to waste away in a matter of moments."

Lindsey laughed and sat on the floor beside the dog. He promptly rolled over, giving her full access to his belly. Lindsey obliged and gave him a tummy rub. He was as content as the cat until he heard food land in his dog bowl. He jumped to his feet and joined Sully in the kitchen with the clear intention of being his sous-chef.

Lindsey relaxed against the couch and admired their tree. It was simple, with a star on top and shatterproof ornaments in red and gold covering the rest of it, because they'd discovered the hard way that Zelda liked to bat the breakable ones across the room.

"So, what's our cover going to be tomorrow at the law office?" Lindsey asked when Sully entered the room, holding a beer for himself and a glass of wine for her.

"They're a family law practice?" he clarified.

He sat down on the floor beside her, and Zelda, who had ignored Lindsey, hopped off the radiator and crossed the room, pausing to stretch, until she reached Sully. With a flick of her tail, she climbed into his lap and promptly fell back to sleep.

"It's a rough life she leads," Lindsey said.

"Truly." Sully sipped his beer and stroked the cat's back. A purr was her only response.

"I don't know. How do you think we should approach the law office?" Lindsey asked.

"Family law means we can pose as a couple separating or divorcing."

Lindsey wrinkled her nose. "I don't like that."

"Adopting?"

She shook her head.

"Okay, how about you're a billionaire and you need me to sign a prenup before we get married."

Lindsey laughed. "Billionaire? I can work with that."

"Seriously though, what are you hoping to find out from Liz Maynard?"

"I don't know," Lindsey said. "Maybe just a little insight into the whole Jackie-Helen dynamic."

Sully sipped his beer, considering his next words. This was one of the things Lindsey loved most about Sully. He always thought about what he was going to say before he said it.

"I know you want to help Helen," he said.

"I feel like a but is coming." Lindsey sipped her wine. It was a robust red, chasing the chill right out of her.

"Of course there is," he said with a smile before he grew serious. "*But*, darling, have you considered the possibility that Helen is guilty?"

Lindsey sighed. "I don't want to."

"I know." He ran his hand across her upper back in a gesture of comfort. "And I wouldn't even suggest it, except Helen married Jackie's ex-husband."

"But she told us about it."

"Only after she knew it wouldn't remain a secret much longer."

"True." Lindsey didn't like that he was right. "I just don't get a murderer vibe off her."

"Who else had as much of a motive to kill Jackie?" Sully asked. "She was married to Jackie's ex and had to keep the marriage a secret because Jackie was so difficult about it. That's a pretty big motive."

"If that's the criteria, then Kenny has just as much of a motive as Helen." Lindsey knew she sounded defensive but she couldn't help it.

"Maybe they're in it together," Sully said.

"I don't see how that's any better," Lindsey protested. She set her glass down on the coffee table as Heathcliff entered the room and sprawled out on her other side, resting his head on her knee.

By the twinkling lights of the tree, Lindsey took a moment to let the love of her little family seep deeply into her bones as she sat with her husband beside her and their pets curled up with them. It was peaceful and cozy, and it felt right all the way down to her soul.

Keeping her marriage a secret, never being able to be in public together, Helen had never had this level of peace with her husband, and Lindsey found that incredibly sad. She also knew that it proved Sully's point that both Helen and Kenny had plenty of reason to be the ones who murdered Jackie.

"When I think back to that night, the night we found Jackie, I just don't see how Helen could have murdered Jackie and then run around the park to appear to be coming from the opposite direction as me. She wasn't even winded," Lindsey said. "She was just strolling down the sidewalk, looking perfectly at ease."

"Because her husband was in the gazebo getting rid of their problem," Sully said. "Then she saw you and called out to you, alerting her husband that he was about to be discovered, so he slammed into you, knocking you down and running away, hoping you didn't see him."

"I didn't see him, that's true," Lindsey admitted. "But I also don't think it was him."

"Why not?"

"The person who knocked me down was younger," Lindsey said.

"But you didn't see them," he reminded her.

"I know, but I watched Kenny at the restaurant," Lindsey said. "He's middle-aged and he walks like it. Whoever hit me from behind was spry. They took off running as if they did it all the time."

"We're looking for a jogger, then?" Sully teased.

"You know what I mean, you can tell when someone is in shape, and while Kenny isn't in bad shape, he's not in sprint-away-as-if-your-life-is-in-danger shape," she said.

"That's fair," Sully said. "Of course, it could be that the person who knocked you down was in the wrong place at the wrong time, and maybe they ran away because they were petrified."

"I feel like they would have come forward if that was the case." Lindsey glanced at him. "Once the adrenaline wore off, there would be no reason for them not to go to Chief Plewicki, unless they couldn't because they were involved."

"Looks like we're going for a prenup," Sully said.

CHAPTER

15

BRIAR CREEK
PUBLIC LIBRARY

Don't forget to take your wedding ring off," Sully said.

"Right." Lindsey twisted off her ring and handed it to him. Sully slipped both rings into the front pocket of his jeans. "That feels weird." Lindsey glanced at her hand. At least she still had her engagement ring on, but it felt oddly light without its companion band.

"I don't like it," Sully agreed. "I feel like my wedding ring is a part of my identity now. Did I tell you that Brady, the little boy who lives at the end of our street, calls me Mr. Library?"

"Seriously?" Lindsey asked. "That's so cute. I love it when I see him and his mom outside of work. Brady's always confused as to why I'm not at the library, as if he thinks I actually live there."

There was a knock on the door, which sent Heathcliff

into a frenzy of barking. Lindsey glanced through the window and saw Robbie at the door. She usually met him in the afternoon at the library, as he liked to swing by and share tea. She hoped nothing amiss had caused him to drop in so early. She crossed the foyer and opened the door, forgetting to warn him.

Heathcliff, seeing one of his favorite people, leapt for the Englishman. Luckily, Robbie knew to brace himself for Heathcliff's hug. He bent over and rubbed Heathcliff's ears until the dog was satisfied, after which Heathcliff trotted out into the yard to do a quick reconnaissance.

"Hi, Robbie, is everything all right?" Lindsey asked.

"No, it's not," he replied as he strode past her into the house. "Morning, Sully."

"Hey." Sully gave Lindsey a concerned look. The generally affable actor did not have his usual carefree smile. "What's wrong? Is Emma okay?"

"No, she's not," Robbie said. "She's been very preoccupied lately, which I assume is because of the body in the gazebo. But this isn't like her normal cases."

"What do you mean?" Lindsey asked.

"It's just a suspicious death, not an actual murder," Robbie said.

"She still has to treat it like one," Lindsey countered.

"Okay, explain this. Emma has never loved the holidays, but this year, she's bonkers for them," he said. "We've been to every single event offered in the town, and judging by our calendar, we're booked through the New Year. It's almost as if she's avoiding me by being busy with me. Does that make sense?"

"No." Lindsey shook her head.

"She probably just has a lot of things to do." Sully gestured between him and Lindsey and said, "As do we."

"Yes, about that." Robbie looked them over. "Where are you off to?"

"We're going to get a prenup," Lindsey said.

Robbie squinted. "Sorry, isn't that horse already out of the barn?"

"We're going to New Haven to speak with the other member of the critique group that Helen and Jackie were in. She works at a family law firm, and we want to find out if she's been in touch with Jackie or can share any insight about the situation," Lindsey explained. She clapped her hands, and Heathcliff trotted across the yard and up the steps into the house. "Be good, buddy."

They all stepped back outside, and Sully locked the door after them.

"Mind if I tag along?" Robbie asked.

"How exactly are we going to explain that you're with us?" Sully asked.

"I'll be your vicar," Robbie said. "People always trust a man of the cloth."

Lindsey laughed. "Why would we bring a vicar to our attorney's office?"

"Because I'm tending to your premarital counseling," Robbie said.

Sully frowned. "Why is this so important to you?"

"Because you're my friends, and I want to help in any way I can."

"Or you want to join us so you can go to Helen and tell her what a help you were and convince her to option her Mallory Quest series to you," Lindsey said.

"That, too," Robbie agreed.

"She's not going to option the books," Lindsey said.

"Of course she is," Robbie said. "I can be very persuasive, especially if I'm seen as being helpful."

"You're not coming in with us," Sully said.

"Why not?" Robbie demanded.

"Because you'll be recognized, and it'll make the entire endeavor weird," Sully said. "Why would we bring our actor friend with us?"

"He's right," Lindsey said. "But you can come along for the ride and wait in the car."

"Like I'm a dog?" Robbie gaped.

"Don't worry, we'll roll down the window for you and you can stick your head out," Sully teased.

"Very funny, Sailor Boy," Robbie said. He followed them outside. "For the record, I'm only going because I have nothing better to do. And we're taking my car, because your truck is an abomination. You're welcome."

The drive into New Haven was blissfully traffic-free. The office building was on a one-way street to the east of the city green, and Robbie managed to find street parking a few buildings down from where the office of Dixon, Carter and Suffield was housed.

Sully led the way up the short flight of stairs, pulling open the heavy door of the attorneys' office and gesturing for Lindsey to go ahead. She strode into the lobby, taking in the chandelier overhead, the marble floor and the hushed environment of the office. Was it quiet because the holidays were coming, or was everyone busy working? She had no idea.

A woman in a cream-colored blouse with a forest green cashmere cardigan over it sat behind a desk in an adjacent room. Her dark hair was scraped into a severe bun at the nape of her neck, and she wore round wire-framed glasses and bright pink lipstick. She glanced up when they stepped into the doorway, and she smiled at them. "May I help you?"

"I hope so," Lindsey said. She glanced at the nameplate on the desk. It read *Elizabeth Maynard*. Bingo! "We were looking for some legal advice for a prenuptial agreement."

"Do you have an appointment?"

"Unfortunately, no," Sully said. "We just drove in from Briar Creek and were hoping we could make one."

"Absolutely. Come on in." Liz half rose and gestured for them to sit down in the chairs in front of her desk. "I'm Liz. Normally, I could have someone meet with you at least for a few minutes, but most of the lawyers are away on holiday, so I likely can't get you in until the beginning of next year. Let's check the schedule."

"Thank you." Lindsey glanced at Sully, and he nodded encouragingly.

They sat down, loosening their jackets, and Liz turned to her computer. "I'll just need some information. Shall we start with your names?"

The front door opened, and they all turned to see Robbie enter the building.

Lindsey made an exasperated face at Sully, who rolled his eyes as if he'd expected this.

"Hi, I'll be right with you . . . oh my God . . . you're Robbie Vine," Liz gasped.

"I thought you were going to wait in the car," Sully said.

"It's cold out there," Robbie protested.

Lindsey sighed. She glanced at Liz, who was sitting with her mouth hanging slightly open and stars in her eyes. Maybe catching her off guard like this was a good thing. Lindsey decided to scrap the entire idea about being a couple looking for advice. She held out her hand to Sully and said, "Ring, please."

"Might as well call it," he agreed. He pulled their rings out of his pocket and handed Lindsey hers.

This seemed to snap Liz out of her stupor. "Wait, you're already married? I thought you wanted a prenup?"

"Yes, we are, and no, we don't." Lindsey nodded. "And I apologize for not being up front with you from the start. We weren't sure how to approach you."

"Me?" Liz glanced from Lindsey to Sully to Robbie. "What could you possibly want with me?"

"Well, Liz, my colleagues were hoping to talk to you on my behalf," Robbie said.

He definitely had all of Liz's interest while Lindsey looked at Sully in complete bewilderment. What was Robbie playing at?

"How could I be of any help to you, Mr. Vine?" Liz asked.

"Call me Robbie," he said. He sat on the corner of her desk and smiled down at her. Liz looked like she might swoon.

"Robbie," she repeated. Her voice was breathy, and her cheeks had the faintest tinge of pink to them. "How can I help you?"

"I want to option the movie rights to the Mallory Quest novels, but Ms. Monroe refuses to speak with me."

"Oh, she'll never sell the option," Liz said decisively. "Helen loathes what Hollywood does to books. She always says the book was better."

"She's not wrong," Lindsey said, and Liz smiled.

"She just hasn't met the iron will of Robbie Vine. Is there anything you can tell me about her that you learned from your time in your critique group with her that might give me an in?" he asked.

"You know I was in her critique group?" Liz asked. She looked flattered.

"Yes, Helen mentioned you," Robbie said. "So, what can you tell me?"

"Nothing. Not one thing." Liz vigorously shook her head. "I can't talk about the critique group."

Sully cocked his head to the side. "Why not?"

"We were sworn to secrecy," Liz said. "Jackie had us sign nondisclosure agreements."

"Well, that seems like it should have ended with Jackie's passing, doesn't it?" Robbie asked.

"What?" Liz's eyes went wide behind her glasses.

"You haven't heard?" Lindsey asked. Liz just stared at her. Lindsey softened her voice and said, "I'm so sorry. Jackie Lewis passed away a few days ago."

"Oh, no. How did she die?" Liz asked. Her eyes welled up, and she reached for a tissue from the holder on her desk.

"She was electrocuted by a holiday display in Briar Creek," Lindsey said. "They're still trying to determine how it happened."

"Wait." Liz rose from her seat and stared them down. "You said you were from Briar Creek. That's where Helen is doing her writer in residence."

"You're aware of that?" Lindsey asked.

"Of course," Liz said. She started to pace in the space behind her desk. She waved her hand to a family portrait of herself with a good-looking man, and three young children all dressed in matching white shirts and jeans, which sat on the bookshelf behind her desk. Lindsey glanced from the picture to Liz, noting that she had aged quite a bit since the picture had been taken. "I stayed in touch with both Jackie and Helen after I left the group. I didn't want to quit, but I was having my third baby and I needed to prioritize my family. Besides, after Melanie died, it just wasn't the same."

"Helen said that she and Jackie couldn't work together after you left," Lindsey said.

"She spoke to you about that?" Liz looked surprised. She sank back down into her seat.

"I'm the director of the library where she is doing her residency."

"Oh." Liz glanced at all of their faces as if putting the puzzle together. Her brow furrowed in concern. "So, Jackie and Helen were in Briar Creek at the same time."

"Yes," Lindsey said.

"Oh, no," Liz moaned. She wrapped her arms around her middle and rocked back and forth. "This is all my fault."

"How do you figure?" Robbie asked.

"I'm the one who told Jackie what Helen was doing," Liz said. "Helen and I were texting a few weeks ago, and that same day Jackie popped into the office during our holiday party and I'd had a glass of wine. I don't normally drink at all, and I'm afraid it made me a bit tipsy and loose with my words." She bit her lip. "I try to never talk about either of them to the other. I knew the minute I mentioned Helen's residency that I'd made a mistake. Jackie has never forgiven Helen for . . . well . . . a variety of things. I should have known she'd go to Briar Creek and try to have a showdown."

"Jackie did cause quite a ruckus at the ugly Christmas sweater party, which I won incidentally," Robbie said.

Sully shot him an exasperated look and Robbie shrugged.

"Don't tell me, let me guess." Liz held up her hand. "Jackie accused Helen of stealing her idea and writing the Mallory Quest series with it."

"Exactly," Sully said. He gave her a considering glance. "Is there any truth to the accusation?"

"None that I could see," Liz said. "I tried to talk Jackie out of her unreasonable take on the situation, but she wouldn't listen, and there was more than just a creative dispute on the table, so I stayed out of it."

"But you stayed in touch with both of them all these years?" Lindsey asked.

"Yeah, I mean, working in a family law office, they all came to me for help over the years. I helped Jackie with her divorce and Melanie's widower with her estate, including the intellectual property on Melanie's unfinished books. Her husband really had no idea what to do. Intellectual property can be sticky. And even Helen came to me when she needed legal advice about a stalker. Spoiler alert, it was Jackie."

"How did you manage to stay friends with both Jackie and Helen?" Lindsey asked. "I would think they'd have forced you to choose sides."

"I believe I was considered a non-threat since I quit writing. They knew I was busy raising my kids. Now that they're all in high school, with the oldest about to start college, I'm looking forward to writing full time again. I even have a proposal making the rounds, and my agent is very excited about it."

"Congratulations," Lindsey said.

"Thank you." Liz beamed. "Keeping in touch with Jackie and Helen was a way to keep my passion alive. I've enjoyed hearing about their careers, despite feeling a bit jealous. Although, it was admittedly easier to hear about Jackie's lesser success than it was Helen's massive triumphs.

To Helen's credit, she never spoke of it unless I asked directly. She's very modest that way."

"How was Jackie's career going?" Lindsey asked.

"Eh." Liz cringed. "She published her intergalactic police procedural books at a small indie press, and they did respectably but were nowhere near as successful as she'd hoped."

"Did Jackie tell you that she was going to confront Helen?" Lindsey asked. "Did she give you any indication that she was going to follow Helen to Briar Creek?"

Liz pushed her glasses up on her nose. She stared at the papers on her desk as if trying to recall the memory of her last meeting with Jackie. She shook her head, clearly frustrated.

"No, the only thing she said that seemed weird was something to the effect that Helen must be suffering from the seven-year itch if she was taking off on her own during the holidays, which is odd because Helen is single," Liz said. "I thought maybe Jackie meant that Helen felt that way about her career? I don't know. It didn't make any sense, and before I could question her, Jackie left the party and I forgot all about it."

"I don't think it's your fault that Jackie found out where Helen was," Lindsey said. "It was in all the papers."

"Still, my confirming it probably didn't help," Liz said. "I feel badly for Jackie. She always seemed to look at life through a lens of lack. Her house wasn't big enough, her car wasn't fancy enough, her career wasn't as successful as she wanted it to be. I don't want to speak ill of her, especially since she's gone, but if I could think of one word to describe her, it would be *dissatisfied*."

"Interesting," Sully said. "Did she feel that everyone else had it better?"

"Yes, but particularly Helen."

Lindsey thought this was understandable, given that it sounded as if Jackie must have found out about Helen's marriage to Kenny. Of course, there was no way to prove that unless Jackie had confided in someone.

"Did Jackie have any other writer friends?" Lindsey asked. "Was there anyone she might have told about going to Briar Creek?"

Liz shook her head. "As far as I know, she didn't have any friends. She went a little sideways during her divorce, and I think her husband kept most of their mutual friends. You know how when people divorce, their friends usually only keep one member of the former couple in their life?"

Lindsey nodded. She had lost a few friends that way in a previous breakup.

The phone on Liz's desk rang. She reached for the receiver. "Excuse me."

Lindsey immediately turned to Sully. "Are you thinking what I'm thinking?"

"She knew," he said.

"Who knew?" Robbie asked.

"We have to go," Lindsey said. "We need to talk to Emma."

"Yes, sir, I'll be right there," Liz said. She hung up the receiver and said, "I'm sorry. I have to go."

"Not at all," Lindsey said. "We've taken enough of your time."

Liz lifted a file off her desk and clutched it to her chest. "If there's a service for Jackie or anything, will you let me know?"

"Of course," Lindsey said. "I'm sorry we brought you such sad news."

Liz sighed. "It is sad, isn't it? I wonder if she had spent her life looking at things with an attitude of gratitude if it might have ended differently."

"It's certainly worth considering," Robbie said.

They made their way to the door, and Liz watched them go with an expression that Lindsey interpreted as regret. Did Liz feel bad for the choices Jackie had made in life? Or was she feeling conflicted for telling Jackie where Helen was? Did she think Helen might have had something to do with Jackie's death?

They left the attorneys' office and headed back into the cold. Lindsey noted a car idling by the curb as its exhaust plumed out into the frigid air. She glanced into the car and saw a young woman in the passenger seat swiftly turn her head away as if to avoid Lindsey's gaze. Lindsey glanced past her at the driver, and her eyes went wide. It was Betty Caruthers. What was she doing here?

Before Lindsey could wave or acknowledge her in any way, Betty gunned the engine and screeched away from the curb, leaving skid marks behind.

CHAPTER

16

BRIAR CREEK
PUBLIC LIBRARY

R emind me why we're here again?" Sully asked.

"Because it's Mayor Cole's first annual staff party for all of the employees of Briar Creek, and we're being supportive. Plus, Emma will be here and I want to talk to her."

"About Betty," he said.

"Yes."

"You don't think it's a coincidence that she was in the same section of New Haven that we were in?" he asked. "It's not that big of a city."

"My gut says she was following us, but why?" Lindsey asked.

"Are you talking about book banner Betty?" Emma asked as she joined them. "Robbie mentioned that you think she was following you."

"It's weird that she was in New Haven in the same place we were at the same time, right?" Lindsey asked.

"As weird as you going to talk to the only other remaining member of Helen's book critique group?" Emma countered with an exaggerated shrug.

"Am I in trouble for that?" Lindsey asked.

"Yes," Emma said. "What were you hoping to accomplish?"

"I wanted to find out what the dynamic was between Helen and Jackie," Lindsey said.

"Because you want to prove that Helen is innocent," Emma said. "I understand that she's a favorite author of yours, but given that the former wife of her husband was electrocuted after the two of them had words, she is very much a person of interest, and you can't try to prove she's innocent. You have to let the investigation unfold as it will."

"Does her husband have an alibi for Jackie's time of death?" Lindsey asked.

"I'm not telling you that," Emma said. "No more investigating. Leave it to the police."

"Busted. I knew she wasn't going to be happy about our visit with Liz Maynard." Robbie appeared at Emma's side and held a steaming cup of cider out to her.

"Thank you." Emma glanced at Sully and Lindsey. "Midge from accounting made her famous pistachio chocolate fudge. I'm only telling you to show you that I'm not mad at you . . . mostly."

"But don't you think Betty—" Lindsey began, but she

was interrupted when the door banged open, and they all turned to see who was making such a boisterous entrance.

"Ho ho ho!" Mayor Cole, dressed as Santa Claus, stepped fully into the room.

"Okay, this was one hundred percent worth coming for." Sully grinned at Lindsey.

"And here I thought being my plus-one was reason enough," she said.

"Always." He kissed the top of her head. "But this is definitely the cherry on top. Ms. Cole dressed as Kris Kringle, there's just no way to prepare for something like this."

Lindsey glanced back at Mayor Cole. She lowered the sack of presents onto the floor and stretched, putting a fist to her back. This outward display of joviality was so incredibly out of character for Mayor Cole that Lindsey couldn't help but wonder what had possessed her to dress up in costume for the party. She wondered if it was because Mayor Cole's predecessor, Mayor Hensen, had always put on a Santa suit for the staff party and Ms. Cole felt that it was a tradition she didn't dare skip. Lindsey would have advised her differently. Instead, she turned back to Emma.

"About Betty . . ." Lindsey began, but Emma shook her head.

"Unless she said or did something more than driving away when she saw you, there's nothing I can do," Emma said. She leveled Lindsey with a look. "And there's nothing you can do either."

"There's something not right there," Lindsey said. "I

thought she was just an overreaching book banner, but why is it she's been going after Helen in particular? She tried to bar her from being our writer in residence, she pushed to be the president of the library's Friends group in a very sketchy election, and she just happened to show up when we were talking to Liz Maynard. Why?"

"None of those things are illegal, nor do they tie her to a murder," Emma said. "There is absolutely no reason for me to question her, and you can't bully her either."

Lindsey put her hand on her chest. "Me? Bully?"

"Yes, you—" Emma began, but Mayor Cole joined them, diverting the conversation.

"I'm sweating in places I didn't even know it was possible to sweat," she said. She pulled the fake beard away from her face and fanned herself with her free hand. "Robbie and Sully, would you mind taking this and handing out gifts to all of the staff? Thanks."

She didn't wait for an answer but thrust her burlap sack at the two of them.

"Well, I guess we've been given our marching orders," Robbie said.

"Happy to help, Mayor," Sully said as he followed Robbie into the fray.

"Subtle you are not," Emma said.

"Eh." Mayor Cole shrugged. "It'll be more of a thrill for the staff to have a gift handed to them by Robbie than me, and Sully will keep him on task. Also, I wanted to warn you two."

"Warn us?" Lindsey asked.

"We've been receiving a lot of calls at the mayor's office for information about Jackie Lewis's death," Mayor Cole said. "We've been able to put them off, saying we can't discuss it until the medical examiner shares his findings, but I find it odd that a marginally successful author is warranting such a steady stream of calls."

"Jackie is from the area, just like Helen. Maybe it's the local-author angle making people curious," Lindsey suggested.

"Maybe, but it feels off," Mayor Cole said. "The callers don't identify themselves as media but rather as concerned citizens, and their angle is that they think Jackie was murdered and that Helen Monroe is guilty."

"Friends of Jackie's?" Emma asked.

"As far as I can tell, Jackie didn't have many if any friends," Lindsey said. "I'd think enemies of Helen is the more likely group."

"Why does a bestselling author have so many enemies?" Emma asked. "That seems wrong."

"Helen based the books in her series off real cases," Lindsey said. "She changed the names and a lot of the particulars in the stories, but if you were a true-crime junkie, you could probably suss out what stories she based her books on. That's why the Campbells loathe her. She wrote about Diana Campbell, and both Jeffrey and Lisa despise her for it."

"How many books are in her Mallory Quest series?" Emma asked.

"Ten." Lindsey had read and loved them all.

Emma nodded. "All right, I want you to talk to Helen

and ask her the name of each true-crime case that she used for the basis of her books and then come up with a list of people that I will then contact. I'd ask her myself, but I suspect Helen will have an easier time talking to you. Also, we're short-staffed due to the holiday and I need to be on patrol."

"So what you're saying is I can help." Lindsey grinned.

"Do not let it go to your head," Emma said. "I'm only asking you because you're the town librarian and this request seems like something you could do without messing it up."

"There's a vote of confidence," Mayor Cole said. "I don't care how you do it, but we're just days from the holidays, and I'd like to have Jackie's death resolved by then. I've got a call into the medical examiner's office, and I'm leaning on him as hard as I can to make a determination of the cause of death."

"And if he determines that it was an accident?" Lindsey asked.

"Then we let it go," Mayor Cole said.

Lindsey and Emma exchanged a look, and Lindsey knew that Emma didn't believe Jackie's death was an accident any more than she did. If it was ruled an accident, then a murderer was going to walk free.

"I know what you're thinking, and I understand," Mayor Cole said. "But can we just take it one step at a time?"

"Now who do we have here? Would these ladies be on the naughty or nice list, Mayor?" Robbie asked as he approached them.

"Do not pull me into your inappropriate speculation," Mayor Cole said.

Sully strode beside Robbie, carrying the bag and looking aggrieved. Lindsey grinned at him.

Robbie shoved his hands into the bag and pulled out two metal water bottles. They were emblazoned with the town logo. Emma and Lindsey took them with cursory thank-yous. Mayor Cole frowned at them. "Hydration is important. Besides, this is a one-size-fits-all sort of gift."

Lindsey was about to thank her with a bit more enthusiasm, when her phone rang. She opened her shoulder bag and took her phone out. It was Helen.

"Hi, Helen, how are you?" she asked. She met Emma's gaze with raised eyebrows.

"Not good," Helen said. "I think someone just tried to murder me."

"What?!" Lindsey cried. "Hang on, the chief is here. I'm putting you on speaker. What happened?"

"Maybe I'm being paranoid, but I was crossing the street and this car came out of nowhere—" Helen paused, and Lindsey could hear her uneven breathing. "I had to jump out of the way and I barely made it—"

Lindsey glanced at Emma. "She said someone just tried to murder her."

"Where are you, Helen?" Emma asked. "Are you safe?"

"Yes, I'm with Kenny," Helen answered. "He saw the whole thing. We're driving to the police station now."

"We'll meet you there," Emma said. She glanced at Mayor Cole. "Great party. Bye."

Mayor Cole waved her on.

Emma strode to the door, pausing in the doorway to turn and look at Lindsey. "Are you coming or what?"

"Oh," Lindsey said. "I'm invited?"

"Only because she's your writer in residence," Emma said. "You can start locking in those true-crime stories we discussed."

"On it." Lindsey turned and kissed Sully's cheek. "I'll check in later."

"Be careful." His blue gaze met and held hers.

"Always." Lindsey darted after Emma with a quick wave at the rest of the partygoers. "Happy holidays, everyone!"

She heard a few people call out the same in return, but she was hurrying to catch up to Emma and didn't look back.

Molly had settled Helen and Kenny on the leather sofa in the chief's office. Helen was holding a cup of hot chocolate as if using it to keep warm, while Kenny had his hand on her upper back, rubbing her shoulders in a soothing circular motion.

"Ms. Monroe, Mr. Lewis," Emma greeted them as she entered the room. She took one of the armchairs and Lindsey took the other.

"Hi, Helen, Kenny." Lindsey sent them a sympathetic look. Helen appeared pale and shaky, and Kenny had tight lines around his eyes and mouth.

"Do you mind if Lindsey sits in?" Emma asked Helen and Kenny.

"No." Helen glanced at Lindsey. "I called you right away because I was hoping you'd meet us here. You've been so kind since I arrived, I consider you . . . a friend."

The word came out awkwardly, as if Helen wasn't used to saying it. Lindsey was touched, but knowing how reserved Helen was, she knew better than to show it.

"Thank you," Lindsey said. "I feel the same, and I'm happy to help in any way that I can."

"We'll get to that," Emma said. "In the meantime, can you tell us what happened?"

Helen took a deep, steadying breath. "I was coming out of the post office. I had small gifts to send to my editor and agent, and I wanted to be sure they arrived in time. I stopped at the crosswalk and looked both ways. I am absolutely positive about that."

"She did," Kenny confirmed. "I was watching her from across the street where I had parked the car." He glanced at Helen with regret. "I should have gone in with you."

"No, I was just dropping them off; there was no need." Helen squeezed his forearm in reassurance. She turned back to Emma. "I stepped out into the crosswalk and was halfway when I heard this horrific roaring noise. I glanced up, and there was a black sedan bearing down on me. It came out of nowhere."

"It did!" Kenny confirmed. "One second the street was clear and the next . . ." He swallowed as if reliving the moment. "The driver was aiming for her. I'm sure of it."

"I managed to jump out of the way but just barely," Helen said. She put down her cup and showed her hands. Her palms were scraped raw. She then pulled aside her coat and revealed the torn fabric of her woolen trousers. Lindsey could see the bloody cuts on her knees, and she gasped. Helen had clearly hit the sidewalk hard.

"You need to have those cleaned," Emma said. "But before you do, can I have Molly take a few pictures for the report?"

"Yes, of course," Helen agreed. "That's why I didn't patch them up yet."

Emma rose from her seat and crossed the room to the door, where she called, "Molly!"

Molly arrived with a digital camera in one hand and a first aid kit in the other. "Ready to assist."

"Excellent." Emma turned back to Helen. "Why don't you go with Molly and we can finish up the report when you get back?"

"All right," Helen agreed.

Kenny helped Helen to her feet. She walked toward Molly, and he went to follow her, but Emma stopped him by putting up her hand. "Not you, Mr. Lewis. I'd like to get your description of events to see if you saw anything different than Helen."

Kenny frowned. He clearly did not like being separated from his wife. "She's already told you everything that happened."

"I'd still like to hear it from you," Emma said. Her tone did not allow for argument.

"You'll be all right?" Kenny asked Helen.

"Yes, don't worry." She patted his hand.

Kenny watched her go with a resigned expression. "She's been through so much. I hate that this is happening to her."

"What is it that you think is happening?" Emma asked.

Kenny slowly sank into his seat. "I think it's obvious. Jackie's behind this."

"Jackie is dead," Emma pointed out. "I don't think she's driving presently."

Kenny waved his hands as if trying to wipe away any argument Emma made. "That's not what I meant."

"Then explain." Emma leaned back in her seat and crossed her arms over her chest.

"I can't," Kenny said. "I just feel like it has something to do with Jackie. There was a news story last night about Jackie's death, and the reporter actually mentioned Jackie's claim that Helen stole her work. It could be a reader heard that and is now trying to seek justice on Jackie's behalf."

"To be clear," Emma said. "You think a reader of Jackie's tried to run Helen down because of some old plagiarism complaints that were proven false in a court of law."

Kenny dropped his head into his hands. "I don't know what to think. I just know that I saw my wife almost killed by a car that was obviously intent upon hitting her."

"All right, let's start there," Emma said. "What did you notice about the car?"

"Black sedan," he said. "Fairly nondescript."

"The driver?"

"I was on the passenger side of the vehicle. I couldn't see them." He sounded equal parts furious and depressed.

"Were there any other witnesses?" Emma asked.

"I don't know," he said. "I rushed to get to Helen. No one came forward while I was helping her up. I was afraid to linger in case the person in the car came back with a gun. My only thought was to get Helen to safety."

"Understandable," Emma said. "One last question. Does Helen have any enemies? Anyone who has made a threat against her recently? A neighbor? A fellow author? A relative with a beef? Anyone?"

"Jackie was the only person who had a problem with Helen that I'm aware of, and she was more than enough," Kenny said.

"If you think of anyone or Helen knows of anyone, I want you to let me know immediately," Emma said. "I'm going to canvass the area in front of the post office where she was almost run down and see if I can come up with any witnesses." She turned to Lindsey. "In the meantime, I want you to get the names of every true-crime case she used as the basis for her novels."

"I'm on it," Lindsey said.

Emma rose from her seat, pulling her jacket back on. "When Helen is all cleaned up, Molly will have her fill out a formal statement, and then you can go."

"Thank you, Chief." Kenny stood as Emma swept out the door.

He resumed his seat, and Lindsey wondered what to say to him. She was really only comfortable talking about books, but there was no way it wouldn't be awkward to ask him who his favorite author was at the moment.

"Helen seems to have become fond of you," he said.

Lindsey smiled. "I'm fond of her, too."

"She doesn't have many friends," he continued. "She doesn't do book tours or any public appearances because, well, Jackie made it impossible."

"It sounds as if it has been a difficult few years," Lindsey said. "Are you certain that Jackie didn't know you were married?"

"Positive," Kenny said. "We were so careful."

Lindsey thought about Liz telling them that Jackie had said something about the seven-year itch. It seemed very on point given that Kenny and Helen had been married for seven years. Jackie had to know. There was no other explanation for her appearance in Briar Creek and her determination to harass Helen.

"I'm back," Helen said as she entered the room. "All photographed and bandaged and I even signed my statement."

"Excellent," Kenny said. "Let's get you home."

"Sorry," Lindsey said. "The chief asked me to get some information from you, Helen."

"It really can't wait?" Kenny asked. He was holding Helen's coat and looked as if he wanted to snatch her up and spirit her out of there as fast as possible. Lindsey understood, but there was no way she was going to tell Emma she hadn't gotten the names of the true crimes that Helen had used to base her novels on. It was the first time

Emma had ever allowed her to assist, and she was not going to blow it.

"No, I'm sorry it can't." Lindsey glanced at Helen. "I'll be quick."

Helen sat back down on the couch. "All right, how can I help you?"

"I need to know the names of every case you've used as a jumping-off point for a book," Lindsey said.

"Ah." Helen nodded. "You think someone from the past is out to kill me."

"Emma is just trying to rule out all possibilities," Lindsey said. "I saw how angry the Campbells were. They might not be the only ones."

"I guess you can start right there," Helen said. "Jeffrey Campbell has probably wanted me dead ever since my first book came out."

CHAPTER

17

BRIAR CREEK
PUBLIC LIBRARY

It didn't take long for Lindsey to get a list of the cases that Helen had used as inspiration to pen her thrillers. She jotted down the pertinent names on a piece of paper and headed back to the library while Kenny took Helen home.

The party at the town hall was wrapping up, and Lindsey's staff, who had attended the party in shifts so that they could also keep the library open, were back at their service areas. After a quick check-in with her staff, Lindsey retreated to her office to search the old crimes and see what had become of the people involved.

The Campbells were easy. Jeffrey had been cleared of all charges when the woman he'd been having an affair with was tied to the murder by a strand of hair the victim had in her hand. She confessed, and he'd been released and become a single father. There were no news stories of him in any of the papers since. Apparently, he'd managed to keep a very low profile.

The perpetrators in Helen's next three novels were similar to actual criminals who were all currently still in prison and most likely would be for life. As far as Lindsey could tell, there was no one in any of those cases who would care that Helen had used elements of the crimes for her mysteries. The next case was a young man accused of killing his abusive father in self-defense. He'd been released and was on probation for several years with mandatory counseling. By all accounts, he'd become a model citizen. Still, he was not in jail, and Helen had modeled a book after his case. Lindsey made a note of his name, Titus Bondurant.

Sarah Alexander was the next case. She'd murdered her twin sister, Sadie, when they were seventeen years old. Sadie had been an honor student, choir singer and football cheerleader, and had received a full scholarship to Yale. The unexpected murder had shocked their small New England town.

No one had considered Sarah as the potential killer since the two sisters had always seemed so close, but Sarah had been consumed with jealousy, and one night, she reached her breaking point. Horrified by what she had done, Sarah assumed her sister's identity and tried to pass herself off as her twin, pretending that she (Sarah) had been murdered in a home invasion gone wrong.

Lindsey read the story with a growing sense of unease. It was hard to even imagine what could drive one sibling to murder another. She thought of her brother, Jack, and felt sick to her stomach at the mere idea of ever harming him. It was unfathomable.

Being the daughter of very wealthy parents, Sarah was given the best defense money could buy. It was obvious that the parents wanted to believe that Sadie was the survivor and that Sarah had been murdered by a home invasion gone wrong, but Sarah's shaky mental state soon cracked under the pressure, and she confessed. There was no other option beyond having her sent to a maximum-security psychiatric hospital. The remaining family members, the parents and a younger sister, had relocated to Florida, clearly trying to put the past behind them.

Lindsey could find no release information for Sarah, and made a note to mention it to Emma. Because Sarah Alexander was a teen at the time of the murder, there were no photos of her. She could be anyone, anywhere. Lindsey shivered.

"What are you doing?"

"Ah!" Lindsey jumped in her seat.

Leaning against the doorjamb was Robbie, holding a tea tray with a teapot, two cups and a plate of biscuits. "I thought you could use a cuppa, given the way you bolted out of the staff party without even a chance to enjoy the spread."

"Thank you." Lindsey gestured for him to take a seat. "How did the rest of the party go?"

"Well enough," he said. "There weren't any crackers with silly paper crowns in them, which was a pity, but otherwise I'd say Mayor Cole was quite successful in her first run as Santa."

Lindsey smiled. "I admire her willingness to step out of her comfort zone for the good of morale."

"Commendable." Robbie poured the tea and handed Lindsey her cup. "What has Emma got you working on that's made you so jumpy?"

"Why do you suppose I'm working for Emma?" Lindsey countered.

"Because she told me so." He sipped his tea. "I ran into her while she was canvassing the area around the post office where Helen was almost run down, and she said she had you doing some research for her."

Lindsey gave him the side-eye. She wasn't sure whether Robbie was just fishing for information or if Emma had actually told him all of that. Either way, she didn't suppose it would hurt to let him know. Maybe he could be of help.

"I'm looking up all of the true-crime cases that Helen used as the basis for her books and checking to see what happened to the people involved. We're trying to determine if any of her subjects are carrying a grudge." Lindsey took a cookie off the tray.

"Well, that's festive, isn't it?" he asked.

"Christmas and murder, what's not to love?" Lindsey toasted him with her cup.

"Do you really think someone tried to murder Helen?" Robbie asked.

"What do you mean?"

"She has to know that she and her husband are the

prime suspects if the medical examiner declares Jackie Lewis's death a homicide," he reasoned. "Do you think she and her husband cooked up the potential hit and run to drum up sympathy and get the speculation off themselves?"

"I don't want to believe that," Lindsey said.

"I hear a *but* in there."

"There's no escaping the fact that Helen and Kenny had the most to gain, namely their freedom, if Jackie was no more; however, I have three potential revenge seekers, and three more names to search, so maybe something substantial will turn up."

"Murdering an author for a fictionalized account of something you did seems a bit extreme," Robbie said. "They have to know they'd get caught and sent back to jail."

"I don't think reasonable people commit murder to begin with, so I don't know that the threat of additional incarceration would sway them away from their purpose," Lindsey said.

"Fair point." Robbie contemplated the situation while he drank his tea. "Assuming there is a killer, how do you propose to draw them out?"

"I have no intention of drawing anyone out," Lindsey protested.

"Seriously?" Robbie set his cup on his saucer with a rattle. "Do you mean to tell me that you're just going to hand this list of names over to Emma and not investigate any of them on your own?"

"That's exactly what I mean," Lindsey said. "Besides, I'm not even done yet. There are more names to go, and it could be that one of them is so obviously it that I won't have to draw them out at all."

"Does it seem likely though? I mean, why now? Why not when they were released from prison?" Robbie asked.

"Because she's accessible now," Lindsey said. "She's our writer in residence. She lives in a fishbowl of a room in our public library, where anyone can reach her. In fact, now that I think about it, maybe we need to cancel the program."

"What? No! Please don't do that." Carrie Rushton stepped into Lindsey's office with a frown of concern creasing her brow.

"Sorry, Carrie," Lindsey apologized. "We're just talking. I have no plans to cancel the residency as of yet."

"No, no. I shouldn't have eavesdropped," Carrie said. "I didn't mean to. It's just that I had such high hopes for the program, but it's been much more controversial than I expected."

"You're not alone on that." Lindsey gestured to the plate of cookies, but Carrie shook her head.

"No, thank you." Carrie held up a current bestseller. "I just came in to pick up a book and let you know that I've officially turned over the running of the Friends of the Library to Betty."

"You were a great president," Lindsey said. "Betty will have a tough time following your lead."

"I doubt that." Betty strode up behind Carrie and sent Lindsey a baleful glance. "Particularly since my first order of business will be to end the writer in residence program immediately."

Carrie gasped. Lindsey frowned. Robbie nibbled his biscuit.

"Isn't that a decision for the board of the Friends?" Lindsey asked.

"No, I've relieved them all of their duties," Betty said.

"You can't!" Carrie protested. "That's not your job. The president of the Friends isn't the queen. You can't just decide to shut programs down and wipe out the board."

"Well, it seems one of us didn't read the bylaws of the Friends group." Betty smirked. "And that would be you. I had my attorney look them over, and he said I can do whatever I want. You can go fetch my tiara now."

"You're horrible!" Carrie seethed.

Betty shrugged. "You might want to go tell your little author friend to pack up. She's outta here."

With that, Betty turned on one spiky heel and strode away. Lindsey had no idea what to make of any of this. Was Betty right? Could she do this? Who was her attorney? She actually went to an attorney? It was definitely time to call an emergency meeting of the Friends.

"We need to loop Milton in," Lindsey said. "He was the president before you, and if anyone knows the bylaws, it's him."

"Seems to me she isn't following what is written in the bylaws but rather she's weaponizing what is not," Robbie said.

"He's right," Carrie said. "I'll call a meeting with the board . . . er . . . former board and see if we can think of how to stop her. With just her toadies as members of the

Friends, I expect her next move will be to disband the group altogether."

"We can't allow that to happen," Lindsey said. She felt a ball of anger burn in her belly. "The library is dependent upon the Friends for so much. We'd be lost without you."

"You're not going to lose us," Carrie said. "Even if I have to call for a new election, I'm not going to let her win. Why is she so determined to ruin the writer's residency and ban books like Helen's thrillers from the library? It's almost as if she has a personal vendetta."

Lindsey glanced back down at the list of true-crime names Helen had given her. Betty Caruthers was not on there, and yet what Carrie had said was true. It was almost as if Betty had some twisted revenge scheme against Helen. But why?

"Call the meeting, Carrie," Lindsey said. "The Friends deserve to know what's happening, and if they decide a new election is in order, then we'll find some loophole in the bylaws that lets you do just that."

"Thank you." Carrie looked infinitely cheered by this plan of action. She left the office, digging her phone out of her handbag as she went.

"What are you thinking?" Robbie asked.

"Carrie is right," Lindsey said. "Betty has been practically targeting Helen. Why?" She held up her list. "Was she one of the crime stories?"

"Maybe not her specifically, but perhaps it was someone that she knew," Robbie said. "Isn't Caruthers her married name?"

"Yes." Lindsey nodded. "We need to know her maiden name and everything else we can find out about her."

Robbie sat upright. "You search the true-crime stories for a connection, and I'll see what I can find out about our Ms. Caruthers."

"Where are you going to search?" Lindsey asked. She was thinking of all the databases the library had access to and which one she could start him on.

"I'm going to the source," Robbie said. "I'm going to speak with her ex-husband."

"How do you think you're going to manage that?" Lindsey asked.

"Um, do you know who I am?" Robbie asked. He struck a pose like an outraged diva, and Lindsey laughed.

"Let me rephrase," Lindsey said. "How do you know how to contact him?"

"He's a money guy in New York." He shrugged.

"And?" Lindsey asked.

"I have a money guy in New York and they all know each other," he said. "Believe me, in three calls I'll know everything about Betty that's worth knowing."

"If you say so." Lindsey turned back to the list of names Helen had given her, while Robbie put down his teacup and took out his phone. He moved into the workroom outside her office, and Lindsey watched him pace as he called "his guy."

The remaining four cases were dead ends. Two of the killers had passed away, one was in a high-security facility in New York, and the fourth had relocated to Australia and never returned. There was no way they were involved. Lindsey started looking wider at the friends and families of the killers and their victims. Were there any sisters, cousins, children, friends of the victims or of the convicted murderers who might want to make Helen suffer, much like the Campbells, for keeping their family tragedy alive through her work, however tangential?

If Betty was connected to any of the families, Lindsey couldn't find her. Perhaps if Robbie discovered her maiden name, Lindsey would be more successful. She put aside the information she'd gathered for Emma. Even though she considered the search for the chief a reference question, she knew she had to do her own library work before she fell impossibly behind.

"No luck as yet." Robbie poked his head in the door. "My guy is going to try some of his colleagues and call me back."

"I struck out, too," Lindsey said. "Let me know if you get a name, and I'll search again."

"You'll be my first call," Robbie said.

"Your first?" Emma popped up behind him, and Robbie yelped.

"After you, of course, love." Robbie leaned down to kiss her, but Emma blocked him with her hand. "What name are you supposed to be getting?"

"Betty Caruthers's maiden name," he said through her fingers.

"Why Betty?" Emma turned to Lindsey, dropping her hand and leaving Robbie off balance.

Lindsey hid her smile as he gripped the doorframe to keep from falling. "Betty stopped by while I was speaking with Carrie Rushton, and she announced her intention to end the writer in residence program, which Carrie noted felt like a personal sort of revenge move. It got us to thinking maybe she's like the Campbells and has an ax to grind with Helen."

"It's a theory," Emma said. "Too bad we won't be following up on it."

"What do you mean?" Lindsey asked. She had a sinking feeling in the pit of her stomach.

"The medical examiner has made a determination in Jackie Lewis's death," Emma said. She looked grim.

"What did he decide?" Robbie asked.

"Jackie Lewis's death was a tragic accident," Emma said. "He said the injuries she sustained were those of a person who was electrocuted, and the damaged string of lights was determined to be the cause of the electrocution."

"But the lights were swapped out," Lindsey protested. "Did he not consider that?"

"He did." Emma rocked up on her toes and back down. "Apparently, several strings of lights from the town's light display have been taken and replaced with damaged or inferior lights. Ernie reported five other strings that had been swapped."

"But what about the fact that the lights were found in Helen's car?" Lindsey asked.

Emma shrugged. "Because four other strings of lights were also swapped, there's no way to prove that the ones in

Helen's car were switched with the ones that caused Jackie's death. Helen insists she doesn't know anything about the lights or how they got in her car, and her mechanic verified that the back hatch has a broken lock and the part is still on order. There was no evidence of her fingerprints on the lights. As far as we know, whoever was doing the light switching dumped them in Helen's car because it was nearby."

"So what does this mean?" Robbie asked.

"It means Jackie's death has been determined to be an accident, so case closed."

"What about the hit and run on Helen?" Lindsey asked.

"Without a hit there's no run. There's no reason to think it was anything more than a speeder who just didn't see her," Emma said.

"You don't believe that," Lindsey said.

"It doesn't matter what I believe," Emma said. "We're dealing in facts, and the fact is Jackie Lewis's death was a tragic accident."

CHAPTER

18

BRIAR CREEK
PUBLIC LIBRARY

Lindsey handed over all of the notes she'd made about the true-crime cases on which Helen had based her books. She was reluctant to part with her work, as it felt unfinished, and Lindsey's librarian need for order resisted leaving things undone.

"So that's it, then?" she asked.

"Yup," Emma said. "I'm on my way to tell Mr. Lewis that he's free to arrange Jackie's funeral. I imagine that's a bit odd for him, but I suspect he'll be relieved to get it done."

"I suppose there's no point in following up on Betty Caruthers, then?" Robbie asked Lindsey.

"Just because she apparently had nothing to do with Jackie's passing doesn't mean there isn't something wrong there," Lindsey said. She glanced at Emma. "As the director of the library, I need to know more about the woman who is single-handedly trying to shut down one of our programs and ban the books of the author doing the program."

It wasn't a request or a defense. It was a statement of fact. Emma nodded. "As far as I'm concerned, that has nothing to do with my investigation, so have at it."

"Go forth and ask questions," Lindsey said to Robbie. She glanced between them and asked, "Sully and I are going to the Christmas carol sing-along tonight at the Blue Anchor. Are you?"

"Wouldn't miss it," Emma said. Her smile was tight, and again Lindsey wondered what was going on with the chief. Before she could ask, Emma kissed Robbie's cheek, spun on her booted heel and left.

"All right, I agree with your assessment. She is being weird," Lindsey said.

Robbie was frowning at the open door, looking bewildered. "Right? I have no idea what's gotten into her. She's been absolutely bizarre about the holiday this year."

"Bizarre how?"

"She seems to have been swept into the holiday spirit, and yet, there's something not quite right about it," he said.

"What do you mean?" Lindsey asked. She peered over his shoulder and watched Emma leave the building as if she were running from a fire.

"Does one generally smile with their teeth gritted?" Robbie asked.

"Not usually," Lindsey said. "Has she been doing that a lot?"

"Yes, and she insisted we hike out into the woods and chop down a tree. *Chop*." He emphasized the word in case Lindsey hadn't registered his dismay. He lifted his hands until they were level with Lindsey's gaze. "These are not the hands of a lumberjack."

"Unless he's playing one on TV," Lindsey countered, and Robbie glared.

"I'm serious," he said. "She's beginning to scare me. Yesterday, she was baking sugar cookies. *Sugar cookies.* My girl does not bake."

"I got it." Lindsey held up one hand in a *stop* gesture. "The question is, why is the chief, who has always been ambivalent about the holidays, suddenly overly, manically excited about this holiday?"

"I have no idea." Robbie shrugged. "And the thing is, she's not enjoying any of it. Except for the ugly Christmas sweaters, because that really is a highlight for her."

"Do you think she's trying to make the holiday more festive for you?" Lindsey asked. She turned back to her desk and snagged a cookie.

"Why?" he asked. He followed her back into the office. "I'm not one to make a big fuss about the season."

"Perhaps she's worried that you're homesick," Lindsey said. "You know, the lack of crackers and paper crowns and all that."

"No." Robbie shook his head. "If I wanted them, I'd have them."

"Well, there's something going on," Lindsey said. "She's definitely on edge and trying to hide it. You don't think . . . nah."

"Think what?" Robbie asked. He picked up his cup and took a sip of the tepid tea. "You can't just leave me hanging."

"You don't think she thinks that you . . . that you might . . ."

"Spit it out." Robbie made a circular gesture with his hand.

"Do you think she thinks that you might ask her to marry you for Christmas, and maybe that's why she's being weird?" Lindsey asked. "Have you two ever talked about it?"

"No." He dropped into the chair as if his legs had given out. "I didn't think either of us were the marrying kind."

"It's just a wild guess," Lindsey said. "I mean, why would she think that if you've never given her any reason to believe you wanted to get married?"

Robbie let out a low moan. He put his hand over his eyes. "I might have inadvertently given her that impression."

"Oh?" Lindsey asked.

"It was just a small thing," Robbie said. "I didn't think anything of it at the time, but looking back, it could be that Emma got the wrong idea."

Lindsey leveled him with a hard stare. "What did you do?"

"I was rehearsing the lines for a play," he said. "And part of it was a proposal."

"Oh, well, she had to know you were rehearsing," Lindsey said.

Robbie shook his head. "I was in the bedroom, practicing my lines, and when I came out, Emma was standing in the living room with the strangest look on her face. At the time, I thought she was thinking about work, but now I'm wondering if she overheard me and thought I was practicing a proposal for her."

"You have to tell her," Lindsey said.

Robbie downed his tea as if it were a magic elixir that could save him. "Tell her what? That my wrenching heartfelt speech about finding my soulmate and wanting to spend the rest of my life with her was just for a play I'm auditioning for in January? You want me to tell her that?"

"What's the alternative?" Lindsey asked.

"Oh my God, I'm going to have to propose," he said. "For real."

Lindsey's eyebrows shot up. "I don't think Emma wants a proposal given out of a misunderstanding. You'd be better served to tell her the truth."

"And hurt her feelings if she's expecting a proposal? What if she gets mad and dumps me?" Robbie looked horrified at the mere idea.

"Looks like you're going to have to make a decision, then," Lindsey said.

"How did this happen?" Robbie dropped his head into his hands. "I'd make a terrible husband. What could she be thinking?"

"That's a big assumption," Lindsey said.

"No, I think it's a fact. I'm a self-involved prat. I'd be a lousy partner," he said.

"Not that part," Lindsey said. "You're being very dramatic about the whole thing and assuming that Emma wants to marry you. Maybe she is being so manic about the holiday and forcing herself to be cheerful because she's afraid you're going to ask her and she doesn't know how to say no. Maybe she doesn't want to get married."

"Not get married?" Robbie blinked. He ran a hand through his reddish blond hair, looking completely confounded. "Why wouldn't she want to marry me?"

"Did you miss the part where you called yourself a self-involved prat?" Lindsey asked.

"No, but . . ." He rose to his feet, his body tight with indignation. "She would be lucky to have me."

Lindsey smiled. Robbie was getting himself all wound up when a conversation with Emma was all that he needed to have to set things straight.

"I have no doubt you would make an excellent husband if you decided to give it your all," Lindsey said. "That being said, Emma has a career in law enforcement that she's worked very hard for, and she may not see a husband fitting into that."

"I have to go." Robbie picked up a cookie and bit it in half with more force than Lindsey thought was warranted. He crammed the rest into his mouth and strode toward the door. "I have some stuff I need to do."

"All right, call me if you hear from your guy." Lindsey moved back around her desk and sat in her chair. She watched as Robbie stomped through the library. She couldn't wait to see what happened at the carol sing-along tonight.

The crafternooners had their own booth at the Blue Anchor for the sing-along. It helped that Mary owned the restaurant and was a founding crafternooner. As Lindsey entered the restaurant, she saw the group huddled in the large booth at the back. She checked her watch. Sully was making his last run on the water taxi to the islands and wouldn't be ashore for another hour.

Nancy and Violet were seated with Mary, who was wearing her Blue Anchor apron, meaning she was likely working through the sing-along. Paula and Mayor Cole were ahead of Lindsey, hanging their coats on the rack beside the booth. Beth had just sent a text that she was waiting for her husband to get home from work so that he could watch their daughter. She hoped to be there soon.

Lindsey strode across the room, looking for Emma or Robbie, but there was no sign of either of them. She wondered if Robbie had figured out what he wanted to do. She hoped she'd been right in her assessment of Emma's behavior. Maybe her forced holiday enthusiasm had nothing to do with Robbie or what she may or may not have overheard. Lindsey shook her head. Either way, something was bothering Emma, and it would be better out than in.

She was halfway across the room when she saw Helen and Kenny sitting in a corner booth. Helen looked pale and shaky and Kenny grim. She pivoted away from her group and went to say hello.

"Helen, Kenny, how are you?" Lindsey asked.

"Confused," Helen admitted. "You heard about the medical examiner's report?"

"I did," Lindsey said. "I assumed you'd think it was good news."

"Because we're no longer suspects?" Helen asked. She shook her head. "Something's not right. I know someone tried to run me down, and I know it has something to do with Jackie."

She and Kenny exchanged an uneasy look.

"I'm surprised to find you out and about," Lindsey said.

"We feel safer being out in public," Kenny admitted. "Sitting in the cottage felt a little too horror movie. We were both jumping out of our skin."

Helen laughed, but it was more a nervous release than a sound full of humor. "We must sound completely paranoid. This is another reason I want to shift from thrillers to more genteel murder mysteries."

"Featuring a small-town librarian on the Connecticut shore?" Lindsey asked. Helen nodded. "Murder is gruesome whether it's a thriller or a cozy. It's the worst thing one human being can do to another."

Kenny raised his glass and toasted Lindsey. "No truer words."

"Will you two be leaving us for the holiday?" Lindsey asked.

"Yes, we're going home to my place in Fairfield

tomorrow," Helen said. "But I'll be back to finish my residency, assuming that Caruthers woman doesn't shut it down."

"You heard about that, too?" Lindsey asked.

"Hard not to when she accosted us on our way into the restaurant," Kenny said. He turned to look at Helen. "She really doesn't like you."

"I know," Helen agreed. "And I have no idea why. You'd think I wrote a novel based on her instead of the Campbells."

"Is it possible that you did?" Lindsey asked. "She was married. Maybe you knew her under her maiden name."

"It's possible," Helen said. "Do we know what her maiden name is?"

"I have a friend doing a search," Lindsey said. "I'll let you know if we find out."

"Thank you," Helen said. "You've been a real friend to me, Lindsey, and I appreciate it."

"No problem," Lindsey said. "I'm just glad you haven't quit the program. If it fails, I doubt we'll be allowed to keep it going."

"I'm not a quitter," Helen said. "I promise to see it through to the end."

"Excellent." Lindsey stepped aside as their waitress arrived with their dinners. "I'll talk to you later. Enjoy your holiday if I don't see you until you get back."

"Merry Christmas," Helen and Kenny said together, and then smiled at each other, and this time there was an ease to it. Maybe being out in public, being surrounded by new friends, was a balm to the traumatic events of the past few days. As Lindsey walked away, she got the feeling they were going to be all right.

She slid into the booth with her friends just as Ian stepped out from behind the bar with a microphone in hand. "All right, let's have a warm-up. Everyone knows the words to 'Jingle Bells,' so I want to hear it!" He cupped his ear and stared the crowd down. Mary grinned at her husband, who was wearing a headband of reindeer antlers with Christmas tree baubles hanging off them. He looked ridiculous in the best possible way.

"And a one, and a two, and a three! *'Jingle bells, jingle bells . . .'*" Ian sang into the mic, and the entire restaurant joined him. Mayor Cole pushed a glass of wine in front of Lindsey, and Nancy slid over a basketful of clam fritters. In that moment, Lindsey felt more holiday spirit than she had in weeks.

While she sipped her wine and nibbled on fritters, Lindsey sang along with her friends and waved at other neighbors and acquaintances around the restaurant. A glance outside and she noticed it was dark and a light snow had begun to fall, but they were cozy inside the Blue Anchor, warmed by good food and friendship.

As the restaurant filled up with more and more people, Ian passed the microphone to a patron and jumped back behind the bar. The singing continued, and when the mic landed at their table, Violet took it up like the actress she was and led everyone into a soul-lifting version of "Silent Night." As the last note lingered on the air, Lindsey felt her heart swell with a sense of peace and contentment, which to her mind was the true gift of the season.

In a blink it was over as the power abruptly went out, collapsing the entire restaurant into darkness held off only by the small tea lights in glass votive holders on each table.

"Don't panic!" Ian shouted over the murmurs of concern, which were growing in volume. "I'm sure it's just a circuit. I'll be right back."

Lindsey saw him grab a flashlight from under the bar and head back into the kitchen. Mary had rejoined them at their table and used her phone as a flashlight to see her way out of the booth. "I'm going to see if I can help."

Lindsey glanced out the window to see if the power outage was just the restaurant or the entire town. She wanted to get home to her pets if it was the entire town, but Sully wasn't here yet. She could see the light display on the town green, so it appeared to be just the restaurant.

She was turning to the others to say as much, when a scream cut through the muted conversations and everyone jerked upright, scanning the room to determine where the scream had come from.

"Help me! Somebody help me!"

Lindsey saw Helen standing beside her booth. She was holding Kenny, who was slumped sideways, clutching his arm.

Lindsey bolted out of her booth and ran across the restaurant. "What happened?"

"I don't know," Helen said. "I went to the restroom, and when I came back, the power went out, and the next thing

I knew, Kenny grunted and slumped against me. I think he's been stabbed."

"Light!" Lindsey cried. Several flashlights from phones appeared over the back of the booth. Lindsey knelt down until she was level with Kenny. His eyes were open but his teeth were gritted in pain.

"Kenny, what happened?" she asked.

"The lights went out and then I felt this stabbing, burning pain in my arm," he said.

"Let us take a look," Helen said as she knelt beside Lindsey.

Kenny slowly removed his hand from his arm. The sleeve of his dress shirt had been slashed, and blood was pouring down his arm. "Oh, no, I'm not good with the sight of bl—"

Kenny fainted, nearly toppling out of the booth. Lindsey and Helen grabbed him, pushing him back into the seat.

"What's going on here?" Emma appeared in the ring of light. Her Maglite blasted into the area, giving them a better look at the situation.

"Kenny's been stabbed," Helen said.

Emma took one look at his arm and immediately spoke into the radio on her shoulder, calling for an ambulance. "Help will be here shortly. In the meantime, let's try and stop the bleeding."

"Here's some clean dish towels." Nancy came charging out of the dark.

"And some duct tape." Violet handed off a roll to Emma.

"Wait, you need to clean it first," Mayor Cole said. She handed Emma a first aid kit.

Just then the lights came back on. Ian and Mary came out of the kitchen singing, "*It's the most wonderful time of the year . . .*"

When the shocked gazes of their customers reached them, they stumbled to a halt. "What happened?" Ian cried.

Marty Bailey, a local who was sitting at the bar, said, "Dude got stabbed." He pointed at Kenny and then continued to eat his dinner before it got cold.

"Stabbed?" Ian cried. He glanced at his wife. "That's never happened before."

"I should hope not," she said. Mary hurried across the room to join them.

Emma cut away Kenny's shirtsleeve and cleaned out the wound, which appeared to be superficial even as it gushed blood. Lindsey glanced away, feeling a bit woozy herself.

The front door opened, and Robbie and Sully entered. As if they caught the panicked vibe right away, their gazes went right to Lindsey and Emma.

"What's happening?" Sully asked as he approached.

"Kenny Lewis was stabbed during a power outage," Lindsey said.

"Accident?" Sully asked.

"I don't see how," Lindsey said.

He put his arm around her and she leaned into him.

"Everything all right, love?" Robbie asked Emma. She was sweating as she tried to tie off Kenny's arm to keep it from bleeding more, but she blinked at him and smiled. It did not meet her eyes.

"Of course everything is fine," Emma said. She glanced around the restaurant as if suddenly aware of everyone staring. "Go back to your meals. Nothing to see here. Looks like a slip of a knife in the dark."

Helen narrowed her eyes at Emma and hissed, "That's not a slip."

"I know that and you know that, but no one else needs to know that," Emma whispered in return. "Do you follow me?"

Helen glanced down at Kenny, who was beginning to rouse. "Yes, of course, you're right."

"Excellent," Emma said. "So, here's what's going to happen. Kenny is going to go in the ambulance to the nearest emergency room to see if he needs stitches. You're going with him and I'm going to follow. I want to stay here and investigate this area and the restaurant, but I want to keep it quiet so that whoever did this thinks that we think it was just an accident. All right?"

Helen nodded. "Yes, absolutely. If anyone asks, it was a silly accident. Perfectly reasonable."

"Excellent." Emma nodded. The doors to the restaurant opened, and two EMTs entered carrying medical bags. "Looks like you're going to get a chance to practice." She stepped back and waved the medical technicians over to join them.

Robbie moved to give the team room, and Sully and Lindsey followed. Lindsey met Helen's gaze and said, "I'll come to the hospital as soon as I can. Text me when you get there."

"Thank you," Helen said. She turned back to Kenny, holding his uninjured hand while the EMTs inspected Emma's work.

The customers in the restaurant resumed eating, and when Kenny was escorted out of the restaurant with Helen beside him, most of them called encouraging words after them. Ian and Mary offered everyone a drink on the house, and the carol singing started back up in earnest. To Lindsey it felt as if everyone was determined to have a good time despite the incident.

Emma turned back to the vacated booth, looking grim. She glanced at Lindsey and said, "Go ahead and say it."

"Say what?" Lindsey asked.

"You know what," Emma said.

"All right, that was no accident," Lindsey said.

"That's what," Emma confirmed.

CHAPTER

19

BRIAR CREEK
PUBLIC LIBRARY

B ut why Kenny?" Emma asked. She kept her voice low to be certain that no one could hear them.

Lindsey shrugged. "Maybe it's been about him the entire time."

Emma put a hand on her forehead and said, "I think my brain is going to explode." She dropped her hand and shook herself from head to toe like a dog shedding water. "All right. First things first. I'm going to examine the booth. Keep everyone clear, if you don't mind."

"Not at all," Lindsey said. She, Sully and Robbie stood shoulder to shoulder pretending to sing carols and chat while Emma crawled around the booth with her hands in blue latex gloves as she searched for a clue as to what had happened here.

After twenty minutes of intense searching, she stood up and joined them as if she'd been chatting with them all along.

"There's nothing," she said. "Whatever was used to stab Mr. Lewis left with the person who did the stabbing."

"What do we know about Kenny?" Lindsey asked.

"Secretly married to Helen, works in insurance, pays his bills on time, and other than the scandal of him leaving his wife for Helen, he is by all accounts a stand-up guy," Emma said. "At least, that's according to his background check."

"So maybe the stabbing wasn't meant for him," Lindsey said.

"Helen said he was sitting alone while she went to the bathroom," Emma said. "Who else could it have been for?"

"It had to be Helen," Sully said. "And whoever did it cut the power without realizing Helen had left her seat. They must have been in a hurry, slashed Kenny and bolted without waiting to see who they hit or what happened."

"If that's true, then it means someone is trying to kill Helen or scare her, and the hit and run was intentional as well," Lindsey said.

"And somehow it's all tied to Jackie Lewis's death," Emma said. "It has to be."

A phone chimed, and Robbie reached into his pocket and pulled out his cell phone. "It's my guy in New York." He slid his thumb across the display and held his phone up to his ear. "Hi, Mick, what's the good word?"

There was a pause, and Emma glanced at Lindsey in question.

"Robbie is following up on information about Betty for me," Lindsey said.

"Oh, right, because you're hoping something in her past will explain her inexplicable hatred of the library," Emma said.

"Essentially." Lindsey shrugged. She glanced at Sully and admitted, "It's a long shot."

"Better than no shot," he countered.

"Thanks, mate, you've been a big help," Robbie said into the phone before he ended the call. "I have some news."

"Which is?" Lindsey prompted him.

"Betty Caruthers's maiden name was Alexander," Robbie said.

Lindsey felt her jaw drop. It was a common last name. There was nothing to get excited about, but she felt in her bones that it meant something.

"How old would Sarah Alexander be now?" she asked Robbie.

"Who is Sarah Alexander?" Emma asked.

"For one of her books, Helen took inspiration from the true story of Sarah Alexander, a teen who murdered her identical twin, Sadie Alexander, by stabbing her fifty-seven times."

Robbie was typing on his phone using both thumbs. "The original case took place in the nineties, May of 1997 to be exact, and they were seventeen years old at the time, so Sarah would be forty-four now."

"Is Betty forty-four?" Sully asked.

"No idea," Robbie answered. "Maybe?" He looked at Emma. "Thoughts?"

"I think I need to go and have a chat with Betty Caruthers," Emma said. She turned to Lindsey. "Is the Alexander case in the notes you gave me?"

"Yes, the book Helen wrote based on the case is entitled *Sister Mine*. If you talk to Betty, you might want to lead with that."

Emma nodded. "I'm going to question the diners here first and see if anyone saw Betty. Let me start with the crafternooners." She left them to go talk to their friends, who had returned to their booth and were singing carols but with much less enthusiasm than before. Lindsey watched as one after another they shook their heads.

"We have to find out if Sarah was let out of the psychiatric hospital." Lindsey glanced at Sully and Robbie. "If she's still there, then it obviously wasn't her, but maybe Betty Alexander is related and seeking revenge for her?"

"I am not loving that scenario," Robbie said.

"Me either," Sully said. He glanced at Lindsey. "Since you're the director of the library, it would be very easy for whoever the killer is to target you. From now until this case is solved, you need to be careful, and I would prefer it if you weren't alone at any given time."

"That's fine with me," Lindsey agreed. A shiver raced up her spine. "And to think with our parents on their cruise and my brother spending the holiday with his wife's family, I thought this was going to be a quiet Christmas."

* * *

Lindsey and Sully went straight to the emergency room of the nearby hospital to see whether Helen needed any help. She was in a curtained room sitting beside Kenny, who had received a neat line of stitches and was now fully bandaged and on pain medicine.

"Thanks for coming." Helen stood as they entered the room. "The physician's assistant said we'll be able to leave soon. Did the chief find anything?"

"No, whoever did this managed to do it without being seen," Sully said.

Helen frowned. "I just don't understand why. I mean, if Jackie were still alive, I'd suspect her, but other than Jackie, I don't know of anyone who would have a motive to harm either of us." She reached down and squeezed her husband's good hand.

"It's a mystery." Kenny smiled wanly at her and shook his head. Clearly, his pain meds were working.

"Emma canvassed the restaurant to see if anyone saw anything, but no one did," Lindsey said. "We did come across an interesting piece of information about Betty Caruthers, however."

"Oh, really?" Helen tipped her head to the side. "You know that woman loathes me for some reason I can't fathom."

"Yes, and now we think we might know why. Robbie asked a friend of his who works in finance in New York if he knew Betty's ex-husband, who also works in finance in New York, because we don't know much about her life before she moved to Briar Creek a few years ago, not even her maiden name."

"All right." Helen frowned as if trying to determine why Lindsey was giving her so much backstory.

"Betty's maiden name is Alexander," Lindsey said.

Helen's eyes went wide. "Do you think . . . could she be . . . whoa."

"What is it, honey?" Kenny asked. "Wait. Alexander. Isn't that the surname of the twin sisters whose case gave you the idea for one of your books?"

"Yes," Helen said. "Sarah and Sadie Alexander, but Sarah was committed to a psychiatric hospital."

"Is there any way Betty could be Sarah?" Lindsey asked.

Helen slumped against the seat back. "I feel like I would have known. On some level, wouldn't I have recognized her?" A shudder racked her body. "No, I don't think Betty could be her, but maybe I'm wrong. Maybe she had a lot of plastic surgery done? Well, this is terrifying."

"We'll know soon enough," Lindsey said. "Emma went to talk to Betty when she finished at the restaurant. She might be with her right now."

"All right, but even if Betty is Sarah, why would she kill Jackie?" Helen asked. "That makes no sense."

"Unless Jackie knew who she really was," Sully said. "Didn't Jackie have a printout of your manuscript? Do you think she was meeting with someone to give it to them?

Could it have been Betty? Was it a part of their plan to humiliate you?"

"It would have succeeded," Helen said. "Seeing an author's rough draft is like catching them in their underwear."

"We assumed Jackie was stealing it for herself," Kenny said. "I thought she'd try to pass it off as her own and get even for what she thinks Helen did to her."

"Which was just ridiculous," Helen said. "And it likely had more to do with your marriage than my work."

"That's what we always thought," Kenny said. "But maybe we were wrong. Maybe she was more jealous about your success than she was about the affair."

Helen rested her elbows on the side of his bed and put her face in her hands. "I am just so tired of all of it. I'm tired of always hiding, keeping my life with you a secret and worrying who might jump out of the shadows at me. I'm just over it. Maybe it's time to quit writing."

"Oh, no," Lindsey said. "Please don't do that. You're a brilliant writer, and it would be a shame if you quit. I think this pivot into a new genre of mystery will be good for you. At least, give it a chance."

Helen nodded. "I'll think about it. In the meantime, Kenny has been discharged, so I'm going to take him back to the cottage. We've decided not to go home for the holidays. He can't drive and I'm too rattled."

"Understandable," Lindsey said. "Do you need any help getting home?"

"No, but thank you," Helen said. "Will you let Emma

know that we've left for the cottage? She said she'd station an officer on the premises for our protection."

"Absolutely," Lindsey agreed.

She and Sully left Helen to help Kenny into his coat. As they stepped out into the mostly vacant parking lot of the hospital, Lindsey glanced at her husband.

"Yes, we can absolutely follow them home if it will make you feel better," he said.

"You know me so well."

Sully pulled her in for a half hug and planted a kiss on her head. "It's not difficult. You always lead with your heart."

They waited in Sully's truck until they saw Helen and an orderly help Kenny into their car. Helen glanced over at the truck, and when she noticed Lindsey, she smiled and waved. Lindsey returned the gestures and was certain she didn't imagine the relief in Helen's relaxed posture. Sully followed them all the way to their cottage.

Once Helen got Kenny inside, Sully and Lindsey left, knowing that Emma would be stopping by any minute. The drive home through Briar Creek was quiet. The village seemed muted, as if holding its breath awaiting the next bad thing that would happen. With Christmas just days away, Lindsey felt as if a pall was leaching the joy out of the holiday. It seemed to her that it was imperative that they solve Jackie's murder and discover who was behind the attacks on Helen and Kenny as swiftly as possible.

Sully pulled into the driveway. Snow had been falling on and off all evening, and there was a light dusting on top of the snow that had fallen the week before. Lindsey stepped out of the truck, and the ice and snow crunched under her boots. Sully reached out a hand to steady her, and together they made their way up the steps to their front door.

A happy bark greeted them, and a black nose was pressed up against the window beside the door, making puffs of hot breath and fogging up the pane.

"Hi, Heathcliff," Lindsey greeted their dog, which sent him into a frenzy of barking.

"Brace yourself," Sully said. He opened the door and Heathcliff bounded out. He ran right past them and down the steps, racing around the yard in paroxysms of joy as he leapt into the air, biting the fat snowflakes as they fell.

"I think we've been replaced in his affections by snow," Sully said with a laugh.

"I can't blame him," Lindsey said. "It really is beautiful."

She glanced across the yard. It was so quiet. As if the night were pulling a blanket over the village after a bad day and tucking it in for some rest. Lindsey was down with that. She clapped her hands, and Heathcliff came running. She and Sully stepped inside with their snow-covered dog right behind them.

While Sully cooked dinner, Lindsey fed Heathcliff and Zelda, who roused herself from her warm cat bed to eat before she returned to her spot and curled back up, clearly not as big a fan of the cold weather as Heathcliff.

It was after dinner, when the dishes were done and Sully had made them each a mug of his special hot chocolate, that they sat in front of the fireplace, watching the flames and discussing the events of the past few days.

"So, the medical examiner determined that Jackie Lewis's death was an accident," Sully said. "But then why is someone going after Helen?"

"I feel like it has to be connected to her books," Lindsey said. "It's the only thing that makes sense. She doesn't have any exes or disputes with her neighbors or beefs with other authors."

"You're sure about that?"

"Positive." Lindsey sipped her cocoa. "I checked."

Sully grinned. "Of course you did."

"Librarian." She shrugged.

Sully lifted his mug and tapped it against hers in silent appreciation.

"I suppose the question is, who would want to harm both Jackie and Helen?" Lindsey asked.

"It has to be someone who knows both of them, which Betty does or did," he said. "If Betty is Sarah or related to the sisters Alexander, it seems most likely to be her, don't you think?"

Lindsey stared into the fire. "That does make sense. It all started when Jackie Lewis came to town. She approached us at the library, and looking back now, I realize she was clearly staking out Helen."

"You did get a bad feeling about her from the start. Then she caused that scene at the sweater party," Sully said.

"Right." Lindsey nodded. "From there it snowballed, forgive the pun—" She paused to gesture out the window, where the snow continued to fall. "To the light ceremony, where the Campbells were visibly upset by Helen's presence, and we overheard Jackie having an argument with Betty Caruthers."

"Right. Jackie was upset that Betty hadn't humiliated Helen as she'd promised to," he said. "It seemed random at the time, but it does indicate that they knew each other. If Betty is tied to the Alexander case, then it makes sense why she'd be in league with Jackie."

"It would. They both had revenge in mind." Lindsey sat up straight. "But who murdered Jackie and why? Did she know too much? Was she going too far and they tried to stop her?"

Sully pondered her questions while he drank his cocoa. "What other cases did Helen write about where the murderer might still be at large and holding a grudge?"

"I went through them all. There was only one other case where the perpetrator was released, but he was a teen who was being horribly abused, and he killed his father in self-defense," Lindsey said. "According to the search I did, he left the state and started over on the West Coast. I don't think he's interested in dredging up the past."

"So that leaves Betty, assuming she's related to the Alexander sisters, or potentially the Campbells, but Emma said they have an alibi for the time of Jackie's death," Sully said.

"Maybe it's all three of them, if they were working together," Lindsey said. "Just like Jackie connected with Betty, Betty could have reached out to the Campbells. We know that Jackie knew about the residency because of Liz, and she knew that Helen and Kenny were married. Her seven-year-itch comment is too on point, given that they've been married for seven years."

"It is suspicious. Wasn't the residency Carrie Rushton's idea?" Sully asked. "If we're casting the net wide, I have to ask if you think Carrie had anything to do with Jackie's death? Could she be involved?"

"No." Lindsey was certain Carrie wasn't. "But I wonder where Carrie got the idea to host the program. Maybe Jackie planted the seed?"

"It's a theory," Sully said. "Maybe she reached out to Carrie with the idea."

Lindsey hopped up from her seat on the couch, setting her cocoa down on the coffee table. "I'm going to text her."

She took her phone off its charging station and scrolled through her contacts. It wasn't ten o'clock yet, so she felt safe in sending a text. She tried to word it casually yet specifically.

Lindsey's phone chimed, and the display lit up as she crossed back to the couch and resumed her seat. It was Carrie. Lindsey opened the message. Carrie wrote that while she'd like to take credit for the idea of the residency, she couldn't since she'd received the suggestion from a seasonal visitor to Briar Creek. She then attached the email.

Lindsey read the friendly message, scanning the short note until she got to the person's name. She read it and slowly lowered the phone into her lap.

"What is it?" Sully asked. "You look shocked."

"Carrie sent me the email from the person who recommended the writer in residence program and suggested Helen as a potential author," Lindsey said. "It was Melanie Starland."

"Wait. Wasn't she the member of the book critique group who passed away over a decade ago?" Sully asked.

"Yes, which means someone used her name to write the email to Carrie," Lindsey said. "And it would have to be someone who knew her and Helen, which leaves Jackie, Helen or Liz."

"Liz had no reason to do it, so we can rule her out," Sully said. "Jackie seems like the most likely culprit."

"But what if it was Helen?" Lindsey asked. "It makes no sense . . . unless it was a way for her to infiltrate the library to study the crafternoon group so she could use us as the basis of her next series." Lindsey looked at Sully and wrinkled her nose. "If that is the case, then I am feeling sorely used."

"There's only one way to find out," Sully said. He pointed to her phone.

"I could call Helen, but I think this is something that needs to be asked face-to-face," Lindsey said. "I want to look her right in the eye when I ask her if she's been playing us all."

CHAPTER

20

BRIAR CREEK
PUBLIC LIBRARY

Lindsey waited until Helen showed up at the library the next morning for her writer shift. She watched from afar as Helen settled into her room then she strolled through the library intent on her purpose.

She knocked on the doorframe and Helen glanced up. There were dark circles under her eyes and she looked tired, but Lindsey was too peeved about being used to be able to manifest much sympathy.

"How is Kenny?"

"Much better," Helen said. "Thanks for asking and thanks for following us home. That meant a lot."

"Of course." Lindsey thought about how different this Helen was from the aloof woman who had first arrived to do her residency. She wondered if she and Helen had started to become friends, but then shoved the thought aside. It wasn't real if Helen had just been using them all as material for her next book. She stepped inside the glassed-in room and closed the door behind her. "I just have one question for you."

"All right, shoot." Helen leaned back in her chair, giving Lindsey her full attention.

"Why did you send an email as Melanie Starland to Carrie Rushton suggesting a writer in residency program to be hosted by our Friends of the Library and featuring you?"

Helen's eyes went wide. Lindsey wondered if she was genuinely shocked or just surprised that she'd been found out.

"I did it so that I could study you and the crafternoon group up close," Helen said. "I was telling the truth when I said I was writing a mystery novel based on the crafternooners. I just let you think that the idea came to me once I got here."

"When instead you planned it long before you arrived."

Helen lowered her head. "I did. I wanted to have a reason to be here every day, observing you all without anyone growing suspicious. A writer in residence seemed like the perfect cover."

"You could have just asked for an interview," Lindsey said. "You could have even joined the crafternooners."

"I wanted to keep my distance," Helen said. "Clearly that hasn't worked out. How did you figure it out?"

"I asked Carrie how she got the idea for the program, and she said she received an email from a seasonal visitor suggesting it. She also forwarded the email to me so I saw the name of the supposed sender."

"Clever." Helen picked up her pen and tapped it on the desk. "What are you going to do now?"

"Meaning?" Lindsey asked.

"Are you going to tell Carrie?"

"I think she deserves to know, don't you?" Lindsey asked.

Helen winced. "Probably. But if it's all the same with you, I'd like to be the one to tell her."

Lindsey crossed her arms over her chest and stared at the toes of her shoes. She didn't want to be petty, but her feelings were a bit tender. She'd genuinely believed that Helen was becoming a friend.

"Tell her this morning," she said. "Or I will."

"Understood." Helen sighed. "Are we okay?"

"I don't know," Lindsey said. "I don't know how to feel about all this. I mean, you had plenty of opportunities to tell us, but you never did."

"When the manuscript showed up in Jackie's hands, I was embarrassed," Helen said. "I didn't know how to admit that I'd read an article about the crafternoon sleuths years ago and thought what a great idea it would be for a mystery novel. It seemed so calculated."

Lindsey raised one eyebrow at her, and Helen had the grace to look embarrassed.

"Who else knew that this was your plan?" Lindsey asked.

"Kenny," Helen said. "And my agent and editor, of course."

"No one else?" Lindsey asked.

"Just Liz, but she wouldn't say anything to anyone," Helen said.

"Yeah, I talked to Liz. You might want to check in with her," Lindsey said. "I think she has some things to tell you."

Helen's eyebrows lifted. "She was in touch with Jackie, too, wasn't she?"

Lindsey nodded.

"She told her about the residency?"

"Apparently."

"Why? Why would she do that?" Helen asked.

"She said she was trying to stay friends with both of you," Lindsey said. "She didn't know that you and Kenny were married, did she?"

"No, we never told anyone," Helen said. "We couldn't risk it."

"I wouldn't be too hard on Liz if I were you," Lindsey said. "It's difficult to make the right choices when you don't have all the information."

Helen met her gaze and nodded. "Point taken. For what it's worth, I really am sorry."

"I'll decide if you're forgiven when I read the manuscript," Lindsey said. Then she smiled, letting Helen know that they were, indeed, okay.

She stepped away from Helen's desk and opened the door to find Betty Caruthers standing on the other side.

Lindsey felt her heart jump, and she glanced over her shoulder at Helen and said, "Get your phone out."

Helen looked past her, and her eyes widened. She pulled her phone out of her bag just as Betty shoved the door open.

"I was the lucky recipient of a visit from the police chief this morning," she snapped.

"Well, you're not in jail, so I'd say it worked out okay for you," Helen said.

"Why would I be in jail?" Betty growled.

"I don't know, *Ms. Alexander*," Lindsey said. "But maybe you could enlighten us."

"So, it was you." Betty turned from Helen to look Lindsey over from head to toe. "You told the chief that my name used to be Alexander."

"Technically, it was someone else, but I was present when she was informed," Lindsey said. "Just like I was outside the law offices of Dixon, Carter and Suffield when you followed us into New Haven."

"I did no such thing. My daughter's therapist's office happens to be on that street, and you can check with them if you don't believe me."

"Fine." Lindsey could let that go. "And your maiden name? It is Alexander, isn't it?"

"You think you're so smart." Betty's lip curled. "My maiden name was Alexander, and yes, I am related to Sadie and Sarah."

Lindsey couldn't believe that Betty admitted it. "How?"

"I'm their younger sister," Betty said.

"Well, I'll be damned," Helen said. "Seraphina."

"It's Beatrice, Betty for short, now." Betty sighed as if she'd been carrying a heavy weight and was finally putting it down. "I changed it as soon as I legally could. But I'm going to tell you, just like I told the chief, I had nothing to do with the car that almost ran you down or the stabbing that took place at the restaurant."

"Why should we believe you?" Lindsey asked. "You clearly have an issue with Helen as you've been trying to end her program and ban her books since she arrived. And honestly, given the amount of true-crime shows and podcasts that have covered your family's tragedy and in great detail, I don't see why Helen's novel, which is vastly different from what actually happened, is the focus of your ire."

"You wouldn't understand." Betty gave Lindsey a dismissive glance. "I'm trying to raise my kids here. I want to give them a fresh start. Having *her* here, bringing all of this attention to her novels and peripherally my family, well, I won't have it. Helen, your book *Sister Mine* makes my past inescapable, and I really hate you for that."

Helen flinched.

"But even so, I would never ever harm you," Betty said. "It took me years to put some distance between myself and my family, and I would never behave in a way that would drag me back into that nightmare."

"That's perfectly reasonable." Helen put her phone down. She clasped her hands in front of her and took a deep breath. "I didn't write *Sister Mine* to hurt anyone. I haven't written any of my novels to cause harm. In part, I write because I'm trying to make sense of the unfathomable. So many innocent people, just like you, are impacted by horrific crimes. In writing my novels, I'm trying to shine a light on mental health care and domestic abuse and other societal issues. I want to open a dialogue about these situations. I want to help, not harm."

The small room was silent except for the sound of the generic industrial clock ticking the seconds as they passed.

"I suppose I can understand that." Betty studied Helen. "When does this residency of yours end?"

"At the end of January. And then I'll be gone," Helen said.

"It's not as soon as I'd like," Betty said. "But at least you'll be leaving. I'll stop trying to ban your books, and I'll reinstate the Friends of the Library board, but when you go, you go for good."

"Fair enough," Helen said.

Betty let out a bitter laugh. "Yeah, in case you haven't noticed, life is never fair." She turned on her heel and swept from the room, leaving the door ajar behind her.

"Well." Helen looked at Lindsey.

"Well, indeed." Lindsey sat in the only other available chair. She leveled Helen with a look. "Do you believe her?"

"Yes." Helen watched Betty through the glass wall as she strode out of the building. "The one thing I remember from all of the cases I researched was the lengths some people would go to for revenge. The Alexander sisters, for example. Do you know what the tipping point was for Sarah that caused her to rage stab her sister?"

"No, I'm not really a true-crime reader," Lindsey said. "I stick to fiction mainly."

"You like the guaranteed good triumphing over evil?" Helen asked.

"Helps me sleep at night." Lindsey crossed one leg over the other.

"For their birthday, the girls were each gifted a very expensive cashmere sweater. Sarah's was blue and Sadie's was pink. Sarah wanted the pink and felt that her parents were showing favoritism by giving Sadie the pink. When Sadie offered to trade, Sarah felt that her sister was rubbing her face in it, so she stabbed her."

"That's horrible," Lindsey said.

"In Sarah's mind, it was the final straw. She felt that Sadie was the favored child, everything went her way, and Sarah couldn't stand it anymore, so she killed her." Helen stared at the top of her desk. She looked weary.

"Do you think that whoever stabbed Kenny was aiming for you?" Lindsey asked. "Do you think they wanted revenge?"

Helen clenched her hands in her lap. Her knuckles were white. "I think so, yes. You've met Kenny. He's the nicest man. He has zero enemies. There's no reason to think that anyone would harm him, unless—"

"Unless they thought that by hurting him it would hurt you," Lindsey said.

"Precisely." Helen closed her eyes. "Or they really did think they were stabbing me in the dark. Idiots."

Lindsey felt the corner of her mouth lift. She really did enjoy Helen's abrasiveness.

"The night that Jackie was killed, where were you going?" Lindsey asked.

"I've already told the police I was walking back to my cottage the same way I always went after eating at the restaurant," Helen said. "I can see how living in a town with one restaurant when you don't cook makes it easy to slip into a routine. Frankly, I was looking forward to going home for a few days just to eat somewhere else. No offense to the Blue Anchor, it's fabulous, but after several weeks, I could use some Italian or even a steak."

"Understandable," Lindsey said. Then she frowned. "Did you go for dinner at the same time every night?"

"More or less," Helen said.

"So, it would be fairly easy for anyone to know your schedule," Lindsey said. "Especially as you were at the library every morning."

"I suppose so," Helen agreed. "Why?"

"If someone, say Jackie, wanted to murder you, it would be simple to learn your schedule and find the perfect time to dispose of you, wouldn't it?" Lindsey asked.

"If I were plotting this as a novel, yes, that's exactly how I'd set up a victim," Helen said. She glanced at Lindsey. "Do you think Jackie was setting me up?"

"I know that you and Kenny think that Jackie didn't know about your marriage, but Jackie said something to Liz about you suffering from a seven-year itch if you felt the need to get away and go do a writer's residency," Lindsey said. "To me that means she knew."

Helen's eyes went wide. "We were so careful. How could she have found out?"

Lindsey shook her head. "I don't know, but as you mentioned the lengths some people would go to for revenge, I feel like Jackie had some plans for you. I think she knew your schedule, and I suspect her electrocution was actually meant for you, but something went horribly wrong with her plan."

Helen put a hand over her chest. "I feel ill."

"I'm not done." Lindsey leaned forward. She made her voice soft when she said, "I also think that Jackie had help. Someone was in the gazebo with her, and they shoved me down those steps when they ran away."

"That makes sense, because after she died someone still tried to run me down and stab me or Kenny to get to me," Helen said.

"They also tried to frame you for Jackie's murder," Lindsey said. "They planted the town's string of lights in your car."

"I've thought about that a lot. There's no way it was random. And if we didn't have a mechanical record of the back hatch's lock being broken, I could be in jail right now." Helen took a steadying breath.

"I think we need to tell the chief what we're thinking, and we need to convince her to help us come up with a way to draw the killer out, or you're never going to be free," Lindsey said.

* * *

No, absolutely not," Emma cried.

Helen and Lindsey were in her office, pleading their case to set up a sting to draw Helen's would-be killer out into the open.

"You know that Jackie's death wasn't an accident," Lindsey said. "It makes no sense."

"I know nothing of the kind," Emma said. "The medical examiner—"

"Got it wrong," Lindsey said. "Jackie was planning to murder Helen."

"What proof do you have?" Emma slammed her hands on her desk in frustration. "I am happy to listen to anything you say, but you have to give me some proof. It can't just be librarian intuition."

"It's more than intuition," Lindsey mumbled.

"Well?" Emma spread her hands wide.

"It's not just Lindsey," Helen said. "I believe it, too. And I have years of researching criminals and their motives to back it up. Also, it's my life at stake, so I feel that our concerns should be taken seriously."

"I do take them seriously," Emma said. "But I have nothing to go on. We have Jackie's phone. There were no texts or messages on it that indicated she was working with anyone else to kill you. We searched her room at the bed-and-breakfast and found nothing but books she bought at the library and several changes of clothes. She didn't have a tablet or a laptop with her. There is literally nothing."

"What about her home residence?" Helen asked.

"We got a warrant and worked with the local police in Jackie's hometown and again found nothing," Emma said. "I'm sorry."

Helen looked at Lindsey, defeat in her gaze. "Well, we tried."

"What if the person who tried to run Helen down and who stabbed Kenny strikes again? Because if they really are trying to kill her, they won't quit," Lindsey said. "And don't you find it weird that a writer like Jackie had nothing in her room at the bed-and-breakfast to indicate she was a writer?" She turned to Helen. "Do writers ever go without taking notes?"

"No, never." Helen looked at Emma. "And I knew Jackie. She was always scribbling ideas on whatever was at hand. Someone, her killer, cleaned up anything she might have left behind."

"Tomorrow is Christmas Eve," Emma said. She glanced between the two of them, clearly struggling with her decision. Then she sighed. "If we're doing this, it has to be tonight at the holiday parade. It's the only reason you would be out, Helen, because you're in the parade on the Friends of the Library float."

"Do you really think whoever is doing this is going to make their move tonight?" Lindsey asked.

"What if they bring a gun?" Helen asked. "I don't want anyone to get hurt—mostly me, but no one else either."

"Don't worry," Emma said. "I'll call in backup from the state troopers to cover the entire parade route. Given that the attempts on your life so far have been electrocution—assuming Jackie's death was really meant for you—hit and run and a sloppy stabbing attempt, I don't think we're dealing with a shooter or someone very good at the art of murder. Not that I'm willing to risk anyone else's life, mind you. No, we'll put your float last so you're by yourself. That should draw the killer out since they clearly prefer to get you alone."

"This is not making me feel good about this, not even a little," Helen said.

"Don't worry," Emma reassured her. "It's not going to be you on the float. It'll be me dressed up as you."

"Oh, I don't think I like that," Lindsey said.

"Well, you didn't expect me to send Helen out there, did you?" Emma asked. "And I'm certainly not sending you. You're not even an officer."

"Robbie is going to freak out," Lindsey said.

"Too bad." Emma glowered. "He's not the boss of me." She turned to Helen. "Now let's get me suited up to look like you."

Helen looked her over with a critical eye. "If you wear my fur-lined coat and matching hat—" Emma made a face, and Helen rolled her eyes. "They're fake. Relax. But the fur is very fluffy and will obscure most of your face. If you wear my signature dark-framed glasses and red lipstick, you might fool them from a distance."

"Excellent." Emma beamed. "You know what? I think this just might work."

"What can I do?" Lindsey asked.

"Stay out of the way," Emma said. Lindsey stared at her. "I mean it. You are not under any circumstances to put yourself in harm's way."

What do you not understand about staying out of the way?" Emma asked. She and Lindsey were waiting in the staging area for the parade.

"I am out of the way," Lindsey argued. "I'm merely providing a buffer between you and anyone else so that no one realizes the chief is dressed up as our writer in residence in an attempt to flush out a killer."

"Fine. As soon as I'm on the float, you skedaddle," Emma said.

They stood silently watching as the school marching bands took their positions amid the veterans' groups, the dancing grannies and the high school cheer squad. Several local businesses, including the Blue Anchor, had floats in the parade. After a quick meeting with Carrie that morning, it was agreed that Emma would be on the float by herself. As a precaution, Emma was wearing a bulletproof vest beneath her fluffy coat. It had to be hot, because even in the frigid temperatures, Lindsey could see that Emma was sweating.

"Are you nervous?" she asked.

Emma tipped her head to the side. "I don't want to answer that."

"Why not?"

"Because if I say I'm actually excited, you'll think there's something wrong with me," she said.

"Nah, that makes sense. You're a cop, catching bad guys is what you do," Lindsey said.

"If this person has been trying to murder Helen and got Jackie by mistake and is still trying for Helen, then, yes, I am all in on locking them up," Emma said. "But it could be that the car that almost hit Helen was an accident, and so could the knife wound Kenny received."

"But it doesn't seem likely," Lindsey said.

"No."

"What is this?" Robbie appeared across the parking lot. He strode toward them, and Emma's eyes went wide.

"He's going to blow my cover," she hissed at Lindsey. "Do something."

"Like what?" Lindsey cried. It was bitterly cold and her nose was running and she could no longer feel her toes.

"I don't know," Emma said. She hurried toward her float. "Stall him."

Lindsey jogged across the lot toward Robbie. "What is Em—"

"You mean *give me* an *M*," Lindsey interrupted very loudly.

"What?" Robbie looked confounded.

"You know, give me an *M*, give me an *E*, give me a double *R* and a *Y*. What does it spell? *Merry!*"

"Is your brain frozen?" Robbie asked.

"Potentially," Lindsey admitted. She slipped her hand

into the crook of his elbow and none too gently yanked him out of earshot. "Emma is undercover."

"Under—" Robbie squawked. He was so loud Lindsey was afraid someone would hear him, so she interrupted him again.

"Under the weather? That's a shame. You should go home." Lindsey gave him a hearty shove.

Robbie spun around and stared at her. "What has gotten into you?"

Lindsey glanced past him to see that the floats and bands and community groups had started to move. The parade was in motion. She had promised to stay out of the way, but she'd be damned if she let Emma and her float out of her sight. "Come on."

There were several state police troopers undercover in the crowd mixed in with the local force, which made Lindsey feel better. Also, Sully had been tapped to be one of the judges and was sitting in the stands with Mayor Cole and several other town residents to pick the best float. Lindsey and Emma had told Sully the plan, and she knew he was using his training as a Navy SEAL to scan the crowd for potential problems.

Lindsey did the same. She was looking for anyone who appeared suspicious. She glanced at Emma on the float. The Friends had rigged it with a desk, where Emma was to sit. As the float meandered down the parade route, she would pose at the desk as if she were writing, while pausing every now and again to wave at the crowd. At the moment she was hunched in the desk chair with her back to Robbie, trying to ignore him as the driver of her flatbed pickup truck moved the float into position.

"What is going on?" Robbie demanded. "Why is Emma up there, pretending to be Helen?"

"Shh!" Lindsey hushed him.

He raised one eyebrow and gestured to the float and said, "Don't use your librarian shusher on me. Why can't you tell me what our chief of po—"

"Robbie, for the love of Christmas, stop talking!" Lindsey barked. She glanced around them to make sure no one could hear him over the sound of the marching bands.

Robbie froze, and Lindsey was jerked back as her arm was still looped with his.

His eyes went wide. "She's bait!"

CHAPTER

21

BRIAR CREEK
PUBLIC LIBRARY

N o, not exactly. She's merely trying to determine whether the knife attack on Kenny and the near miss with the car that almost hit Helen were just accidents or if there is someone out to murder Helen," Lindsey said.

"Right," Robbie cried. "Bait!" He shrugged Lindsey's arm out of his and strode toward the float.

"Robbie, don't!" Lindsey cried. It was too late.

He was up alongside the slow-moving flatbed truck, waving his arm at Emma. She hunkered deeper into her faux fur, ignoring him.

"I know you can see me, love," Robbie said.

Lindsey glanced wildly around, hoping the crowd wasn't aware of what was happening. She turned back to the float to see Robbie hoist himself up onto the flatbed. Oh, no! He was going to ruin everything.

"What are you doing?" Emma cried. "Get down!"

"And what? Stand on the sidelines and watch you get harmed in the line of duty?" Robbie cried. "Absolutely not!"

"You are messing everything up," Emma hissed. "I have the situation under control."

"Really, because so far, and correct me if I'm wrong, the person who has been doing really bad things has used electrocution, a car, and a knife to try and harm their victim. And now you're standing on a float in the middle of a bloody parade, giving them a clear shot! Are you really that desperate to avoid marrying me?"

"Marry you?" Emma cried. "What are you talking about? We've never discussed marriage."

"I know!" Robbie retorted. "But I know you heard me rehearsing for a new play the other night, and there was a very wrenching proposal in that monologue, and I crushed it if I do say so myself, but I think you heard me and you've been freaking out ever since."

Emma's jaw dropped. "You were rehearsing . . . for a play?"

"Yes!"

"So, you don't want to marry me?" Emma asked.

"Um, hey, you two." Lindsey cleared her throat. The float was next in line to start down Main Street. "I know you need to talk, but now is not the best—"

"It's not that I don't want to exactly . . ." Robbie waffled.

"Oh my God, I am so relieved!" Emma jumped up and grabbed him around the neck in a hug that strangled. "I don't want to marry you either!"

"You don't?" Robbie blinked.

"No!" she cried. Realizing she might sound a bit too enthusiastic, Emma pulled back and cupped his face with her gloved hands. "I love you, quite desperately, but I am just not the marrying kind."

Robbie blinked, and then a slow grin spread across his face. "But you do love me?"

"Like crazy!" Emma assured him.

Lindsey clapped her hands. "Okay, you're on the route now. Wrap it up."

"Oy, we're having a moment here!" Robbie spun around to frown at her.

It was at that exact moment that a torch landed on the floor of the flatbed and rolled across it, igniting everything in its path. Robbie let out a yelp, and Emma shoved him to the side of the truck and leapt after him. They tumbled to the pavement not a moment too soon, as within seconds the fire spread across the very flammable Friends of the Library display, engulfing the float in flames.

People screamed and ran. The driver of the truck shut off the engine and jumped to safety. The town fire trucks, which were decked out in holiday cheer and placed at the end of the parade, roared forward to deal with the fire.

"Where did the torch come from?" Emma asked Lindsey.

"Over there. I'm sure of it." Lindsey pointed to a thin spot in the crowd. The person with the torch had clearly sent people scattering when they lit it.

"The person ran that way! Toward the park! They're

wearing a long black coat and dark gray hat!" Jeanette Palmer pushed her way out of the crowd and pointed down the street.

"Get to Sully," Emma ordered Lindsey. She yanked off her furry hat and coat, dropping them on the ground, and started to run.

Lindsey and Robbie exchanged a glance and ran after her, catching up to her at the town green. The park was deserted, as the parade had staggered to a halt and the attendees were looking for their participants as the firefighters dealt with the burning truck and everyone filmed the chaos with their phones.

Emma glanced at the two of them and rolled her eyes. "I told you to find Sully."

"He's on his way." Lindsey knew this with a certainty that she couldn't explain.

"Stay in the shadows," Emma ordered as she led them around the perimeter of the gazebo.

"What do we do if we see them?" Robbie asked.

"You tell me and then you get out of the way," Emma said.

"Mercy, you're sexy when you're in charge," Robbie said.

"Inappropriate in the moment," Emma snapped.

"Sorry." He held up his hands in apology.

"No talking!" Emma ordered, and then she disappeared around a large tree.

"We're supposed to follow her, right?" Robbie asked.

"Yeah, absolutely," Lindsey bluffed.

They hurried after Emma, who darted and dashed

around the park, checking every nook and cranny. Finally, she stopped, stepping into the light. "They're not here."

"Chief!" Officer Kirkland strode across the green toward them. Lindsey noticed that Sully was right behind him.

When they reached them, Sully gave her a quick hug. "All right?"

"I'm fine," she said. "I wasn't on the float."

"I saw it go up in flames, and my heart about stopped," Sully said. "Jeanette Palmer told us she directed you to the park."

"She did but we were too late," Lindsey said. "Whoever it was got away."

Sully looked at Emma. "Do you think they saw you and realized you weren't Helen?"

"If they did, then she's in trouble." Emma stared at him for a beat and then turned to Kirkland. "Helen lives at 34 Sycamore. Where's your car?"

"Right there!" Kirkland pointed to a squad car parked beside the park.

"Great! You drive!" Emma and Kirkland ran across the park and ducked into the police car. In seconds, the lights were flashing and sirens were wailing as they shot away from the parade chaos and headed to Helen's house.

"Do you think whoever threw that torch onto the float is at Helen's right now?" Robbie asked.

"I don't know," Lindsey said. She took her phone out of her pocket and called Helen. It rang and rang. "She's not answering. Emma and Kirkland might need support."

Her gaze searched Sully's and he said, "I'm parked right there. Let's go."

"Don't even think about leaving me behind." Robbie strode after them. "The woman I am not going to marry could be running into danger."

Lindsey smiled and said, "Come on, then."

Sully fired up his old truck, and they shot through town on the way to Helen's cottage. When they arrived, they saw Kirkland's squad car and the unmarked police car, where Emma had stationed an officer, parked in front. The house was dark, and there was no sign of any of the officers.

"I have a very bad feeling about this," Robbie said.

"Do you think they walked into a trap?" Lindsey asked Sully.

His gaze was narrowed on the house. She knew he had done special ops in the military and was tapping into that training right now.

"Maybe," he said. "Whoever is doing these random acts of violence against Helen very specifically has her as their target. The question is who and why?"

"Revenge? Money? Jealousy? A secret?" Robbie rattled off guesses. "It seems like the person with the most reason to harm Helen is Jackie, but she's dead."

"Unless we've been looking at it wrong and there is someone who wanted both Jackie and Helen dead." Lindsey felt as if the earth moved under her feet. How had she not seen it before? "Who told us in her office that she was jealous of both Jackie and Helen, but more Helen than Jackie?"

"Their critique partner Liz Maynard." Sully frowned.

Robbie looked confused. "That can't be. She was so nice and completely enamored of me, which is a testament to her good taste."

Sully rolled his eyes, and Lindsey resisted the urge to do the same.

"Do you really think jealousy is driving Liz to do this?" Sully asked. "And why after all this time? What changed that Liz suddenly feels the need to kill her former critique partners?"

"Robbie said it," Lindsey answered. "If it's not jealousy, it has to be one of the other motives. She wouldn't get money from their deaths, and revenge doesn't work because neither of them did anything to her, so if it isn't jealousy, it has to be a secret. What would Liz want to keep a secret so desperately that she'd kill her old writing partners?"

"Do you remember when we visited her in the law office and she told us that she'd helped all of the members of the critique group in different ways?" Sully asked.

"Yes!" Lindsey nodded. "She said she helped Helen with her stalker, which was weirdly Jackie, who she assisted with her divorce, and Melanie's widower with her estate, including the intellectual property on Melanie's unfinished books. She knows all of their secrets and has access to everything."

"Most importantly Melanie's unfinished work," Sully said.

"And if she decided to help herself to that material, the

only people who would know that the material wasn't hers would be Helen and Jackie."

"She's a plagiarizer!" Robbie gasped. "And she seemed so nice."

"I'm going to check things out," Sully said. "You two stay here."

Lindsey looked at him and then at Robbie. "It's like he hasn't been married to me for two years."

"Right?" Robbie agreed.

Sully sighed. "Fine but stay out of sight."

The three of them climbed out of the truck cab. It was cold and Lindsey burrowed into her coat, pulling her scarf tight around her neck and tugging her hat low. Holiday lights decorated most of the houses on the street. The light snow that had been falling had ceased, but the air was cold and damp and carried the woodsmoke of fireplaces, which added to the festive feeling in the air.

As they crept up to Helen's cottage, Lindsey saw several cars parked along the curb, but there was no way to tell if one belonged to Liz or not since they had no idea what she drove.

"Wait here," Sully said.

"No." Robbie shook his head. "I'm going with you."

Sully glanced at him, and a look of understanding passed between them. Sully gave him a quick nod. He turned to Lindsey, who said, "Don't worry. I will stay out of sight. In fact, I can't feel my toes. I'm going to wait in the truck. Please be careful."

"We will." Sully kissed her forehead and handed her the keys. "Turn on the engine if you get too cold."

He and Robbie jogged across the street, and Lindsey watched them with a pit of dread in her stomach. She climbed back into the passenger seat of the truck and prepared to wait.

She stared at the house until she feared her eyes were drying out. Why wasn't anything happening? Had something gone wrong? Why hadn't she put Sully on speakerphone before they parted? Damn it.

She shifted restlessly in her seat. Maybe she could just go peek in a window. That wouldn't be so bad, would it? She hopped out of the truck before she changed her mind. She was about to quietly close the door, when someone punched her in the back from behind. Lindsey caught herself on the doorframe. She glanced over her shoulder and saw Liz standing there holding a lethal-looking kitchen knife.

"Don't even think about it." Liz slapped the phone out of Lindsey's gloved hand. "Get in. Start driving."

"Where's Helen? And Kenny?" Lindsey demanded, refusing to move.

"Get. In." Liz shoved the knife in Lindsey's face, dangerously close to her eye. Lindsey climbed in.

She slid across the bench seat into the driver's seat. She held up her hands. "I don't have—"

"Yeah, no," Liz said. "I saw your husband hand you the keys. Let's go."

Lindsey fumbled to get the keys into the ignition. She glanced at the house, desperate to see anyone. "What did you do?"

"In two seconds, I will stab you and leave you to bleed out. Now drive."

Lindsey turned the engine on and pulled away from the curb. She glanced at the house as they passed. It was still dark. There was no sign of life. She thought she might be ill.

"You murdered Jackie," Lindsey said. "Why?"

"I don't know what you're talking about. The medical examiner declared it an accident," Liz said.

"He was wrong."

Liz shrugged.

"If I'm going to die, I think that makes it my business," Lindsey said.

"Your death, just like Jackie's and Helen's, will also be an accident," Liz said. "Sorry not sorry."

Lindsey felt woozy. "Helen is dead?"

"She should be by now." Liz unfastened her black coat and pushed the dark gray hat back on her head. Her face was shiny with sweat, and her skin was flushed a deep pink as if from exertion.

"Why?" Lindsey asked. "Why would you kill two people who considered you their friend?"

"They're not my friends," Liz said. "Did either of them reach out to me when I had to quit the critique group? Did they offer to help me? No. I had to sit on the sidelines and watch their successes, knowing that I was just as good a writer if not better than them."

"So, you killed them because they both got published?" Lindsey asked. "Why not just keep writing so you could get published, too?"

"Oh, I'm getting published." Liz smiled at her but it didn't reach her eyes. Lindsey shivered and turned back to the road. "That proposal I told you about when you visited my office? Well, I've been offered a major deal for it. Do you know what that is?"

"In publishing, it means over half a million," Lindsey said.

"Exactly," Liz said. "It's going to change my life."

"Then why murder Jackie and Helen?" Lindsey asked. "I would think you'd want to flaunt your success and rub their noses in it, unless of course you can't."

Liz said nothing. She turned and stared out the front window. "Drive faster."

Lindsey gasped. They'd been right. There was only one reason Liz wouldn't want to brag about her success to her former partners. And only one reason why she'd feel compelled to murder the last two remaining members of her critique group. "The book you sold isn't yours, is it?"

"Yes, it is." Liz glared at her.

"And the only two people who know it isn't yours are Jackie and Helen, because they were in your critique group," Lindsey concluded. "Which means the book must belong to the late Melanie Starland."

"Shut up! She's dead. She can't own anything," Liz snapped.

"That's why you had to kill them," Lindsey said. "Because they would have said something. They would have called you out for stealing her work."

"I didn't steal it!" Liz cried. "I found it. When her husband came to the office with her files and laptop, looking for clarification on intellectual property, it was just this half-baked, half-written idea. I took it and made it into a compelling novel. It would never have existed without me. It's mine."

"That's why you did it," Lindsey said. "You sent Jackie after Helen knowing there would be an altercation. Then you murdered Jackie in the gazebo but tried to frame Helen for it by planting Helen's manuscript on Jackie. That's why you were in the gazebo."

"I was doing Helen a favor. Her new idea is terrible," Liz said.

Lindsey gasped. "You were the person who pushed me down, aren't you?"

"You shouldn't have been there," Liz snapped. "Everything was going perfectly until you showed up."

"Seriously? Did you think if Helen went to jail for Jackie's murder, she wouldn't notice that you'd ripped off Melanie's manuscript? They have libraries in prisons, you know."

"Stop talking!" Liz waved the knife at her, but Lindsey wasn't finished.

"When Helen didn't get arrested because the medical

examiner declared it an accident, you knew you had to murder Helen, too. So it was you who tried to run her down and stabbed Kenny in the dark, thinking it was her. So now what? Is your plan to stage a murder-suicide for Helen and Kenny?"

"I'm not talking about this anymore," Liz said. "You can't make me."

Liz started to whistle. She was so calm and collected, it made Lindsey more frightened than when Liz had shoved the knife in her face. When Liz didn't need Lindsey to drive anymore, Lindsey knew exactly what Liz had planned. Liz was going to kill her unless Lindsey acted fast.

As soon as the road was wide enough, Lindsey pulled a sharp U-turn, slamming Liz up against the door and giving herself the opportunity to grab Liz by the wrist and bang her hand against the dashboard until she dropped the knife.

"Look out!" Liz screamed.

Lindsey had swerved into the opposite lane and was on a collision course with a delivery truck. She yanked the wheel back into her own lane, slamming Liz against the door again. When Liz bent down to retrieve the knife, Lindsey stepped on the brakes. Liz's head bounced off the dashboard, and she clapped a hand to her forehead, which was gushing blood.

"What are you doing?" Liz screamed. "You'll get us both killed."

"What do I care if you're going to kill me anyway?" Lindsey yelled.

She stomped on the gas and kept the truck veering from

side to side to keep Liz off balance as she raced back to Helen's cottage. As soon as it was in sight, she slammed on the brakes. She was moments too late and rammed the picket fence, sending Liz up against the dashboard. In seconds, Lindsey had unclipped her seatbelt and opened her door, jumping from the driver's seat and running toward the house.

"Sully!" she cried as she ran. "Robbie! Emma!"

The house was dark. But she could hear the sound of someone banging on metal. She ran to the basement doors in the side yard. There was a piece of firewood jammed in the handles, keeping it shut. She pulled it out and the doors burst open. Emma, Kirkland, Robbie, Sully and Barnes, the officer who'd been watching the house, poured out.

"The gas!" Emma cried. "Everyone get away from the house. Call an ambulance!"

She ran to the back door. Emma hit it with one booted foot. The distinctive smell of natural gas mushroomed out. Emma yanked her scarf up over her nose and dove inside, with Kirkland and Barnes on her heels.

Robbie was on the phone with the 911 dispatcher. They all stared at the back of the house until Kirkland appeared with Kenny draped over his shoulders in a fireman hold and Emma and Barnes carrying Helen between them.

"They're alive!" Emma yelled. "But just barely."

"That's how Liz was going to kill them," Lindsey said. She turned to Sully. "Liz! I left her in your truck!"

She broke into a run and Sully followed her. They raced around to the front of the house to find Liz, trying to back the truck out of the picket fence Lindsey had planted it in. The wheels spun, and she stomped harder on the gas. The truck roared, backing up mere inches and pulling the fence with it.

"Sorry about that," Lindsey said.

"It's okay," Sully said. "If you're okay, it's okay."

He strode forward and yanked open the door on the driver's side. None too gently, he shoved Liz across the seat and stepped on the brake. Shifting the truck into park, he grabbed Liz by the scruff of her coat and hauled her out of the truck before she could reach her knife.

Liz flailed and clawed, which was useless with her gloves on. She bucked and tried to kick him, but Sully held her away from him until Emma appeared around the side of the house. In seconds, she had Liz face down on the ground with her knee in her back and cuffs on her wrists.

The sound of sirens grew louder, and Lindsey looked at Emma. "Is Helen . . . ?"

"She and Mr. Lewis are coming around," Emma said.

"Thank goodness." Lindsey felt her knees sag with relief.

Emma glanced down at Liz and then back at Lindsey. "And this person is?"

"Liz Maynard, the other member of their critique group," Lindsey said. "Apparently, she helped herself to the work in progress of their late member, Melanie Starland, and signed a major deal for it, but because she knew that Helen and Jackie would recognize the work as Melanie's, she had to remove them from the equation before the deal went public."

"You can't prove anything," Liz growled.

"Oh, I think we can," Emma said. She hauled Liz up by the arm and walked her over to the squad car. She placed her in the back seat and shut the door. "Let me get this straight. All of this was over a book deal?"

"Yup." Lindsey nodded.

Emma muttered an oath, and Lindsey couldn't have agreed more.

CHAPTER

22

BRIAR CREEK
PUBLIC LIBRARY

M erry Christmas!" Nancy and Violet entered the library
together just as Paula unlocked the doors. A flurry of
patrons came in behind them, and Beth switched on the
wireless speaker that played soft holiday background music. She was decked out as an elf, from the jingle bell on the
tip of her hat to her pointy shoes, and planned to pass out
candy canes to any children who stopped by.

A tradition of hosting a Christmas Eve open house for
the community had started at the library a few years
ago. The library was only open from nine until noon, giving their regular patrons a chance to duck in and check out
materials for the days they were closed and to bring goodies
to share.

Nancy had a full tray of assorted cookies, and Violet

held a large carafe of hot cider. The crafternooners were having an informal gathering during the open house since the library would be closing early, before their usual time to meet. Their shared lunch was now on a buffet table in the middle of the library and was less of a meal and more party food, like Beth's bruschetta and Violet's green chile soufflé.

Paula was working the circulation desk and handed out a paper ornament—that their teen activity group had crafted and decorated the library with—for each item checked out.

The open house grew louder and more boisterous as more patrons stopped by bringing more food. Lindsey leaned against the circulation desk, greeting everyone as they entered the building. She was happy to see all of their smiling faces, but the excitement of the previous evening had kept her from sleeping, and only the caffeine from the three cups of coffee she'd already had was keeping her upright.

"Have some cider." Violet handed her a thick paper cup.

"And a cookie." Nancy gave her a napkin with a coconut-encrusted cookie on top.

"Thank you." Lindsey dutifully took a sip and a bite.

Mayor Cole entered the library and joined them. "They're predicting a big snowstorm tonight. I'm glad the library is closing early."

"Me, too," Lindsey said. "Honestly, I think I might sleep until the New Year."

"Before you enter your torpor," Nancy said. "What happened at Helen Monroe's cottage last night?"

"I heard she killed her husband," Violet said. "Who was actually Jackie Lewis's ex-husband. Did you know?"

"I knew." Lindsey took another bite of cookie and a sip of cider.

"She didn't kill him," Mayor Cole said.

"Are we seriously talking about murder on a holiday?" Paula asked.

"Yes," Beth said. "I missed it all. You have to tell me everything."

"Wait for me!" Mary hurried into the library, carrying a vat of chowder and a basket of fresh rolls. "I have so many questions."

"All right, but I have to sit down." Lindsey moved over to the section of the library with the cushy chairs. The crafternooners joined her, all except for Paula, who had already heard everything during setup that morning.

Lindsey told them everything that had happened the night before and how Liz Maynard had planned the murders of both Jackie Lewis and Helen Monroe, all so she could steal a half-written novel from the member of their critique group who had passed away ten years before.

"Unbelievable," Nancy said.

"And I thought the theater was competitive." Violet shook her head.

"I'm just glad that she was caught," Mayor Cole said. "And that no one else was hurt. When I think of a house full of natural gas and what could have happened. It's a nightmare."

"I'll say," Helen Monroe agreed as she joined them.

"Helen, what are you doing here?" Lindsey asked. "Shouldn't you be resting?"

Helen shrugged. "I'm the writer in residence; how could I not be here to wish everyone a happy holiday?"

"We would have understood," Beth said. "Is Kenny all right?"

Helen pointed over at the refreshment table, where Kenny was talking to Milton and Robbie. Judging by how animated he was with his arms gesturing wildly, he was either recounting the events of the night before or trying to land a plane.

"I think he's just getting to the part where Liz showed up and knocked us out," Helen said. "I knew her for almost two decades and had no idea she had such a violent streak."

"Apparently, Jackie didn't either," Emma said as she joined them.

"I have a question," Mary said. "How did she manage to trap you all in the basement?"

"It was simple," Emma said. "The basement was the only unlocked entry into the house. Kirkland and I met up with Officer Barnes, who was getting concerned when her call to the house went unanswered. We were headed into the basement, when Sully and Robbie appeared and joined us. As soon as the last of us went down the steps, Liz slammed the doors shut and barricaded them with a piece of firewood in the handles. I expect she was hoping the gas would do us in as well, and she'd come back and move the wood to make it look like a horrible accident."

"Either that or she was going to blow the entire house up," Mayor Cole said. They all looked at her. "Sorry. Just speculating."

Lindsey shivered at the mere idea that she could have lost her husband and friends in one horrific instant.

"I can't stay long, as Kenny and I are going home for Christmas," Helen said. "But I'll be back after the New Year to resume my residency." She glanced at Lindsey. "Assuming that's all right."

"Of course," Lindsey said.

Helen turned to the crafternooners. "I have a confession to make, and I hope you'll all forgive me."

Lindsey watched as her friends collectively turned puzzled gazes upon Helen. Lindsey waved at Paula, signaling for her to join them. She knew what Helen was going to say, and Paula deserved to be a part of it.

"What is it?" Paula asked as she joined them.

"I was just making a confession," Helen said. She glanced around the group, making eye contact with each of them. "I owe you an apology. I didn't come to Briar Creek just to be your writer in residence. I came because of all of you."

"Us?" Nancy looked bewildered.

"I wanted to get away from the ultra-dark thriller books based on true crimes that I've been writing," Helen said. "I wanted to write a series that had more of a sense of community, more heart, if you will."

"So you're going to write more traditional mysteries?" Violet asked. "Like Agatha Christie?"

"Yes, exactly." Helen nodded.

"Oh, I love those," Mary said. "They're my comfort reads."

"Me, too," Paula said. "Good triumphing over evil and all that."

Lindsey exchanged a knowing look with Helen, who smiled.

"The thing is," Helen said, "I was looking for inspiration when I read a news article about an intrepid bunch of amateur sleuths who were crafternooners that met at a library on the Connecticut shore, and I thought, that's what I'm looking for!"

The group was silent, processing what Helen had said.

"Of course, if you hate the idea, I will scrap it. And obviously if someone objects to being characterized in the books, I will absolutely keep them out, but . . . um . . . what do you think?"

"Do you mean you're writing a mystery about us?" Beth asked.

"Yes," Helen said.

"We're the amateur sleuths?" Mary clarified.

Helen nodded.

"This is awesome!" Paula said.

"Well, I for one think it's genius," Violet agreed.

The rest of the group nodded enthusiastically.

"So, you're all okay with it?" Helen asked.

More nods.

Lindsey glanced at Nancy, who had yet to say anything. "What do you think, Nancy? Are you on board with this?"

"Are you kidding?" Nancy cried. Her bright blue eyes sparkled with glee. "We're going to be famous!"

Crafternoon Guide

Looking to have your own holiday crafternoon? Well, here are some book discussion questions, a craft, and recipes for *A Christmas Memory* to get you started. Happy holidays!

Readers Guide for
A Christmas Memory

by Truman Capote

1. What does "fruitcake weather" mean in the story?

2. Why does his friend call him Buddy? What is the relationship between Buddy and his friend?

3. What object do Buddy and his friend give each other for Christmas? What do they represent?

4. How does the story's time period impact the characters' lives?

5. What does the buggy represent to the narrator?

6. Would you consider the story happy or sad? Why?

7. What happens to Buddy at the end of the story?

Craft
Paper Circle Ornaments

20 paper circles of the same size*
Pencil
Glue stick or hot glue gun
Ribbon
Yarn needle

On the back of each circle, draw a triangle that extends to the edges. With the picture side of each circle face up, gently fold the edges up along the triangle lines to create tabs. Each circle should look like a flat triangle with three rounded edges, folded up. Hot glue the folded edges of a circle to another circle's folded edge. Repeat to create a chain of 10 in a straight line, then glue the ends of the chain together to form a ring. Hot glue two tabs of five circles together to form a dome. This is the top of the ornament. Repeat with the remaining five pieces to create a second dome, which is the bottom. Attach the ring of circles so the tabs align with the top and bottom domes, and hot glue to secure all the tabs, creating a sphere. Let it dry. Use a large needle to put a hole in one of the tabs and draw the ribbon through, tying it in a loop. Hang on your tree!

*The paper circles can be from anything book-related. For a book club, it could be photocopies of the book covers that the club read during the year. They would just need to be rendered small enough to fit in the cut-out circles.

Recipes

FRUITCAKE COOKIES

1¾ cups all-purpose flour

½ teaspoon baking soda

¼ teaspoon salt

1 cup packed light brown sugar

6 tablespoons butter, softened

2 tablespoons shortening

1 large egg, room temperature

1 cup pitted prunes, chopped

1 cup golden raisins

½ cup candied cherries, chopped

½ cup shredded sweetened coconut

3 ounces white chocolate candy coating

Preheat oven to 375°F. Line cookie sheets with parchment paper. In a medium bowl, combine the flour, baking soda and salt. Set aside. In a large bowl, with an electric mixer, slowly blend the brown sugar, butter and shortening until well incorporated, then raise the speed to high and beat until creamy. At a low speed, mix in the egg until well blended. Add the flour mixture, prunes, raisins, cherries and coconut until just blended. Drop the dough by rounded tablespoons, 2 inches apart, onto the cookie sheet. Bake 10 to 12 minutes, or until golden brown on the edges. Set aside to cool completely. In a saucepan, melt the white chocolate and use a fork to drizzle over the tops of the cookies and allow to harden. Makes 3 dozen.

GREEN CHILE SOUFFLÉ

2 (4-ounce) cans chopped green chiles
¾ pound Monterey Jack, grated
¾ pound cheddar, grated
4 eggs, separated
⅔ cup evaporated milk
1 tablespoon flour
½ teaspoon salt

Preheat oven to 325°F. Grease a 9 x 13-inch glass baking dish. In a large bowl, mix the chiles and cheeses. In a medium bowl, beat the egg whites with an electric mixer until stiff peaks form. In another medium bowl, whisk the yolks just enough to break them up. Combine the milk, flour, and salt with the yolks. Spread the chile and cheese mixture along the bottom of the baking dish. Fold the yolk mixture into the egg whites and pour over the chiles and cheese. Mix together with a fork until just blended. Bake 30 minutes, or until a knife inserted in the middle comes out clean.

Acknowledgments

Many thanks to my team: Kate Seaver, Amanda Maurer, Christina Hogrebe, Kim Salina I, Kaila Mundell-Hill, Stacy Edwards and Christie Conlee. I can't thank you all enough for the work you do behind the scenes to make these books shine and to get them into the hands of the readers. Best Team Ever!

Shout-out to *all* the librarians! This series is for you. I hope I do justice to the incredible work you do every day—despite the many challenges—making the world a better place for us all.

For my readers, how can I thank you? You have supported this series from the very first day, and I am so very grateful for you! Here's to more library lover's adventures for us all!

As always, much love to my dudes—Chris Hansen Orf, Beckett Orf and Wyatt Orf. I couldn't do what I do without your support. It means everything to me.

Keep reading for an excerpt from
Jenn McKinlay's novel . . .

LOVE AT FIRST BOOK

Available from Berkley Romance!

E m, are you all right?" Samantha Gale, my very best friend, answered her phone on the fourth ring. Her voice was rough with sleep and it belatedly occurred to me that nine o'clock in the morning in Finn's Hollow, Ireland, was four o'clock in the morning in Oak Bluffs, Martha's Vineyard.

"Oh, I'm sorry. Damn it, I woke you up, didn't I?" I asked, feeling awful about it.

"No, it's fine," Sam said. "I told you when you left that I'm always here for you." There was a low grumbling in the background and she added, "And Ben says he's here for you, too."

That made me laugh. Sam and Ben had become couple goals for me. Not that I thought I'd ever find anything like the connection they'd made, but they kept the pilot light of my innermost hope aflame.

"Thank you and Ben," I said. "I'm going to hang up now. Forget I ever called."

"Emily Allen, don't you dare," Sam said. Now she sounded fully awake. *Oops.*

"No, really I—" I began but she interrupted me.

"Tell me why you're calling, otherwise I'll worry." There was more grumbling in the background. Sam laughed and said, "Ben says he's begging you to tell me so that I don't drive him crazy with speculation."

I grinned. She would, too. Then I grew serious.

Glancing around the Last Chapter, the quaint bookshop in which I was presently standing, I noted objectively that it was a booklover's dream come true. A three-story stone building chock-full of books with a small café, where the scent of fresh-brewed coffee, berry-filled scones, and cinnamon pastry permeated the air. I felt myself lean in that direction as if the delicious aromas were reeling me in.

One of the employees had unlocked the front door of the shop, and I had trailed in behind a handful of customers who'd been waiting. I'd been agog ever since.

This was it. The bookshop where I'd be working for the next year. My heart was pounding and my palms were sweaty. The black wool turtleneck sweater I was wearing, in an attempt to defeat the early November chill, felt as if it were choking me and I was quite sure the pain spearing through my head meant I was having an aneurysm.

"I'm supposed to meet my boss in a few minutes, and I think I'm having a heart attack or potentially a stroke," I said.

There was a beat of silence then Sam said, "Tell me your symptoms."

I listed them all and she noted each one with an "uh-huh," which told me nothing whatsoever as to what she thought about my condition. I was three thousand miles away and starting a new job in a bookshop, having put my career as a librarian on Martha's Vineyard on hold to chase some crazy fantasy where I traveled to a foreign destination and lived a life full of adventure.

"I think I'm going to throw up," I groaned.

"Inhale," Sam said. "You know the drill—in for eight seconds, hold for four, out for eight."

I sucked in a breath. *Ouch.* "I can't. It makes my head throb. See? Aneurysm."

"Or a lack-of-caffeine headache," she said. "Have you had coffee yet?"

Come to think of it, I had not. I'd been too nervous to make any before I left my cottage this morning so the potential for this skull splitter to be from coffee deprivation seemed likely.

"No," I said. "And I see where you're going, but I still have brutal nausea and I'm sweating. I bet I have a fever. Maybe it's food poisoning from the airplane food last night. I had the beef stroganoff."

"You ate airplane food?" Sam sounded as incredulous as if I'd confessed to eating ice cream off the bathroom floor. She was a professional chef, so not a big surprise.

"I know, I know," I said. "It's pure preservatives. I'll likely be dead within the hour."

There was a lengthy pause where I imagined Sam was practicing her last words to me, wanting to get them just right.

"Em, you know I love you like a sister, right?" she asked.

Well, that didn't sound like the beginning of a vow of friendship into the afterlife.

"I do," I said. "I also know that's how you'd start a sentence I'm not going to like."

"You're panicking, Em," Sam said. Her voice was full of empathy. "And you and I both know that bout of hypochondria you dealt with last summer was how you coped with your unhappiness."

"But I'm not unhappy," I protested. "I'm living the dream in a quaint village in County Kerry where the green is the greenest green I've ever seen and there's a sheep staring at me over the top of every stone wall. Seriously, I'm drowning in picturesque charm, which is probably why I'm about to keel over dead."

A sound came from my phone that resembled someone stepping on a duck.

"Are you laughing at me?" I asked. Rude but understandable.

"No, never," Sam said. She cleared her throat. "I just think you might be freaking out because it's your first day at your new job."

"I'm not," I protested. I was. I absolutely was. "I just think I need to come home before they discover I have some highly contagious pox or plague and I'm quarantined in a thatched stone cottage to live out my days in a fairy-infested forest, talking to the trees and hedgehogs while farming for potatoes."

"Have you ever considered that you read too much?" Sam asked.

"No!" I cried and I heard Ben, also a librarian and formerly my boss, protest as well.

Sam laughed. She enjoyed goading us.

"Just think, if I leave now, we can meet for coffee and pastries at the Grape tomorrow morning."

"While I'd love to see you, you know that, you have to stay in Ireland and see your journey through," Sam said. "If you go home now your mother will guilt you into never leaving again, not to mention clobber you with the dreaded 'I told you so.'"

"Fair point." I sighed. I glanced at the display on my phone. My mother had already called five times and texted twelve and I hadn't even been in Ireland for twenty-four hours yet. I'd let her know I'd arrived safely, but I knew that wasn't what her messages were about.

My mother had made it clear that she expected me to continue in the role of her caregiver, a position I'd assumed when my father left several years ago. Were she incapable of caring for herself, I'd understand, but there was absolutely nothing wrong with her except a scorching case of toxic narcissism. I tabled the mom problem to deal with the one at hand.

"I still think I might pass out and then I'll likely lose the job and this entire conversation becomes moot," I said.

"You won't," Sam said. "Find a place to sit down. Can you do that?"

"Okay." I was standing in the stacks—well, more accurately, hiding. The shelves were dark wood, long and tall and stuffed with books. They comforted me. Scattered randomly amid the shelving units were step stools. I found one and sat down.

"Are you sitting?" Sam asked.

"Yes."

"Good, now put your head between your knees," she ordered.

"Um." I was wearing a formfitting, gray wool pencil skirt. I tried to maneuver my head down. No luck. The skirt was too snug. The closest I could get was to look over my knees at my very cute black ankle boots. "Sorry, Sam, nothing is getting between these knees. Not even a hot Irishman."

Sam chuckled, but over that I heard a strangled noise behind me and I straightened up and turned around to see a man in jeans and an Aran sweater, holding his fist to his mouth, looking as if he was choking. He had thick, wavy black hair and blue eyes so dark they were almost the same shade as his hair. Also, if I wasn't mistaken, he was my new boss.